Rancho Alviso

ZaneDoe

ISBN: 1-4537-3996-3
ISBN-13: 9781453739969

dedication: In Gratitude, I Dedicate This Book To Joseph, Seven And The Odiferous Puppy. And, To Lena And Sonora Who Live The Real Meaning Of Family.

Chapter 1

No Potatoes

The old adobe hotel with its reputation for fine dining—fine dining in accordance with the tastes of the locals, that is—is well loved, *and not* just by the locals. Those who come upon Rancho Alviso either by accident, desperation, or otherwise, fall in love with the ambience and the accommodating staff as well as the food. Rancho Alviso possesses a natural charm one could not easily fabricate and lays claim to a history that is speculatively legendary: Billy the Kid bunked at the Alviso, as did Pat Garrett—looking for Billy no doubt. President Roosevelt dined at the Alviso—if you ask which President Roosevelt, the best answer you will get is "the one with the glasses." It is claimed that Georgia O'Keefe stayed more than once in the little adobe separate from the hotel. A prominent musician is said to have taken his last breath in room number 3. So go the many tales, or truths, about this ranch that came into being over a hundred years ago on three hundred rough-cut acres. Though the ranch and land have since been reduced in size, Alviso still defiantly claims its ground, its influence and its permanency. Every weathered wall, uneven walkway, clinging vine and twisted gray-bark tree proclaims its history and resolutely its future.

Mesquite Grilled Steak
Cactus Salad
Fresh Rosemary Potatoes

"*How!*" Buck pointed to the sign. "Oh man, potatoes. That's what I need, potatoes. Real potatoes, not those fuckin' flakes."

How glanced over at the sign but said nothing in response.

"*Really man*, let's stop." Buck was hungry. Eating potatoes suddenly seemed crucial, a necessary food he couldn't bear to pass up. Buck's demand was actually more of a plea or desperate suggestion since How—short for Howard and one takes their life in their hands if they were to ever call him

Howie—made the decisions. How was in charge, the boss, and of the two deserved the title and position.

"We're not stopping. We got alotta ground to cover before we start thinking about our stomachs." How was stuck with Buck—not his first choice to be on the run with but it just happened to turn out that way.

"Come on, How. I'm hungry. I'm really fuckin' hungry, man. We're out in the middle of nowhere. There's no one for a hundred miles. I'm really hungry…"

"No one for a hundred miles? Then who's running the restaurant, Buck, and how the fuck do you know who is around for a hundred miles?" How was not interested in accommodating Buck's whims but he also was hungry and therefore pulled onto the dirt parking lot of the hotel. If they could make it a quick meal without drawing attention to themselves, they would be on their way with little time lost.

Buck jumped out of the truck like he was going to a whorehouse. How wasn't so enthusiastic. Acting on the side of caution first and foremost, he scanned the parking lot and the surrounding area before catching up to Buck. A bell clanged their arrival and Rosa greeted them with a rather strained smile. She moved slowly from behind the immense ornately carved dark-wood counter that must have been as old as the building itself and led them at a leisurely pace to a table in the small antiquated restaurant. Rosa handed them each a menu, gave a brief smile and an "enjoy" then headed back to her station behind the counter and to her book. Buck was impressed with his "choice" of eating establishment. This was better than a Denny's.

"Nice, huh? Good choice, huh? I made a good pick," Buck said, bouncing his head around, proud of himself and eager to order.

How remained cautious. He surveyed the room, taking notice of each person, before feeling comfortable enough to scan the menu—there were only three other people in the restaurant.

"I'm so hungry, man. Potatoes, I could order just potatoes. Bring me a *great big plate* of them potatoes." Buck smiled as his eyes foraged for service.

"Yeah, I know already," How replied with haste. He didn't like how Buck felt the need to express how he felt or what he wanted or was thinking at any given moment; it made How nervous. Buck just blurted out whatever popped into his head without much, if any, forethought, which only made Buck a bigger risk for How and his plans.

"What are you going to order, How?" Buck asked, attempting to rush things along.

"Here she comes, just order."

Scarlet approached the table with pen and pad ready. She was soft spoken and gracious. How spoke first.

"I'll take a cup of coffee. Sugar. I don't see a hamburger on the menu, can I get a hamburger, or a cheeseburger?"

"It's the dinner menu but I'm sure Roberto will make one for you. How would you like that done, sir?"

"Ahh, medium; medium would be fine, thanks. Does it come with anything?"

"Soup or salad tonight."

"What about fries, you have those right?"

"No, I'm sorry. We make everything from scratch and we're all out of potatoes, sir."

Buck looked like someone had punched him in his ravenous stomach. His eyes opened wide, his head jutted out and his mouth shot open as How had feared it might. "You don't have potatoes? *Your sign says potatoes!*"

She was taken aback by his quick and dramatic response, and even more by the volume of his voice.

"I'm sorry, sir, we ran out yesterday——" before she could finish Buck cut her off with a display of what only could be described as an adolescent tantrum, raging about the posted sign that deceived him into the restaurant and insisting that she was lying—*he knew that they had potatoes.* Then, the worst, he began making threats. The unstable partner brought about all the unwanted attention How had feared.

Scarlet turned quickly, leaving the table to get Roberto. Buck frightened her; she'd been frightened by a customer before and the outcome wasn't pleasant. She didn't want a repeat.

The intimate eating establishment held 12 tables; three were now occupied. Spanish guitar music played softly in the background and all was serene until the two showed up. An older woman sipping on a glass of sangria was staring at the new arrivals. She sat alone with no one to keep her attention so they were.

"What are *you* lookin' at!" Buck hollered to the innocent onlooker. She quickly diverted her eyes. She meant no harm. He turned back to How and justified his anger. "I want potatoes, man. It's bullshit that they don't have 'em. They just don't wanna bother cuz it's me," Buck said in true chip-on-the-shoulder fashion.

"Because it's you? They don't even know who you are. Don't be an asshole and quit drawing attention, you moron. Hell, she might be going to call the police right now. Who cares about some fucking potatoes? We just want to eat and *get outta here* without any problems." How kept his eyes on the kitchen door, pondering if he should get up and leave as fast as possible.

With alarm, Scarlet relayed what transpired at the table; she wanted Roberto to make them leave. The last hostile customers Scarlet had encountered ended their meal with a fistfight.

"No, no. I'll go out and talk to them," Robert responded with no sense of worry or urgency in his voice. "It's about potatoes, that's all."

"This guy is not right, Roberto," she warned. "Be careful." She had a bad feeling and didn't believe a few words from Roberto would sooth the situation.

"Where is Roberto going?" Rosa asked, entering the kitchen through the lobby door.

"Problem customer," Scarlet answered. "I have a bad feeling, Rosa."

Rosa grabbed an apple and left back to the lobby without concern.

"Sir, we are out of potatoes. We have a nice Spanish rice with——-"

"You have potatoes on the sign and I *want* potatoes." Buck craned his neck upward and stared at Roberto like a dog in a stand off.

"I'm sorry; we're all out of potatoes."

"If you don't have 'em then why'd you put 'em on your sign?" Buck maintained his stare as if it put power to his words.

How was about ready to leave. Everyone was now watching the disgruntled potato lover including Scarlet hidden behind the kitchen door.

"Sir, we have no potatoes. You'll have to go somewhere else for potatoes." Roberto felt the incident ridiculous and petty and he turned to head back to the kitchen. Shocking everyone, including How, Buck jumped from his seat and grabbed Roberto by the shirt. Scarlet scurried through the kitchen and yelled for Rosa. Just then, Jeff, a familiar drifter who had been lingering in the area waiting for a ride, entered the dining room. He had worked for Roberto several times, found him a decent and fair man, and decided that maybe he could work for a bed and meals for a week or so, rest up then continue on with his precarious journey.

"Hey man! Get your hands off him," Jeff's shout was more threatening than his hippie-style appearance.

The situation was escalating before How's eyes. Fear kicked in, fear of going back to prison and How was on his feet with gun in hand. Everyone, including Buck—who had no idea How possessed the gun—froze in place. Heads didn't move, only eyes ping-ponged from person to person. Scarlet had come through the kitchen door into the dining room, and like the others, she stood silent, frozen in place—but only for a minute then turned to run. Buck quickly let go of Roberto and caught Scarlet before she reached the kitchen door. Roberto immediately responded.

"Hold it!" How shouted, his gun pointed at Roberto. Roberto, Buck and Scarlet all stopped in their tracks. Buck gave How a quick glance and proceeded to hold on to Scarlet, pulling her up against him. The scenario was blatantly obvious to How—they screwed up and if he didn't come up with something quickly, and effective, he just lost his freedom.

Jeff took a step back, ready to bolt out the door and go for help. His attempt was stopped by the angry demands of How who ordered everyone to the center back of the restaurant, away from the front entrance and the hallway to the kitchen. How was angry and it added to the potency of his demands but he was only angry with Buck and the situation Buck got them into. He held no bad feelings towards anyone lined up before him; they just had the misfortune, as did he, of Buck's company.

Buck looked anxious. "Now what, How?"

How now felt like turning the gun on Buck for using his name aloud. If anyone was able to call the police, they now had his name. If he had left Buck behind initially, he'd be on his way and not in this predicament but he bought into Buck's pleas and now had major buyer's remorse.

Rosa peered through the archway from the front entrance.

"Get over with the others!" How shouted while wondering who else might be in the restaurant or lobby. He had Buck do a quick check. "Make it fast and get back in here."

"There's no one else here," Roberto informed.

There they all stood, lined up in front of the back tables and How wasn't sure what to do. His rage at Buck preoccupied him for the moment as everyone waited for his next move.

"We tie em up?" Buck looked at How for confirmation.

"I should have left you behind, you fuck up." He didn't want to hurt these people, he hated seeing their scared faces. This was Buck's fault. He'd rather see their fear on Buck's face. How pointed the gun at Buck. He pondered having them tie Buck up. How would move on and leave these people in peace. Leave the fox now defenseless to the chickens.

"Whattaya doin'?" Buck questioned, confused with a bit of fear on his face—which, of course, pleased How. Buck was tough only with backup. One option ran through How's mind: He could walk away—just back his way out of the restaurant and leave, head towards a destination unknown to Buck. Buck didn't have a gun. Let them call the police and put Buck back where he actually did belong. This plan of action became more appealing by the second. How smiled from the thought which seemed to confuse the highly dependent Buck even more.

"Well, How...what?" Buck had an on-hold expression.

How looked at each faultless person before him. They all stared back displaying more confidence than Buck. He had contempt for Buck, not these innocent bystanders. At that moment, to fire a shot in Buck's direction would be therapeutic. How decided to depart from the situation and leave Buck to face the music of his own demise. He stepped backwards under the archway to the lobby then rushed out the lobby doors, jumped into the truck, started it up and laughed. This was the happiest How had felt in years. His joy lasted but only a minute or two, literally. Another car was pulling into the parking lot. He turned off the engine and rushed back into the restaurant. Oddly, no one had moved much. They looked like a group of befuddled tourists. His gun up and once again aimed, How ordered everyone into the kitchen, including Buck.

The bells on the front door rang. They all remained quiet.

"Hellllllloooo?" said the voice of an older man. How wasn't confident to hand the gun over to Buck while he played hotel employee and informed the arrivals that the establishment was closed. Buck wasn't sensible and How didn't want anyone to get hurt.

"Buck, go out there and tell them the restaurant is closed," How ordered in a tight, low and very stern voice.

Surprisingly, no one but Scarlet looked as frightened as Buck and no one looked as though they were going to fight the current situation. They all stood side by side in the kitchen in a rather comfortable stance. How thought that maybe they believed this new arrival meant help.

"Give me the gun, How."

"Just go tell them the place is closed *and hurry the fuck up* and look like you own the place." How had little faith in Buck's abilities but had no choice at the moment. "And, lock the front door when they leave." While they waited for Buck's return How couldn't help himself, and he apologized for the incident. He requested their temporary cooperation then reassured them that no one was going to be hurt—it would all be over soon. There was no response other than a smile from Agnes, the woman who sat alone at the table, the woman Buck had yelled at earlier.

Buck entered the kitchen with a bewildered look on his face and the unexpected proclamation, "They want to eat."

"*No shit.* I told you to tell them the place is closed. You *fucking* moron!" How's frustration was mounting and his temper rising.

"The sign said open and they came in to eat," Buck repeated the obvious.

"You *fucking* moron!" How took a deep breath. These names didn't phase Buck in the least, as if they were familiar tags his whole life. It was clear that Buck couldn't handle the predicament. How didn't trust Buck holding the gun on their captives if he went to the lobby to try to remedy the situation himself. "Then go seat them. Take their order. Act normal, Buck. Just be calm and go seat them." How tried to control his anger, however, he was beginning to feel like a defeated man. It was apparent that any plan that included Buck was doomed to failure.

"*Me?*" Buck looked panicked.

"Yeah, *you*," and he added in a low voice, "You absolute dumb fuck."

How could think of no plan other than to get them fed and on their way. They were more than likely tourists; tourists would have no idea how the restaurant is normally run or who ran it. But, Buck just stood there shooting his eyes around those in the kitchen.

"I told you, *go seat them.*" How's steely and unyielding glare left no doubt in Buck's mind that he was serious. "*Now!*" he ordered, raising the volume and intensity of his command. "*And don't draw any attention by being an idiot!*"

Buck stood there looking at How like a just hired employee: uneasy, clueless and waiting for further instructions. How only stared back with his tempered rage visible to all. Buck hesitated but left to seat the hungry couple as ordered. He was back in no time, standing just inside the kitchen door looking more nervous than he had before the judge in court.

"Did you give them a menu?" Rosa surprised everyone by speaking up. "They're at the front counter."

Buck raced back out to retrieve menus for the customers and was immediately back through the kitchen door.

"*Go,*" insisted How.

"Go *what?*" Buck questioned.

"Go take their order."

"Fuck this, How. I'm not a waiter——"

How cut him off. "You're the fucking idiot that got us into this fucked up predicament." How stared directly into Buck's eyes and stated his regret with clenched teeth, "*I should have left you.*" How stretched his neck and rustle his shoulders to try to help calm himself then took a large audible breath and continued. "I'm *pissed,* Buck; too pissed to play around with this shit. You *fucked it up* with your little tirade over potatoes, now you gotta play this out so we can get out of here. We need some lead time. Just take their order, don't draw attention to anything. *Just do it.*"

Nobody moved.

"Okay, okay. Chill." Buck appeared to give in, but added, "Shouldn't one of these women do it?" It was his last attempt.

"No."

"Okay," he said nervously. "Where's one of the order things; I need somethin' anna pen."

Scarlet handed him an order pad and pen from her apron pocket.

"What do I tell them?" Buck asked, reluctant to leave the kitchen. Under other circumstances, How would have been amused by the rattled "tough guy" before him.

"Ask them," corrected Scarlet. "Ask them what they would like for dinner. Everything's on the menu. It won't be difficult."

As Buck left the kitchen How added with clenched teeth, "And remember Buck, we're out of *fucking potatoes*." Agnes responded with a low snicker which surprised How due the present state of affairs.

"If you want to sit down, any of you, go ahead," How offered. There were several chairs close to the group. Rosa sat down first; Bernard and Katherine followed.

Buck indeed was not a waiter. He lacked good judgment even at this crucial juncture and without a smile or a degree of hospitality, Buck abruptly asked the elderly couple, "Whata ya wanna eat?" Perhaps the happy tourists thought Buck's crude manner was the way of the local culture and they responded to him politely as if he were a normal happy-faced and accommodating waiter.

Buck gave the order to the waiting Roberto who then confused matters for Buck by asking if the couple wanted salads.

"I don't know."

"Go ask them," demanded How. "*Smile*. Be a waiter. Don't let on to anything, Buck."

Roberto began pulling items for the couple's order from one of the refrigerators, going about his job as if nothing were out of the norm. This again confused How, though he was relieved that he was not, so far, meeting resistance.

Buck was back. "One wants a salad and, ah, the other one wants French fries." Buck looked down at his order pad. "Coffee, they both want coffee." He thought for a second then remembered, "You don't have any fries, no *fucking potatoes*. Or *you better not*."

"We don't have fries," Roberto answered without looking up.

"They're old, they don't eat fries," Buck protested. "Just give em both salads."

"I'm old and I eat French fries," Agnes quietly contributed.

How smiled. He liked Agnes right off. He wasn't sure who she reminded him of but from first eye contact she rubbed him the right way.

"What kind of dressing do they want?" Scarlet asked.

"*Fuck!*" and Buck snatched back the pad and pen he had just gladly tossed down. Evidently, he didn't believe that he could remember their dressing choice and he needed to write it down. When Buck returned How immediately instructed him to go back to the front door, lock it and make sure that the closed sign was up.

Scarlet got up from her chair to prepare the two salads. She was the only one in the kitchen who appeared frightened; everyone else seemed to be taking the unfortunate incident in stride. Noticing Scarlet's apprehensive disposition, Agnes offered to make the salads. "Just tell me where everything is." She had been a guest for a while and knew which ingredients went into the salads; she just didn't know where they were located in the kitchen. She could have taken an obvious guess, but she felt it better to ask. Scarlet pointed to one of the refrigerators and then sat back down in the chair at the table next to her mother-in-law, Rosa. Agnes was ready to go to work—eager to make the salads, eager to help out in any way. Agnes was just eager to feel useful or needed once again and she wasn't particular in what means or manner she achieved that status.

"You go out there and serve it," Buck instructed Scarlet. How was quick to correct him.

"*You're* serving, *not* anyone else." How was adamant. Buck once again donned a look of panic. And again, a very amusing sight for How—if not for the dire circumstances. How wasn't comfortable having Scarlet out of his sight. She was the only one displaying fear and was an obvious risk. She might slip up or intentionally inform the guests of the situation, making matters dangerous for everyone concerned.

"*I'm not a fucking waiter,*" Buck announced at an almost squeaky volume. Committing crimes seem to be easy for Buck but waiting tables, *that* was too much for him to handle. He was as nervous as if he were presenting to a critical crowd instead of two friendly seniors sitting at a table only wanting to eat.

"*You* finish serving, Buck. Take their money...*when they're done...you* escort them out the door. *And make sure you lock the door behind them.*"

Agnes put ranch dressing on the salads and promptly handed them to Buck for delivery, adding, "Do they have their silverware?"

"Here." Scarlet handed him two sets of silverware wrapped in napkins.

"Do they have water? What are they drinking?" added Agnes.

"*I told you, coffee.*" Buck sounded and looked as though he was about to come unglued. The kitchen was quiet.

"Cream? Sugar?" Agnes questioned.

"It's on the table already." Rosa settled that issue.

"Hurry up. Go on. Go serve 'em—food, coffee, whatever." How spoke to Buck as if he was reprimanding a child and Buck's criminal ambiance was waning fast in front of his captives. He left the kitchen with his hands full and was soon back.

"Okay, they need water and the coffee."

How kept the facial expression and stance of one who was tough and in control, more for the benefit of Buck than the passive kitchen prisoners. Buck vacillated from aggressive tough-guy to bewildered child. He was unstable in all ways a human could be unstable. For the moment, as Buck played waiter, he was the bewildered child, which was the easiest to deal with. How had thought about going out the back door, leaving Buck, leaving him to clean up his own mess. But How honestly feared for the safety of the innocents who were willingly helping him at this point, though not fully understanding why they were calmly cooperating, How appreciated that they were. With the exception of Scarlet, staff and guests alike were basically behaving as if they were on How's team. It was Buck and Scarlet who were nervous for wholly different reasons—Scarlet's distress was understandable, Buck's was puerile—he was afraid of waiting tables. The others were getting on with business, preparing the couple's order in true restaurateur fashion.

If How's impromptu plan somehow failed, which didn't seem likely since it only entailed getting two people fed and on their way, he would have to make his escape and let the fate of the others take its course. He got this far and fully intended on going all the way. How could not survive even a short stint back in prison so he would do what he needed to do.

Chapter 2
Buck Failed...

Buck failed to lock the front door and to turn the sign as he was so menacingly instructed. As so often happens, one or two vehicles in a parking lot inspire others to join. The bell on the front door clanged again as the next hungry travelers entered. Buck looked at the new diners as if they were the police with handcuffs extended. He turned with the coffee pot in hand and made haste back to the kitchen.

"*Fuck,* How, more people. We need to get the hell outta here. *We gotta move!*"

All in the kitchen heard the bell.

"Buck, listen to me, *you gotta calm down*...take their orders," How said with an affected tone of a serene man without a worry.

Buck wasn't having it. It was time to run.

Calmly, How made show of his gun again and Buck was relieved—How finally came to his senses: with everyone tied up tight, they could be long gone before anyone could contact the authorities. Buck was eager for the escape—until How pointed the gun at him.

"*What the fuck ya doin' now, How?*" Buck muffled his yell of confusion.

It seemed sensible to How for them to just continue as they were, particularly since the others were compliant. "You take their order, just like with the first table."

"I'm outta here, this is fucking stupid, How," Buck complained as he threw the pad and pen against the counter.

How pulled the keys to the truck from his pocket. With the keys in one hand and the gun in the other he aimed his words at Buck, "I'd just as soon put a bullet through your fucking stupid head...dump you out back at this point. You didn't lock the fucking door. You didn't put the closed sign up. This is your fault, again Buck, and you're going to make it right by waiting on the next table." He was stuck, in a situation tagged by Buck's stupidity. Like with the first table, if they could just get them fed and gone with the cooperation of the staff and guests, How and Buck could soon be on their way.

How maintained a calm confident composure which may have been why the others, except for Buck and Scarlet, seemed undaunted by the additional customers.

The bell clanged again.

"They'll be customers all night if you don't lock that door," added Rosa.

"Go back out there and seat the people," How insisted with his gun still raised. Buck reluctantly complied.

Out of view, Agnes smiled then asked, "Is he *a friend* of yours?" sounding like a grandmother about to scold How for his poor choice in friends.

"What is your name?" How asked her.

"Agnes, and yours?" she responded politely.

"Well, Agnes, he's not my friend—just an unfortunate burden. You're welcome to him."

"*Oh,* no *thank you,*" Agnes snapped back, which caused How to crack a smile.

He then turned to face everyone in the kitchen. "Help get these people served. Get them fed and safely out of here. No one is going to get hurt if you just go along until these people are out of here and then we're gone. No one gets hurt." How waited for a response but no one said a thing. "Just go along with me." He hesitated for a few seconds then added, "I apologize. Everything will be fine with your cooperation. I appreciate it." He exchanged looks with each person. Still no one spoke. How found the situation quite strange, not for the present scenario of two escaped convicts taking over the restaurant, holding people captive at gun point, but for the relatively docile and cooperative demeanor of his prisoners. Yet, How didn't have time for the brain-teaser; How had to be in the moment to make sure that he safely got out of there and to try his best that no one got hurt, particularly with Buck in his charge.

They also thought of Buck as a dimwitted danger and therefore truly depended upon How to keep him in control and them safe.

Roberto spoke up, "We can go along, just don't pull anything on us— and try to keep your…" he hesitated, "*friend* under control."

Buck entered the kitchen before How could respond to Roberto and in a singsong voice Buck announced, "Well, they want some of those potatoes on your menu. It's on your fucking sign, 'rosemary potatoes.' Pisses me off, man, and I bet they're gunna to be pissed off too." Buck picked the pen and order pad up off the floor.

The bell clanged once more.

"You didn't put the closed sign up, did you? You didn't lock the door." How knew he had to get rid of Buck when this was all over. He needed to lose him somewhere, somehow.

"Fuck. Sorry." Buck was rocking from foot to foot looking not just nervous but antsy which was making everyone in the kitchen on edge.

Rosa spoke her words of wisdom. "Probably better that he didn't. That would draw attention to any local. They'd be calling me or the sheriff to see what was wrong."

"She's right," added Roberto.

How was now worried about locals coming in. Buck's presence and demeanor would no doubt alarm any local who might stop by.

"Agnes, can you wait tables?"

"Yes, I can wait tables; I can wait on all of the tables," she answered with enthusiasm.

How knew that this wasn't going to be over quickly.

"Can you all get me through the next few hours and I'll," he corrected himself, "we'll be gone. I don't want to hurt anyone. Just help me out here."

No one was paying attention to How's gun at this point. Buck seemed the bigger threat as he bounced back and forth. The clang of the bell and the sound of customers seemed to wind Buck up and he looked as though he was about to spring.

Everyone verbally agreed to pitch in, with Agnes acting as if it were the opening night of her own restaurant—everyone but Rosa. (As far as Rosa was concerned the two intruders could have the place. It was her business and her home since childhood, but ever since her husband, Roberto Sr., died and her son and daughter-in-law took over, she felt akin to an old house cat—there just because she'd always been there, a living fixture at the Alviso. The business had lost its luster and appeal for Rosa. Her hopes and dreams for a future faded years ago and she felt as though she merely existed; living was something she did in her past.) Rosa sat at the table resting her chin in her palm saying nothing.

Buck was confined to the kitchen, glad to be relieved of waiter duty yet ridiculously preoccupied with getting his tip from the first table.

How kept a close eye on everyone and things were moving along smoothly with Agnes happily taking orders and chatting-it-up with customers; she was in her element.

"The plates are hot," Roberto warned as Agnes whisked the plates away in a hurry to fill her orders.

The clang of the front door bell was heard again.

"You always this busy?" How directed his question to Rosa.

"No," she answered with an indifferent tone. That's all she said, no explanation—just a plain no.

Enough time had passed, in How's opinion, that he felt the closed sign could go up without creating suspicion with the locals and the process of clearing the restaurant out could begin.

How asked Rosa if he could trust her to put the closed sign up so they could get this over with. She agreed in silence. Without a word, Rosa got up from her chair and methodically left the kitchen to flip the sign over. How stepped to the side of the door to monitor the apathetic older woman. She flipped the sign around to read closed, stopped at the desk to grab a mint from the basket then continued at her leisurely pace back to the kitchen, right past How, to sit in the same chair at the table.

"What's for dessert?" Agnes asked.

"Flan," answered Scarlet. "Just tell them that all we have is flan and we are about out of that."

Clang went the bell. Rosa looked up at How, "I turned the sign but I can't lock the door; the customers have to leave."

Just then Agnes rushed into the kitchen to gleefully inform the crew, "We're getting busy, really busy." Oddly, she thought the news would delight Rosa and Roberto. Agnes exclaimed, "I think it's because it's snowing outside."

"How, it's snowing; we gotta get the fuck outta here." Buck panicked.

"That's why we're busy," explained Rosa.

"And it's going to get busier," Scarlet added.

"Why?" How looked out the door to the lobby where he could see through the front window. Indeed it was snowing and yes, the parking lot was scattered with vehicles. Buck peered over his shoulder to look into the lobby as well, straining to see through the front window.

"Because there is nowhere else for them to go or stay if the roads get bad," answered Roberto. He knew that, closed sign or not, travelers would be stopping for either a meal, a room or safe harbor in the parking lot.

"Look at all those cars, How. A fucking RV just pulled up!" Buck cried out as though announcing that the place was on fire. *"We gotta get goin', How. We gotta get outta here NOW! Come on. Let's book. Now, How. We gotta go now. Come on, How."*

"Ya know, ya wouldn't draw much attention if ya left now," the drifter expressed his observation.

"Go see how bad the snow is." How needed to think without Buck staring at him like a child needing to use the bathroom.

"We always open up in a snow storm," Roberto informed. "And, the sheriff will be checking the roads for stranded travelers if it really starts coming down and they'll get towed or brought here." For all its years Alviso, Rancho Alviso to be exact, has been known to accommodate wayward travelers particularly in the fast and heavy snowstorms common to the high elevations of New Mexico. "You close the doors and that will certainly draw the attention of any locals and, sorry to tell ya, the sheriff."

"More people are pulling into the parking lot, Roberto. It's snowing hard; it's really coming down," Agnes trumpeted with glee; she could not have been more pleased. Agnes could keep her job for at least a few more hours. This was wholly exciting and she was an active part of it. Foremost, Agnes was needed and Agnes was a part of something and Agnes would not spend her evening alone.

How realized that his control over the situation was weakening, if not already void. The truck wasn't a four-wheel drive so it was useless in heavy snow. How pulled his gun back out, just to have it in view and to temporarily exert what power he may have left in the situation. He had no desire to use it on anyone, except maybe Buck. He needed to keep the ambiance of control though panic was seeping into his calm demeanor. He didn't want to hurt anyone. He didn't want to fire his gun at anyone but he wasn't going to go back to prison if he could help it in any way. How figured he could exit out the back, get to his truck and before the snow got too deep make his getaway. In a somewhat nonchalant manner, How stepped to the back kitchen door, placed his hand on the door knob.

"Don't leave the other one here." Katherine surprised How. She spoke so quietly but How heard her as if she had shouted. Her face was gentle and kind and much to How's remorse, displaying fear. To see the fear on her face was disturbing: he was responsible for that fear. The others turned their attention to How and Katherine.

"Aye!" A new voice was heard at the kitchen door to the lobby.

"Sheriff Shelton," said Roberto loudly. How's gun quickly fell to his side then into the back waistband of his pants"

"Busy night: the snow is really falling, that cash register's going to be a *ringing*, Roberto. Ching cha ching cha ching!" Sheriff Shelton joked. The rather odd scene of several people sitting around the kitchen didn't seem to catch the sheriff's attention as out of place. "Hey, Jeff," the sheriff continued, "guess I won't find *you* on the road tonight."

Jeff shook his head and answered, "No, I'll be helping Roberto and Scarlet out tonight."

"Good. You could use a job." He laughed in a way that might offend most but not Jeff. They had a mutual understanding: Sheriff Shelton was very familiar with Jeff as a harmless soul who drifted in and out of the area—likable though scraggly and sometimes an eyesore. Jeff was familiar with Sheriff Shelton as the man with the local authority whose stature and position allowed him to be a bully but he chose not to.

"Well, hope you make a fortune tonight." The sheriff lifted his hand in a wave and left back out the door.

All eyes were on How. He wondered if they were protecting the sheriff with their silence or him. Either way, his heart was beating like a chased jackrabbit.

"Okay, we have two orders of chicken enchiladas. Two of the cactus salads; they want to give it a try," she said eager and enthusiastic. "Oh, and two coffees—cream and sugar. And, the cream and sugar are on the table," she remembered aloud. Agnes gave the order like an old pro. No one moved; they waited for a response from How.

"Better feed the customers." Those words were like a starting gun and as How leaned against the wall, taking deep breaths still with the overwhelming feeling to run out the door and take his chances in the snow, the kitchen went to work.

Buck charged through the lobby door. He was in another panic. "How, the snow is comin' down an' there are all kinds of people in the parking lot. *I think I saw a fucking cop, How.*"

"How," Agnes interrupted as though Buck and his newest panic were irrelevant. How turned to look at Agnes. "We need another waitress, or waiter."

A brief silence followed.

"I ain't waiting those tables, How. There's a fucking cop out there," Buck insisted in a frenzied grumble.

"I can help with the tables," Katherine offered.

"I can wait the tables." Scarlet got up from her chair.

"I think I can do tables better than preparing food," Katherine pointed out to scarlet. "Let me wait the tables. I think it will go a lot smoother that way, don't you?" Katherine quietly yet convincingly questioned.

Scarlet agreed.

Everyone but Rosa was up and either helping or ready to help. Bernard's manner was just as modest as his wife's, Katherine. He went about helping by making the drinks looking like a volunteer at a Kiwanis Club event. Scarlet made the salads, repeatedly looking up at How as she worked. Roberto did the cooking, with assistance from Jeff, as though How and his gun weren't there. Katherine and Agnes waited tables as though it had been their regular and longtime job.

It was How and Buck who were nursing fear—How's fear covert and Buck's on full display—his transparency had How again worried that Buck might blow what was at the moment a working situation.

How sat down at the table next to Rosa who seemed very unaffected by any of the happenings in the kitchen or elsewhere in the establishment. In fact, Rosa looked bored but Rosa typically looked bored because, on the most part, Rosa was bored. She often thought about her funeral. She thought about the last gathering and whom she wanted to be there and who likely would *indeed be there.* She decorated the chapel in her mind with white roses, envisioned her everlasting outfit and wondered where she would purchase it. She was tired of the restaurant; tired of the hotel; tired of her mild-mannered daughter-in-law who chose to give her no grandchildren. She saw her son going down the same path as she. He had lost his luster, in her opinion. He used to snowmobile and go to car shows. He helped a friend build a magnificent boat and they once had lofty plans for that boat. He bragged of plans to build a spacious cabin for scarlet and himself. When his father died, Roberto believed it was his responsibility to take up residence at Alviso and help run the business. He wanted to relieve his mother of the burden particularly during her grieving period, but the grieving period never seemed to end as she felt the loss of her beloved husband daily. Scarlet had no objection to moving to Alviso and seemed unaffected by the change, however, as time went on Roberto lost that adventurous spark his mother had admired and so reminded her of his father.

It was Roberto Sr.'s idea to turn Alviso into a business, which started out more like a small bed and breakfast long before the concept became so very popular and Rancho Alviso was a unique operation. Roberto Sr.'s love of people, his upbeat personality and cheerful vitality made Alviso a success. His enthusiasm was contagious and Rosa supported his efforts, always. If Roberto was happy then Rosa was happy. He eventually expanded both the hotel and the restaurant. Alviso was buzzing with life and Roberto's dreams. He was filled with surprises and new ideas. Roberto always had a plan for the future though dying wasn't one of them. After his passing, everything ran the same, thanks to Roberto Jr., but Alviso was not the same.

Rosa wasn't as gregarious as Roberto Sr. and the people—travelers and tourists—didn't hold her interest as they did Roberto Sr. Where Roberto loved listening to their stories, their chatter just bored Rosa and she did her best not to roll her eyes and walk away mid-story. She learned to stare at the bridge of the gabber's nose so as to appear that she was paying attention while her thoughts roamed elsewhere. She could listen to people talk about their RVs, the weather, where they had been or where they were going and the road conditions for about five minutes—and even that was pushing it. Alviso wasn't anywhere near the same since Roberto left her.

Everything was running smoothly. Agnes and Katherine were making well-deserved tips, which added to their enthusiasm for their unexpected occupation. Buck would periodically man the front door, nervously checking the people status. He'd be gone for a few minutes then be back in the kitchen where he was not wanted. He stayed on an even neurotic balance until someone wanted a room. Buck was rushing through the door again in a fury of panic.

"I'll take care of it," Rosa responded in a voice one had to strain to hear. She calmly rose to remedy the new dilemma. As she passed How, he stopped her.

"Look, everything is running smoothly. Don't do anything to mess this up and we'll be out of here. I promise." How tried to sound stern, sincere and maybe a bit threatening. It had no affect on Rosa; she didn't fear How. She merely looked up at him and with a bit of annoyance detected in her voice said, "Don't worry" then continued at an unhurried pace to take care of business. How somehow trusted Rosa, though it didn't make a lot of sense to trust someone you were holding prisoner, yet, at this point he had to trust her—he had to trust them all; there wasn't much choice. How had more faith in their ability to pull off this impromptu scam than he did in Buck's ability to successfully do much of anything. Regardless, How still needed to keep a vigilant eye on everyone, including Rosa, and kept a path clear to the back door just in case. Scarlet worried How and he watched her closer than the others. Likewise, Scarlet kept her focus on How since he was the one giving the orders and the one with the gun. Scarlet feared How's gun, any gun for that matter, including Roberto's. Buck truly frightened her but under the authority of How she believed no one would get hurt. It didn't take a genius to figure out that the two were running from the law and therefore desperate, however, Scarlet witnessed how it all got started and therefore believed that How was doing what he felt he had to do under the circumstances. She anticipated they would be gone by sunrise and all she needed to do was follow along until then.

The storm deposited numerous patrons at the Alviso and both the restaurant and hotel were full. It didn't take many to fill Alviso and it was now beyond capacity with people waiting for a table and kind patrons sharing tables with strangers, who wouldn't be strangers for long. The parking lot provided a place for campers and RVs to set up for the night. The place was buzzing with activity with people socializing both inside and outside. Rosa sold several post cards that had been in the rack so long that most were faded, though she didn't think the customers could tell. She sold out of the Mexican blankets that had been stacked in the large adobe nicho behind the counter and asked Roberto to go to the cellar to get more. How watched as Roberto pulled up on an iron latch, lifting a heavy panel of the wooden floor that opened to the cellar. The cellar door camouflaged so well that How had stood on it earlier without detection. Roberto climbed down an aged lodge pole ladder, flipped the light switch to on (which allowed How to get a good look at the cellar) and retrieved an armful of Mexican blankets caked with dust. The panel door disappeared into the floor once closed.

Rosa gave Roberto a smile of delight as he placed the blankets on the bench behind the counter, the type of smile that he hadn't seen in a very long time. She was pleased with the sales and found a certain thrill in selling items that had been hanging around the Alviso for so long. Rosa discreetly shook the dust off the blankets then neatly placed the folded blankets into the large nicho as they had been displayed earlier.

"I have over fifty dollars in tips," beamed Agnes. She pulled a wad of bills from her apron. With hopes of an encore she cheerfully asked, "They'll be here in the morning for breakfast too, don't you think?"

Roberto hadn't given the prospect much thought. He too believed that come sunrise the dastardly duo would be on their way. He turned to How. "She's right. They'll be here tomorrow for breakfast too." Fully aware that the influx of people would more than likely be at the Alviso beyond breakfast, Roberto knew that their predicament would be extended—with no apparent extended plan in sight.

There were no government-sponsored snowplows to clear the roads in that small mountain town. Sometimes a local would generously plow if they were in the mood but locals counted on their four-wheel drive vehicles or just waited for those who dared to brave the road to eventually clear a path. Roberto discovered from past such scenarios that travelers gathered together enjoyed the camaraderie and were in no hurry to risk the roads to be on their way. They would patiently wait for the sunshine to melt a path, or for some other means to open the road for them while they socialized and enjoyed their time away from home in a new environment among fellow travelers.

"If the roads aren't cleared, they'll be here another day or so," Roberto added. He wasn't sure how this new information would impact his captor. How stared up at the ceiling, took deep breaths and nervously tapped his foot. He couldn't risk getting stuck or drawing attention by being one of the few, if not the only, vehicle on the road.

Even with the overload of adrenaline, How was getting sleepy. Buck wasn't. He was hyper, per usual, and unpredictable. How needed to stay alert; he couldn't leave Buck in charge. He asked Bernard for a cup of coffee and tried his best to come up with some kind of plan as he watched those in the kitchen diligently keeping things going—chopping, pouring, mixing and cooking.

"We need another pot of coffee made," Katherine shouted to Bernard as she passed by. Agnes stuck her head through the opened door and repeated the request for more coffee. She stopped a few seconds to observe Buck who stood rocking from foot to foot, staring at How. He made her anxious.

Buck wanted to know How's plan to get them out of there. How responded with a stare that was overflowing with contempt and Buck took it as a cue to back off; he pulled a chair from the table and sat down.

"Go help out front," How ordered with a steady stare.

"Why?" Buck snapped back. "The old lady's doin' it" and he continued to stare at How, waiting for a response. How said nothing. He was preoccupied, struggling for a plan. He had to get further than this place. He wasn't going back to prison, not this soon.

The night continued to be busy, busier than Rosa had recalled in a very long time. It stirred something in her, she wasn't sure what, but whatever it was she was enjoying it; she was even enjoying chatting with the customers. They seemed sincerely interested in what she had to say and their stories spiked interest instead of annoyance. She thought of how Roberto Sr. would have loved this busy night and how pleased he would have been with her for socializing like she was. He certainly would have been delighted by the sales. She now knew what stirred in her: it was Roberto Sr. She expected him to be rounding the corner any minute with a huge satisfied smile on his face eager to accommodate the next customer.

How was having a hard time staying awake. He slumped down onto one of the kitchen chairs next to Buck who was fidgeting and acting jumpy which in turn was making the others in the kitchen uneasy. Attention was diverted to Rosa as she entered the kitchen, looking more energetic than hours earlier. Rosa announced that she was going to lock the front door: the restaurant was emptying out; the rooms were full; it was time to close. "It's going to be busy tomorrow and everyone needs their rest." With this said, she turned and left the kitchen.

Rosa courteously waited for the last customer to leave. She locked the front door, making sure that the sign read Closed with the No Vacancy sign alongside it then sauntered off to go to bed for the night. How assumed that she had left to close up and would return, but Rosa never return.

Roberto began cleaning up. Bernard and Jeff looked at the stack of dishes with no desire to wash a single one; the night's activities had finally gotten to them and they were tired. Agnes and Katherine cleared all the tables then blissfully counted their tips.

"*Hey,*" Buck intruded with a shout. "*The tip* off that first table *is mine.*"

How was delighted to see that both Agnes and Katherine only paused but a few seconds to acknowledge Buck's demand then ignore Buck altogether. They continued to add up their tips with no indication that they were willing to share their booty with the woefully inadequate convict waiter.

All but Rosa were now gathered in the kitchen. How got up to check the lobby, then checked the restaurant. No Rosa.

"She went to bed," Roberto confidently informed How. "Don't worry. She went to get some sleep, nothing else. If she were going to turn you in she would have done it long ago." Roberto knew his mother well. She had become predictable. She rarely, if ever, surprised Roberto anymore. He pretty much knew what she would say or do in any given situation.

Now what? How couldn't stop thinking, *Now what?*

Buck wanted to escape. He believed everyone outside the hotel would soon be asleep.

"Come on, How. We got the gun; we can blaze our way outta here! Why we sittin' here?"

The two-wheel drive truck wouldn't make it safely through the parked campers and RVs in the parking lot much less down the steep and winding snow packed road. Buck lived in a criminal fantasy world and How couldn't give him or his ramblings any kind of serious consideration. How was on his own to come up with their next step, and hated it.

While Roberto prepped for the breakfast rush to come, the others finished up the cleaning. How couldn't keep everybody awake until the next day. He didn't belief he could keep himself awake until morning. *What now? What now? What now?* ran through his head like a mantra. He had no answer, no plan. So far it had been a spur-of-the-moment ordeal. He could think of nothing to do to securely rescue himself out of this situation. Unlike Buck, a scenario even close to this one had never been entertained in his life plan. He never fathomed ever being in prison. An escaped convict was another unimaginable life development. Living the life of an outlaw was a new and undesired experience. He had to wing it as he went. Learn on the road.

How walked across the kitchen, opened the back door then stepped outside into the cold and quiet of the snow filled night. He leaned against the wall with his gun held loosely in his tired hand, feeling defeated and watching the snow fall delicately onto his shoes. *How did my life end up like this?* Fair or not, he knew the answer.

How dared to walk a few yards into the darkness leaving those in the kitchen out of his view and control. He brushed the snow from a boulder then sat down letting the cool flakes settle on and around him. His thoughts went to Ronnie. He wasn't sorry as he remembered the gratitude and peace last shown in Ronnie's eyes. His half-cocked smile remembered as if it were yesterday. Ronnie was trapped, but was able to find an escape—with the help of How. Now, How was trapped. Although an entirely different situation, How felt Ronnie's escape route preferable to prison. He took a long deep breath of the night's cold air, filling his lungs, savoring the sensation and feeling relieved at that moment to be alone.

"Can I help?" asked a sympathetic and gentle voice.

How stood up. He couldn't help but give her his smile. He started back towards the open door framing Agnes's motherly stance.

"I'm sorry for all of this, Agnes," he said as one would to a friend.

"I know; don't worry, son." She waited for him to reach the door then added in a whisper, "I think your friend is asleep at the table. He scares us, How. Do you mind me calling you How?"

How strange this all was to How and now his captives were calling him by his first name. "You can call me anything you like—you deserve it," he answered.

"If you leave, will we be safe with him here, How?"

How stepped inside the kitchen. Buck was slumped onto the table. Those in the kitchen could easily overtake him, yet they didn't. How turned to Agnes and muttered, "I could shoot him?"

"Yes you could," Agnes responded with a smile.

How walked to the center of the kitchen. Agnes followed behind. The kitchen work was done and everything was quiet. How could read inside the virtual bubbles above everyone's head: "Sleep." How pondered tying Buck up, leaving him behind and to the care of the sheriff. He tried to remember just what he had told Buck about where he intended to go or who he intended to contact for help. He couldn't remember. But could How trust those standing sleepy before him. Would they allow him the time to maneuver the truck through the snow and be on his way? They hadn't given him any reason so far not to trust them, quite the contrary. But if his truck became stuck in the snow, he was doomed. There was nowhere for him to go but back to Rancho Alviso and by then it might be too late.

"I'll sleep in the restaurant," Jeff announced, looking at How for confirmation.

"We all need to sleep," Roberto commented, also with his eyes fixed on How.

How needed more time to figure out his plan. He felt anxious and guilty—worried and relieved that he made it this far without anyone getting hurt or him getting caught. His captives had kept him from certain return to incarceration so far; surely he could trust them. Yet, if one decided that they had enough and had the clear opportunity to not return to another stint in the kitchen, supervised by a gun-wielding escaped convict, then he'd be back in prison for what would be, more than likely, the remainder of his life.

"Okay, this is what we're going to do." This was the only plan he could come up with. "The men are going to sleep in the cellar. The women can go to their beds. I don't want to hurt anybody, but if you push me you give me no choice. Don't push me. Go along with me for a while longer. Look, I'm sorry about all this, ya know, but I don't have a choice at the moment." How looked at each woman and each nodded their head in agreement, even Scarlet, though How was still apprehensive about Scarlet.

"Well, we don't want a blood bath, How. We'll do as you say," Agnes said, sounding quite sincere. How knew, of all those he held his prisoner, Agnes certainly did not believe he would provoke nor be capable of a "blood bath." He gave her a steady questioning stare but Agnes looked away.

"Can I get blankets and pillows for the men?" Scarlet asked.

How hadn't thought about that aspect of sleeping.

"Agnes can get the blankets and pillows," How responded, then, Buck woke up.

"We takin' off?" he asked How as he quickly rose to his feet.

"You're sleeping in the cellar with the other men," How answered.

"Why the fuck r' we stayin' the night here, How? Let's get the fuck outta here. All those people'll be sleepin'."

How pondered Buck's idea; it wasn't such a bad idea: leave while everyone slept. It gave him pause; but not visibly since if he were to decide to do so, he did not want the others to know and he wasn't taking Buck.

"Do you have a four-wheel drive?" asked Roberto and How shook his head no. "I need to get the cash out of the register and close up," Roberto added, hoping that he had made his point by reminding How of the more than likely impassable road conditions. Roberto was deeply concerned about a possible confrontation. If there was one, he didn't want Sheriff Shelton to get hurt. He had no doubt Buck would do damage to the sheriff and he worried that under hopeless circumstances, How might be compelled to do harm to enable his escape.

Buck's eyes popped open. He wanted the cash from the register. "We'll be taking the register," Buck said to Roberto though his focus was still steady on How.

"You're not touching the register," How was quick to respond.

"I don't want the fuckin' register, I want what's in it," Buck enlightened.

How instructed Katherine to turn out the front lights, make sure that the entrance door was locked and to bring the money from the register to the kitchen. She left without hesitation to do as instructed though she was back in the doorway a minute later. She didn't know how to open the register. Her question interrupted the tension building in the kitchen due to Buck's sense of entitlement to the Alviso's cash. Roberto explained how to open the register to Katherine while How pondered why Roberto would bring their attention to the cash in the register. If Roberto believed that the money would expedite their journey out of there then why warn him about the grim road conditions. This puzzle made How more attentive and more focused on Roberto.

The kitchen was silent again until Roberto expressed his need to use the bathroom—another particular How hadn't put into the equation: everyone would need to use the bathroom, including himself.

"Okay, go." He glanced at everyone as they stood next to Roberto by the grill. "When Roberto is done then anyone else who needs to, go use the bathroom. One at a time." No one said anything. As How looked at his line of victims by the grill, he considered that maybe it was time for him to take off, take the tease of cash from the register and flee. Risk the roads. Just get out of there. He was going to force Bernard, a man in his later years, to sleep in the dusty cellar. He was holding a gun, telling adults that they could use the bathroom one at a time: necessary under the circumstances, yet genuinely shameful. His shame was dancing with fatigue, and anger. Though he did not start this boondoggle or want any part of it, he quickly became the overlord of this fiasco...and it was becoming more and more unbearable. How feared that this was just the beginning of his victimization of others. He had made victims of people that even within the very short and frantic time he actually liked. They were his first victims but would they be the last—particularly running with Buck. Only Agnes found this whole fiasco a high point in her existence and was enjoying her new gun-appointed job as a waitress.

How watched with shame as Bernard walked back from the bathroom to sit on a chair in the kitchen. Bernard noticed his watchful eyes and nodded to How donning a grin. How felt miserable but Bernard didn't seem to. Again, How was, for that moment, loathing himself. Katherine entered the kitchen with the money from the register in a paper bag.

"Here's the money, How," she said.

"Give it to Roberto."

"*No!*" Buck shouted then jumped up to grab the bag.

How pulled his gun into view. "*Don't you dare.*" He was not going to let Buck take his desire for the money any further. He turned toward Katherine. "Go ahead, give the money to Roberto."

"How, man, *whatta ya fuckin' doin'? You crazy? We need that money, man.*"

Buck looked as if he were going to jump Katherine as she passed by to give the bag of money to Roberto. How stepped a few feet closer to Buck, lifted his gun to point directly at Buck's head. He instructed Roberto to open the cellar door and in a voice and manner that startled everyone in the kitchen, How ordered Buck into the cellar. At first Buck didn't budge, he just stared at How, not unlike a resistant child being told to go to his room. How then loudly explained to Buck, for all to hear, how his journey would be made a lot easier without him around—that making him disappear would be easy—no one would know nor miss him. He then convincingly direct-ed Buck to the cellar door. Buck obeyed with only minor verbal resistance. There was a hushed relief in the kitchen once Buck was in the cellar with the cellar door shut and latched.

Roberto stood by the bag of cash on the cutting board. Nothing was said. How himself didn't know what to say, or what to do. He was in charge and a lot was at stake—not at least his own life and freedom—and he didn't know what to do. Agnes was somewhere retrieving blankets and pillows which brought to mind the need for a change in sleeping arrangements, and a reminder of his personal need for sleep.

"Is there any way that he could get out of that cellar?" How asked.

Roberto calmly answered, "I could put the table on the door, but it's not really necessary. He could dig out, but that would take at least two weeks." Roberto gave a slight grin. He was convinced that How didn't want anyone getting hurt and locking Buck in the cellar was further proof for Roberto.

The kitchen was silent and everyone was motionless—a freeze-frame of a nightmare that How would give most anything to wake up from. It was so much like the feeling that overwhelmed How when first in prison—stag-gered in an unexpected and strange world where his next step was a mystery. It took time for the reality to sink in, even with every inch of his environ-ment validating his new reality, How functioned in a bad-dream state for some time.

Agnes was taking longer than he anticipated. How decided to move closer to the kitchen back door not far from where Jeff sat slumped on the floor against the wall, sound asleep. Bernard was also asleep—tucked at the waist at the table with his head resting on his hand. Katherine sat across from him—next to Scarlet—thumbing through a magazine. How watched with remorse as he waited for Agnes to return.

Agnes entered through the door from the lobby. "This is all that I could find; but, there are those Mexican blankets by the front desk." She looked over at Roberto to confirm that it was okay to use them. Roberto nodded permission. Agnes noticed Jeff asleep on the floor and immediately aided his comfort with a pillow and a blanket. She looked at How, waiting for instructions. He had none, and Agnes could see that How was in as much need of rest as the others. As though the reins had been handed to her, Agnes excused herself to those still awake then asked How to step outside with her, "Please."

He did.

"Listen, How," she started, sounding like a mother giving her son the what-for, "I don't know what you did, or what that other boy did, but I know, or I believe, that you don't want to hurt any of us." The door was partially open and How kept an eye on the goings on in the kitchen as he listened to Agnes. She continued, "I don't know about the other guy, that Buck who I am sure is nothing but shame to his family. I believe he *will* hurt us, How. We all know that you just want to get on your way. No one is going to turn you in. I know that, How. I am certain of it." She waited a few seconds for confirmation that How believed her but he didn't respond. "If anyone tried to turn you in, I would stop them. I promise you. I will stop them."

"Why are you telling me this?"

"Because we all need to sleep, including you," Agnes answered assuming a more severe tone. "We need to curl up and get some rest. As I'm sure you've noticed, I'm not so young, How. Neither is Bernard or Katherine. We can't stay up all night, and from the looks of it, neither can you. We all will be better off if we get some sleep. Agree?"

"What do you want me to do?" He *was* tired and feeling trounced both physically and emotionally.

Agnes's expression suddenly changed. She appeared, in an instant, panicked.

"Where is the other one? Buck?"

"We locked him in the cellar." How was pleased to relieve her worry.

"Well, that was a good idea, How—a very good idea, yes. That's a good place for him." She continued, "Okay now, just let us all sleep, including you. You need to sleep, How. I promise I won't let anyone call the police." Agnes was sincere and fully intended to keep her promise to How. If How had faith in anyone at that moment, if he trusted anyone under these bizarre circumstances, it was Agnes. He was tired—tired in every way a human could be tired. A respite, an escape into sleep would be a godsend for How.

"Okay," is all How could think to say. And that's all he had to say for Agnes to be on her way. She was back in the kitchen going about setting up beds for the evening. Scarlet helped pull cushions from the restaurant seating. They grabbed the dusty Mexican blankets from the lobby and proceeded to set up what looked like a slumber party in the kitchen.

"How?" Agnes wanted to know how she could fix his bed for the evening but How waved her off. He would prop himself in a chair, lean against the wall and see if sleep would happened

Rosa and Buck were first up come the next morning. Rosa entered the kitchen rosy cheeked and ready for work. Buck's muffled shouts and banging on the cellar door woke Jeff. Soon all rose from their makeshift beds while How remained sound asleep with his gun resting on his lap. They tried not to wake him as they went about their morning routines, as routine as after being held captive could be. Katherine and Bernard left the kitchen. They went to their hotel room to get washed, brush their teeth and ready themselves for the busy day and when they returned Katherine announced that the travelers were stirring and would be at the door soon.

Scarlet notified Roberto that she was leaving to take a shower and change her clothing. Not only did How distrust Scarlet, but Roberto and Rosa also worried that Scarlet might do something to throw a stick in the spokes of what had so far been a fairly smoothly running wheel of events. Roberto looked to Rosa for her reaction, and took better notice of Rosa's face—Rosa was wearing blush and it looked as though she may have applied lightly colored lipstick. She raised an eyebrow at Roberto then strictly told Scarlet that she didn't have time to shower and change.

"But I have to, Rosa," Scarlet protested.

"You need to help." Rosa wasn't going to chance Scarlet going or calling for help.

Scarlet continued to plead her case to Rosa and Roberto. Her lamenting eventually awoke How. It took a minute for him to gather his senses, to remember where he was and when he did he realized just how vulnerable he had been. He could have been easily overtaken by the group or awakened to the sheriff. How sat motionless, with only his eyes moving about, watching in amazed gratitude. To appease Scarlet, Rosa accompanied her to the house so that Scarlet could shower and change.

While surveying the kitchen activity, How noticed that the bag of money was now gone. The door to the cellar was still closed and latched from the night before. Agnes and Jeff were folding blankets and removing the bedding. Katherine and Bernard looked refreshed and How noted their change of clothing. They appeared ready to work. How was again flushed with shame. He then became aware of Buck's banging on the cellar door and, like the others, ignored it.

"Good morning, How. Would you like a cup of coffee?" asked Agnes. "I'm just about to make a pot. We'll be opening the doors soon. We're going to be busy this morning, busy like last night. Those tables will be full..." and she talked on, her delight unmistakable.

Chapter 3
Katherine Was Correct...

Katherine was correct. The customers were stacking up at the door then lined up in the lobby waiting to be seated. There weren't enough chairs or tables to accommodate the hungry and sociable crowd. Roberto gathered what chairs he could find but it was the customers themselves that readied the dining room. They brought in folding chairs and even a few folding tables. They were ready to eat, and to socialize. Their friendly chatter and blatant sense of community was the saving grace for the diminutive kitchen staff. No one was pounding the table for hurried service or for menus. They passed the few menus about like one passes a greeting card to be signed and some never bothered to even take a look—they knew what they wanted whether it was on the menu or not. Maybe a wave here and there for more coffee, and some even brought their own favorite coffee in a thermos. Bernard's newly acquired coffee-making skills weren't pushed to the limit.

"Roberto." Jeff caught the rushed and efficient Roberto's attention. Roberto gave a quick look Jeff's way, indicating his lack of free time to chat. "Let me make the next omelet," Jeff said like a child asks to throw the ball.

"Have you made an omelet before, Jeff?"

"I've been watching you. Let me give a try. If I fuck it up, I'll scramble it," Jeff answered then took a few steps closer to the stove. He had been helping Roberto by chopping and retrieving while keeping a steady eye each time Roberto worked an omelet.

"When I get an order for one, it's yours. Until then, you mix the batter...."

How watched everyone do their job in the kitchen without ambivalence, as if the ill-fated circumstances of his, and Buck's, presence didn't exist. With the exception of the periodic bangs and pleas from Buck—and the added staff—nothing appeared out of the ordinary. How again pondered if this should be his time to make an escape, with the new day, the roads might be passable. Once he was gone, Roberto could call the sheriff to remove the blight of Buck.

He needed to check the condition of the solitary road that roller-coast-ered through the mountain and passed Rancho Alviso, the only road to, and the lifeline for, Rancho Alviso. Without notice, How exited the kitchen back door and at a hurried pace he rounded the hotel, crossed the parking lot void of people and stood at the side of the road. There were clear tracks where cars had passed. The sun was shining. Cloudy, but the sun was still shining through and no snow falling. As How assessed the success of tackling the road, several people began mingling in the parking lot. He could hear them talking, shouting over to each other. He hurried back, looking down, trying to pass through them without drawing attention to himself or getting caught in the friendly morning chatter.

"Hey Buddy." How felt a hand on his shoulder. "Where you comin' from?" asked Sheriff Shelton. How's stomach felt like two muscle men had just pulled on each side of the knot. He wanted to give a quick calm response but his mind went blank. "Well, enjoy your stay here at the Alviso-great group of people here." He gave a friendly slap to the back of How's shoulder. Rosa was standing outside the front doors. She had watched through the lobby window as Sheriff Shelton approached How in the parking lot and was quick to step out to run interference if necessary.

"Good morning, Sheriff," Rosa sang out to beckon him her way.

"Rosa, you can call me Jack. You don't have to call me Sheriff." He laughed and as he stepped up to Rosa he put his large hand on her up-per shoulder. "I've told you that a hundred times; call me Jack, Rosa. We're friends right?"

"That's Linda's boy," Rosa said, pointing to How.

"Linda's boy, huh," Sheriff Shelton responded, having no idea who Lin-da was—nor did Rosa.

"He's helping us out around here," Rosa informed, then emphasized, "He's a good boy, Sheriff. He's real good help."

The sheriff turned to How and yelled over, "How long ya gunna be here?"

How struggled to give a quick and calm answer but, again, his mind went blank as his heart beat a bruise in his chest.

"He's here helping out, Sheriff, just to help us out—help Roberto. We have a lot of work that needs to be done here," Rosa answered in place of How's silence. "You gunna come help us out, Sheriff? You wanna pick up a paint brush?" Rosa looked up at Sheriff Shelton with raised eyebrows as though waiting for an answer.

"We'll be seeing ya later, Linda's Boy," Sheriff Shelton shouted out to How, lifting his hand in a wave then turning back to follow Rosa through the lobby doors.

How exhaled a sigh of relief so deep that he needed to sit down. He jogged through the parking lot, quickly out of view, bracing himself against the chipped adobe wall where he slid down to a seated position. His heart was still racing as he wiped the sweat breaking through his cold forehead. He could leave now. Rosa knowingly, or unknowingly, opened the door for his safe exit. He didn't need to hide but could walk across the parking lot in plain view—he was Linda's boy, just helping out at the Alviso. How would just get into his truck and drive off as if running an errand.

He thought about going inside to get Buck from the cellar and off their hands then both could flee while the sheriff was preoccupied inside with Rosa. *Maybe, just maybe, nothing would be said and we could be on our way.* But the other side of the coin came into question: why would they protect him... why *would* they keep silent. Why have they protected him? Why have they kept silent? His head was swirling and the thought of prison was escalating his panic. *Was Rosa covering for him to protect him or to protect the sheriff?* With How outside and Buck secured in the cellar she had ample time to secure the doors and inform the sheriff of their presence. He jumped to his feet. He had to do something, now.

How slowly opened the kitchen door to go unnoticed and observe what was going on: Roberto was cooking with Jeff assisting; Bernard was drying silverware; Scarlet was at the table but How couldn't distinguish what she was doing. Agnes, Rosa and Katherine were nowhere in sight. Rosa could be tending to the lobby and the other two waiting tables. How had to make a decision. If Rosa *was* setting him up, he had little time. How could be a sitting duck; he knew Buck was.

How burst threw the door, pulling back his jacket to reveal his control by virtue of his gun. Only Scarlet took notice, and scarcely reacted. He rushed for the door to the lobby but before he could reach the door Rosa and the sheriff pushed through it. Rosa's eyes doubled in size at the sight of How's exposed gun. He spun around in a snap, quickly closing his jacket.

"Well excuse me everyone," the sheriff said in a loud gregarious voice. He passed How and the others as he made his way to the bathroom.

How felt as though his hammering heart and knotted stomach had joined forces.

Rosa stepped up to How and in a surprisingly stern voice said, "You are Linda's boy now, How, helping us out around here." She stared directly into How's eyes. "If you want to go, then take your friend and go. But if you are going to stay, then you stop it with the gun and help out. Quit trying to scare us with your gun. We have guns too, you know. We are not afraid." As Rosa turned to leave the kitchen she clearly announced for all to hear, "If we wanted to, Mr. Man, we would have already turned you in."

The Sheriff took the route through the kitchen to depart. "Looks like you could add on to your restaurant, Roberto, and hire more staff here; we get more travelers every year," the sheriff said as he stood atop the cellar door. It was the sheriff's placement that had everyone stopping what they were doing to listen to his off the cuff business advice. "Well, it looks like you've already hired some help." He looked at Jeff then back at Roberto. "So, how's Jeff here as a cook?" Before Roberto could respond the sheriff stepped up to Jeff and asked, "Now isn't this better? We can call ya a sous chef instead of a bum," and laughed his way out of the kitchen.

Anxious stares ping-ponged around the kitchen. Roberto let out a whistle of relief, then a snicker from the tension of the close call. In little time the kitchen was back in full swing with Katherine and Agnes coming in and out of the doors like figures on a Swiss clock.

How walked over to the cellar door, unlatched it and pulled it open. Buck had found the light and a magazine—one to his liking that Roberto had stashed in the cellar. He warned Buck that he needed to remain quiet since the sheriff was coming in and out of the kitchen. Buck warned How that he needed to use the bathroom and that he wanted something to eat and drink.

Scarlet offered to make Buck a sandwich.

How asked if she had a bucket, one that they didn't want.

"What do you need a bucket for?" Scarlet asked as she handed him the thin plastic empty bucket.

"Can I get a soda in a can or bottle?" How asked, not answering the question regarding the bucket. She got one from the refrigerator.

How placed the sandwich and soda in the bucket.

"Are you lowering his food down in the bucket?" Scarlet asked. How nodded a yes and she grabbed a napkin off the table to place in the bucket. How opened the cellar door and lowered the bucket down to Buck.

"I have to piss, man," Buck complained. How indicated the sheriff and quickly closed the cellar door, latched it, then took a seat at the table next to Scarlet.

After a few minutes, Scarlet asked, "You're not going to let him use the bathroom?"

"He has a bucket," How answered without apology. He had to think and having Buck out and about only hindered everything from the thinking process to the others' ability to work without worry.

"Do you want me to make you something to eat?"

His panic and anxiety began to wane. He looked at Scarlet for a moment then again at those busy in the kitchen. The whole scenario before him became even more fantastic and surreal.

"If you don't mind," How answered.

"I don't mind," she said, pausing to look at How before getting up from the table. He looked rather gentle to Scarlet at that moment, but he was a criminal and carried a gun and she kept that in mind. She didn't ask him what he wanted to eat, she just grabbed Jeff's fresh omelet miscalculation, added toast and placed it in front of him. "Would you like a cup of coffee?" she added, though she didn't wait for an answer. Assuming that he would, she poured him a cup and placed it next to his plate. In true waitress fashion, Scarlet asked if he wanted cream or sugar. He wanted both.

"Hey, Linda's boy," the sheriff shouted through the half-opened door. "We could use your help out here." The sheriff gave a quick and friendly smile then backed out the door.

Scarlet's eyes met How's and she questioned in a hushed voice, "Linda's boy?"

As How saw the present situation, the ball was no longer in his court. He took a few seconds to take another fixed look at Scarlet then raised his eyebrows and gave a cocked smile. She had been the one How least trusted, the one who concerned him most, but now, the timorous member of the crew looked at ease, was compliant and calm. All that had taken place, and was happening now, was an in-the-moment absurd experience for How. Nothing had happened in his life to prepare him for this dichotomy of events—the behavior of his captives being the most perplexing of it all.

How headed for the lobby.

A couple of travelers had taken on the task of helping a fellow traveler change a tire on his RV. The snow caused unforeseen problems for the older men and several gave up with advice to wait for the roads to clear and "call a professional." The slippery and wet snow was taking its toll on all involved, even Sheriff Shelton, who was no fawn himself. Naturally, they sought the help of Linda's boy who was younger and strong and most likely better equipped to brave the job...and, was Rosa's hired hand, helping out at the Alviso.

Nothing, from the moment How stepped through the doors of Alviso, felt so bizarre and surreal—and so unexpected—as working side by side with the jovial sheriff. The sheriff chatted away and occasionally gave How a pat on the back for his efforts and ultimate success in changing the tire.

"Please, both of you, come in and have a cup of coffee," demanded the grateful traveler whose name was also Howard. He opened the door to his RV and waited for the two to enter.

"Thank you but I have things to do inside." How backed away from the two men.

"I'm the sheriff," Sheriff Shelton said with a laugh, "as if you couldn't tell." He extended his hand and added, "Jack or Sheriff Shelton. I answer to either, or just Sheriff. Most people around here just call me Sheriff." Howard accepted his hand in a manly shake and introduced himself. The sheriff turned to How and yelled, "Come on, have a cup of coffee with us—warm up." How didn't respond; he pretended, while rushing away, that he didn't hear the sheriff's invite. Sheriff Shelton hollered out, "Hey, what's your name?" How reached the front doors and quickly entered the busy lobby without answering.

Most of the travelers were leaving the comfort of the restaurant. The sun was shining and they were heading to their vehicles contemplating their travels. The breakfast rush was over and as How entered the kitchen Katherine and Agnes were again happily counting their tips. Their morning jobs were not yet over but they couldn't wait to pour out their spoils from their apron pockets to see where they stood so far.

How didn't walk into a kitchen occupied by frighten captives, but a kitchen going about its business without seeming to have concern for anything but the task at hand. He was in deeper than he imagined and was burdened in ways not imagined—even a few hours prior. How took a seat at the table. Only Scarlet acknowledged his presence back in the kitchen with a few-seconds glance.

"This gentleman would like to say thank you," Rosa said, speaking louder than usual to get How's attention without having to use his real name.

"My name is Howard, ma'am," Howard politely informed then looked to How and said, "I wanted to thank you for your help. Can I pay you?" The sheriff stepped in between Howard and Rosa. Rosa could see the panic rising in How's eyes as he remained seated and silent.

"You don't need to pay him," Rosa interjected. "We pay our employees a good pay to help out around here."

"I'd be happy to pay you a little extra something for your trouble. I know puttin' wheels on isn't part of your job," Howard offered.

Rosa reached for Howard's arm and gave it a tug to indicate it was time to leave the kitchen. She asked him if he would like some coffee before he went on his way, asked in order to get attention off of How.

"So what's Linda's boy's name?" asked the sheriff still staring at the silent How. He expected How to answer but Rosa shouted from the door, "Mick. Come on Sheriff. I'm sure you're needed somewhere other than the kitchen." And with that rather forceful response, he turned and followed Rosa and Howard into the lobby.

"Mick?" repeated Scarlet.

How looked up at Scarlet and smiled. He actually wanted to laugh. His presence at the Alviso was taking on a life of its own and he was losing complete control of it...and, for the time being—he didn't mind. And so it went.

Using the fear of Sheriff Shelton and a bottle of screw-top wine as the most persuasive considerations, How successfully convinced Buck to stay put in the cellar for another day and a half. How, now Mick, had dubious opportunity to make his get away, and though the thought repeatedly raced through his brain, he stayed put. Rosa and Scarlet played the major part in his decision. He understood the Rosa factor: she actually did need his help and he was more than willing to give it. Rosa felt for years that Roberto Jr. had been burdened and unhappy with his obligations at the Alviso. With all his time and efforts spent trying to catch up on the never-ending work required at the Alviso, and with the lack of funds to hire help, Rosa knew that the Alviso was draining the life out of Roberto. Though it made little sense under the circumstances—introducing oneself with a gun, holding others prisoner and taking over a business should hardly warrant trust—Rosa trusted How...and she needed him. But when it came to Scarlet, How was at a loss as to what compelled him to want to spend more time with her. If he had been attracted to her, even though she was married, then it would make some sense, except How didn't find Scarlet attractive. She was rather wispy and plain. She didn't stand out, in fact, she seemed to make it a point to step into the background.

"Mick. *Mick!*" Roberto shouted. "*How!*" he shouted again, only louder, and this time he got a response. "You better get used to your new name, *Mick*," Roberto reminded.

"Yeah, right. Sorry."

"Pull hard, away from the wall," Roberto instructed. The large extended branch proved to be too much for one man and they both hollered over to Jeff who was picking up debris around the parking lot. With Mick and Jeff pulling on the rope tied to the branch, Roberto was able to saw it from the base and have it fall to the ground without hitting the wall or any other weathered adobe structure.

It was late March and at such an elevation the town might receive a few more snowy days but it was most likely that the recent heavy snowstorm would be the last for the season. Spring and summer brought the majority of the tourists and travelers to the Alviso, therefore it was time to ready the grounds for the anticipated guests. How's timing couldn't have been better, as far as Rosa was concerned—and Roberto was beginning to agree with his mother.

"Jeff," Roberto said as he settled his feet back onto the ground. Jeff was helping How drag the twelve-foot branch. "We'll get this. Mick and I'll get the branch. You go back and help or just hang out around Buck." Roberto would understand if Jeff would rather not, but as a new employee, which Jeff was happy to be, he hoped that Jeff would take the request as an order and follow along. Everyone would have preferred to keep Buck locked in the cellar but they eventually had to let him out. Buck didn't mind making the cellar his room for the remainder of his stay, which everyone found peculiar nonetheless elated to have him safely tucked away below the kitchen at night—particularly since they could lock the cellar door if they so chose, and they did. Buck agreed to chop wood around back. It was Rosa's idea since no one else would have trusted Buck with an ax. And, no one wanted to be near Buck with an ax, except How—with a gun—but Rosa needed How's help elsewhere at the Alviso.

"No problem," said Jeff in his typical lackadaisical manner. He headed off across the parking lot, stopped, turned to Roberto and yelled, "You got workers comp n' case I get an ax through the noggin?" then continued on his way. Roberto looked at How, as if to ask how likely that scenario might be.

"Don't worry," How assured. "Unless he's in a panic or his temper has flared, he's shouldn't be a problem."

"I can't believe Rosa gave him an ax," Roberto commented as he wrapped the rope around his arm for a sturdier grip.

"You call your mother Rosa?" How was curious.

"What do you mean?" Roberto was perplexed by the question.

"I mean instead of Mom or Mother or something."

"Oh." Roberto got it. "Yeah, it's easier because everyone calls her Rosa, the guests, the town—everyone calls her Rosa so I call her Rosa too. I've called her Rosa since I was a kid. I grew up in a business, home but also a business. I heard everyone else call her Rosa." He thought for a second then added, "Scarlet called her Mom for a while but it didn't last." They quit talking and began dragging the heavy branch away from the building and around back to salvage for firewood.

"I need a fucking chainsaw, man," Buck complained to Jeff. "Here, you try choppin' all this shit. It's too much work. How many fireplaces do they have in this place anyway?" Buck tossed the ax to Jeff who stood back and let it hit the ground. Buck walked away, disappearing through the back kitchen door without saying another word. Jeff took it upon himself to continue what Buck started.

"Where's Buck?" Roberto scanned the area with a worried look on his face.

"He wanted a chainsaw——"

Roberto cut him off. "Yeah, right," he quipped, shaking his head.

"Yeah, he wanted a chainsaw," Jeff continued. "This is too much work. He gave up and went to the kitchen." Roberto's mouth twisted in obvious annoyance as his head continued to shake a disapproving no. "Well, a chainsaw would be easier, Roberto," Jeff said in a low voice then swung at the oddly shaped small trunk sitting atop a larger barrel shaped trunk.

Buck was nowhere to be seen. Roberto asked Scarlet if she knew where he was and she pointed to the cellar door. He walked over, opened the door and called out Buck's name. He received a delayed response.

"Yeah," Buck said with a tone of disinterest.

"I don't care if you're in the cellar or out, but this cellar door has to be locked. You can't open it randomly, ya know. It's dangerous in the kitchen, so I'm going to lock it. Knock when you want it open."

"Go ahead n' lock it," Buck shouted back.

Agnes smiled.

There was no prodding Agnes to stay on at the Alviso; it was a given that she wanted to stay. Rosa was hoping that Bernard and Katherine would also remain for two reasons: They were helpful. And, she wasn't sure if she could trust them to keep silent about Alviso's recently acquired outlaw handymen. Fortunately, there wasn't much prodding to keep the duo on as well—free room and board which, for Bernard and Katherine, was a much needed extended vacation at the right price. In debt, Bernard reluctantly sold his bookstore in Los Alamos—an act he regretted daily. They had no children, therefore no grandchildren and the two felt rather lost—Bernard more so than Katherine. A bit like Agnes, yet not with the same severity, Bernard and Katherine were traveling in an effort to find something that sparked their interest and would give design to their rather abandoned lives. The unexpected excitement at the Alviso was slowly but surely pulling Bernard out of his bout with what Katherine insisted was "depression."

Everyone was curious about what occupied Buck's time down in the cellar, though no one wanted to ask. They knew that he had a chair, a table, a decently comfortable mattress and he had lighting—and, something of interest that occupied his time. He seemed to have mellowed somewhat and everyone attributed it to whatever he was doing in the cellar. Mostly, they were relieved that he was satisfied to remain below ground the majority of the time and not among them. Buck hadn't gained much favor since the first night when making a scene over the potatoes, or lack there of. How had become one of the group but Buck was merely tolerated.

"How," Agnes spoke as soon as he entered the kitchen. "Roberto locked Buck in the cellar," she said with a smile.

"You better get used to calling me Mick." How added light-heartedly, "Help me get used to it myself."

"Where'd you come up with Mick, Rosa?" Roberto asked as he sat down across from her with a cup of coffee. She was thumbing through a magazine that a traveler had left so many nights ago.

"I don't know. It's a good American name, a white man's name. Right? An Irish name, right?" she answered and questioned.

"A white man's name?" Roberto mocked and laughed while looking up at How.

"So what's my last name?" How asked Rosa.

"I'll leave that up to you," she answered with indifference and continued to look through her magazine.

"Mick McGillicuddy," suggested Agnes. "I've never known anybody with the name McGillicuddy."

"Mick Jones," added Roberto.

"Well, what's Linda's last name," How asked Rosa.

"Linda who?" she responded in all seriousness, making both Roberto and How grin.

"I'm Linda's boy, right?" How reminded. "I should have the same last name."

"I don't know a Linda." Rosa looked up at How and smiled. "Mick, our Mick, you'll have to pick your own last name."

Three weeks had passed since How and Buck commandeered the Alviso. Sheriff Shelton stopped by on a somewhat regular basis. How was Mick who was quite handy to Roberto and Rosa; Buck was mysteriously occupied in the cellar; Agnes was the quintessential hostess and waitress; Katherine and Bernard were feeling better in general and were loving their long walks and helping out at the Alviso. Rosa was busy tallying up chores to be done—

picking out colors of paint, filling her head with landscaping projects and wondering if either Mick or Buck had any artistic talent since she had always wanted a mural in the lobby. Whatever Rosa was up to was just fine with Roberto; he hadn't seen his mother this animated in years. Jeff was delighted and relieved to have a job which gave him a roof over his head with delicious and reliable meals among people he actually liked. Scarlet just went along with whatever transpired at the Alviso with few if any questions—other than why did How change his name but Buck didn't.

Chapter 4

Fuck! Fuck!

"Fuck! Fuck!" The sentiment blared from the cellar. *"Fuckin' A! Damn… fuck…"* and so it went until Roberto lifted the cellar door.

"You okay?" Roberto shouted down to what was now a well-lighted cellar room.

"Man, fuckin' A! I cut my fucking hand. I cut it real bad," Buck shouted up to Roberto. "I'm bleeding like fuck. *Fuck!*"

Buck was indeed cut badly and was dripping blood onto the light colored, lodge-pole ladder as he ascended with much one-handed difficulty. Roberto gave assistance, trying not to get Buck's blood on himself, while yelling for Scarlet to bring him a towel. Buck usually popped out of the cellar like a prairie dog out of its hole but this time he looked faint, moving slowly. He grabbed onto and leaned against Roberto as he climbed out of his hole. Buck looked vulnerable instead of the crazy-eyed criminal.

"What the hell did you do?" Roberto demanded as he wrapped the towel around Buck's left hand.

"Oh God." Scarlet winced; the sight of blood made her queasy and she backed away.

"I cut my hand open, man." Buck moved to one of the kitchen chairs. "I fuckin' cut it bad."

Agnes entered the kitchen and the blood-soaked towel immediately caught her attention but instead of recoiling, like Scarlet, or standing in place (considering who was bleeding and the gamut of scenarios that could have accompanied the wound) she rushed to Buck's side to offer her assistance.

"I cut my fucking hand," Buck said like a child would tell his mother that he bumped his head, though adding the F word—which he retracted immediately. "Sorry about the fuck word," he said looking up at Agnes, surprising everyone listening.

'That's okay, Buck," she responded very much like a mom. "Let me see your hand; let me see the cut," she insisted and he complied, unwrapping the towel to expose the deep, red split across his palm. *"How did you do that?"*

"With a knife...it sliced right open." Buck stared at his palm.

"What I mean is, how did you cut yourself like that with a knife?" Agnes queried again.

"It slipped. The knife just sliced open my fucking hand," he answered twitching his face as the pain increased.

Roberto stared at the large opening on Buck's palm. "We have a first aid kit; I'll go get it."

"Well, we need to get this cleaned or rinsed, Roberto, but this is going to definitely need stitches," Agnes insisted and with that information Scarlet left the room for fear that Agnes was going to sew Buck up right there in the kitchen.

"I'll get the kit," and Roberto left, replaced by Rosa. Buck didn't wait for Rosa to ask what all the blood was about; he told her right off that he cut his hand with a knife.

"Doing what?" Rosa naturally asked, which is what Agnes was asking in the first place.

"I was carving. I pushed into the wood then the knife slipped, cut open my hand," Buck dutifully explained.

"Carving what?" Rosa inquired further.

"A piece of wood." He looked away. (Out of boredom, Buck began carving on one of the wood poles framing the cellar. He quickly became intrigued, and impressed, by the results. He thoroughly enjoyed this new creative venture but wasn't sure that Rosa would be all that happy to find the cellar structure carved up with Buck's artistic attempt at human and animal faces.)

"You rinse that cut in the sink over there," Rosa said looking in the direction of the kitchen sink. Buck did as he was told.

They stood around the sink watching the gap in Buck's palm well with blood continuously. Roberto arrived with the first aid kit only to realize that nothing within that kit was going to satisfy such a cut. Everyone watching, including Roberto, stood silent while Buck made intermittent aching sounds. Jeff walked in and joined the silent observers.

"You guys got a doctor 'round here?" Buck broke the silence.

No one answered.

Buck looked at each face, hoping someone had some suggestion before he bled out.

"How, man, I'm bleeding to death over here," Buck cried out to How as he entered the kitchen.

"Call me Mick. Don't call me How anymore," he was quick to respond then stepped up to look at Buck's hand. He looked around at the others expecting someone to explain.

"I gotta get to a doctor, How."

"Mick."

"Mick, I gotta get to a doctor." Buck began to panic.

"There's no doctor around here…is there?" Jeff commented and questioned.

"Not nearby," Roberto said while looking at How.

"Well, I'm sure someone can take you to a doctor, Buck, and your hand will heal nicely back in prison." How recognized the severity of the cut but also the severity of the situation.

"The doctor's not gunna know nothin'," Buck insisted. "He'll just sew me up an' I'm outta there."

"He has a point," Agnes agreed. "How would the doctor know that he's a bad man?"

How smiled.

"He wouldn't know that he's supposed to be behind bars," she continued.

Her comment also had Roberto smiling.

"Who knows if there's not some bulletin or something and the doctor's not going to treat him pro bono…." How rattled off several reasons why taking Buck to the doctor was not a good idea, his own survival being his greatest concern.

"Take him to Frances," Rosa said. "She'll fix him up and he'll be fine."

"Who's Frances?" Agnes asked but Rosa didn't answer as she walked across and out of the kitchen.

"She's a nurse, a retired nurse," Roberto explained.

"She won't suspect anything?"

"Not Frances," Jeff answered, head tilted with half a smile. "Frances can fix anybody, anything, up. She does you a favor, you do her a favor." He looked at Roberto. "How old is she now?"

"I don't know," Roberto answered with a shrug that immediately had Buck thinking that she was nearing a hundred with shaky hands and bad eyes. He was about to voice his objection until a glance up at How, whose expression denoted more irritation than compassion, changed his mind. Buck was feeling quite vulnerable at that moment.

"Should we give her a call?" Agnes felt that they should rush things along. "You should quit rinsing it, Buck. Wrap it. Let me do it for you," and she grabbed another relatively clean towel—one without blood—and tightly wrapped it around Buck's cupped hand.

"No. She rarely answers her phone. We'll just take him there." Roberto grabbed the keys to his truck from the hook and Buck, How and Jeff followed him out the kitchen back door.

"I'll keep an eye on things," Agnes called out as they left.

"What if she's not there?" Buck worried, rushing to keep pace with Roberto.

"We'll find her. She's in town somewhere, at someone's house."

Roberto drove. Buck sat in the middle with How by the door and Jeff in the bed of the truck.

The truck bounced down a muddy road until they came to a fence made of the trunks of slender trees, all lined up like bark-clad soldiers, side by side, straight and held in place by rusted baling wire.

"That's a long stick fence," Buck remarked.

"Goat fencing," informed Roberto.

"Goat fence? A goat would eat that fence, wouldn't it? Goats eat bark don't they? and they'd eat that fence raw," Buck observed and scanned the area looking for goats.

"Some call it coyote fencing," Roberto added. Buck still looked perplexed.

Roberto honked the horn several times as the truck idled by the fence. They waited about five minutes and Roberto honked his horn a few more times. The wood gate stationed at the front of the adobe wall that encircled the front yard opened and out came Frances with the cadence of a college girl. She was old, alright, in her late-eighties although her walk, her posture and attitude defied her age. She waved an invite to Roberto. He turned off the engine and got out of the truck, alone, to talk to Frances. He explained that a new hire—"You hired some help, well good for you"—had badly cut his hand and he believed that it needed stitches.

"Bring him in and I'll take a look." Frances asked Roberto to give her a few minutes to get ready. Roberto knew what she was referring to. She needed to put her pet away, her "dog," before she could welcome anyone into her home. All three passengers were watching, curious about the delay. When Frances appeared at the gate once more, Roberto waved the others to come.

They filed through the old wood gate into a garden that was more like a jungle, just the way Frances loved it. The house was small and was built by Frances and her now deceased husband. There was a large fireplace in the main room. The kitchen was off to one side, few windows and a tiny hall that led to two small rooms and a bathroom. Frances instructed Buck to sit at the kitchen table where she unwrapped the blood-soaked towel to examine the cut. She looked up at Buck and asked with a smile, "Are you brave?" He looked at the others then nodded a yes. "Good," she said and left to retrieve her medical supplies. Suspecting what was to come, both Roberto and Jeff excused themselves to go outside. How stayed. Not because he might get some perverse pleasure out of seeing Buck have a needle pulled through his already aching palm but to make sure that Buck behaved and that Frances was safe.

Frances returned with her bag of medical supplies. The bag looked as old as she. She rinsed the wound with a solution that had Buck's eyes wide as saucers. She calmly left the table to prepare something at the kitchen counter. Returning with a hypodermic needle, Frances inserted the needle at the corner of the wound while Buck squeezed his eyes shut so hard that his cheeks near hit his eyelashes. When Frances pulled the forceps then needle with the needle driver from her bag, How turned his back to the scene and stepped up to the window to feast his eyes on something more appealing. There were a few unpleasant sounds yelped from Buck's mouth but he held steady and Frances successfully repaired his gaping wound. She applied a topical antibiotic then handed Buck a bottle of antibiotics to take at regular intervals.

"These are for *fish*," Buck exclaimed as he observed the caricature of a happy fish wearing a nurse's hat swimming across the plastic bottle.

"Yes they are and you need to take them as I instructed," Frances responded. She casually put her supplies back in her bag.

"But they're for a fish, not a people," Buck protested. Frances ignored him as she left to put her bag away. "How," Buck shouted over to How.

He turned. "It's Mick." He gave Buck a stern-eye warning. "My name is Mick so don't call me How again…not one more time. Mick. Got it?"

"Yeah, Mick; I gotcha." Buck was back to his original issue. "These are for fish not people," he complained holding up the bottle to show How the fish from the nursing academy.

"Yes, sir," Frances causally chimed in. "That's a fish on the bottle but unless you want to be swimming with the fishes, take those as I told you." She paused for a second to look at How then emphasized, "He needs to take the pills in the bottle faithfully." How nodded that he understood. She then asked, "Where is Roberto?"

"He stepped outside," How answered.

"What is your name again?" she asked How.

"Mick," he promptly replied.

"Mick what and from where?"

How wondered why she was asking him particulars and not Buck, but immediately relieved that the inquisition was not directed at Buck. How hesitated; he hadn't been given a last name as of yet and wasn't sure if he should make one up on the spot. Fortunately, Roberto interrupted by entering through the front door.

"I haven't been formally introduced to your friends, Roberto," Frances reprimanded in jest.

"I'm sorry, Frances." Roberto raised his hand in Buck's direction. "Our wounded here is Buck."

"Buck who," she asked, with a steady stare at Buck as he held his wounded hand.

Buck whipped his nervous stare up at How, searching for an answer.

"You mean his last name?" Roberto quickly asked then gave a name. "Buck Flanagan." Then Roberto turned to How. "And this is Mick Jones. Jeff, you know Jeff and who knows what his last name is." Roberto gave a light laugh and Frances responded in kind. Everyone knew Jeff and knew Jeff as just Jeff. She didn't care what his last name was.

"Well, Buck Flanagan and Mick Jones and Roberto, I'm going to have to shoo all of you along. I have things to do…" and she walked the three to the front door. As she said goodbye and was closing the front door, a grunting sound startled Buck. He turned to look inside the house but Frances at once shut the door and latched it.

"So how's it feel?" Jeff asked as he examined the splint and bandaged hand.

"It's numb," Buck responded and they all got back to their designated seats in the truck.

"So, I'm Mick Jones and he's Buck Flanagan," How commented.

"Fuck, I can't even spell my last name. I shoulda been Jones," Buck complained.

How smiled. He had a point. He would have to brand the name and spelling into Buck's brain quickly.

"Where'd you come up with those names?" How wondered.

"Don't ask me." Roberto thought for a few seconds then added, "Well you guys don't look like a Martinez or Sanchez and there's nobody with those names around this area. Why, you don't want those names?"

"They're fine. I can easily be Mick Jones." How glanced over at Roberto. "I'll just have to teach Buck how to spell his name."

"Or give me the Jones name and you take the other one, the Flaniman or whatever it was."

"Flanagan," How corrected.

"Okay, Miiiiick," Buck responded. "Mick Jones, the easy name." And they bounced down the bumpy dirt road back to the Alviso.

As soon as they arrived everyone, except for Scarlet, wanted to see Buck's sutured hand. When that short-lived event was done Rosa wondered aloud if Buck knew how to paint.

"Well, who can't paint, shit." Buck laughed. "You take a brush, *dunk it in a can and paint.*"

"Can you paint a picture?" Rosa asked Buck directly.

He thought for a moment, looking quite serious, then answered, "I don't know. Maybe. What do you want me to paint?" He knew he was pretty good at carving so maybe he'd be a pretty good painter too.

Rosa pointed to the wall in the lobby to which Buck looked perplexed and responded, "You want me to paint a wall?" Rosa nodded yes. Of course, Rosa wanted him to paint a picture on the wall but Buck thought that by pointing to the plain wall that Rosa wanted a picture of a plain wall. "That wall right there?" Again Rosa nodded a yes. This exchange continued to the amusement of both Roberto and How. They were letting it continue to see how far it would go while holding back their urge to laugh aloud. Before all could be resolved, in walked Scarlet holding the hand of a little girl. All turned. No one had seen this little girl before and quickly wondered who she was and why Scarlet was walking her by the hand.

"This is Gracie," Scarlet said. "Gracie, this is my husband Roberto..." and Scarlet introduced each person in the lobby to Gracie, even remembering that How was now Mick. "We're going to walk down to see Fionn's horse. I think he has a pony too...and a burro." She looked down at Gracie and asked, "That would be nice wouldn't it? Would you like to see a pony?" Little Gracie gave a shy nod then turned her body towards Scarlet. The stares from the strangers seemed to make her uncomfortable. Scarlet and Gracie exited out the lobby doors leaving all to wonder where she found this little girl.

"Here," How handed Buck a small piece of paper. "Keep this in your pocket, memorize it." Buck read the writing on the paper before slipping it into his pocket, *Buck Flanagan.* "How's your hand?" How added.

It's sore," he answered holding his hand up in display.

"You taking the antibiotics?"

"Those fish pills?" Buck shook his head. "Yeah, I'm taking them just like the old lady said to."

"Man, Buck. Her name is Frances. Show some respect."

"I didn't mean any disrespect. I couldn't remember her name."

"Do you want me to write it down on the paper for you?" How asked with sarcasm but Buck took the comment as sincere and took the paper from his pocket, handing it over to How to add Frances's name. How did and Buck put the paper back into his pocket.

"What are you doing?" How naturally inquired.

"Well, Mick," Buck paused to add emphasis to the fact that he remembered How's new name. "I'm going to draw some pictures, see if Rosa likes 'em, wants one on the lobby wall."

"I didn't know you were such an artist, Buck."

"I guess I am," he said with a smile then picked up the notebook.

"Where you going?"

"To the cellar. Agnes calls it my artist's den. I'm goin' to my artist's den." Before How could say anything else Buck was through the kitchen door and on his way to the cellar. Agnes's description was quite accurate. Buck had pieces of wood in various stages of expression and now sketches hanging on the walls. Buck's newly discovered talent was becoming somewhat of a mild obsession and had soothed the edge off of Buck: a relief to those at the Alviso. Agnes was a constant with praise and encouragement. She was certain that Buck had little supervision or guidance when growing up and all he needed all along was direction, focus and encouragement. She shared her theory with How in search of some substantiation but How knew nothing of Buck's childhood and wasn't in full agreement with Agnes's simplistic theory, that art was the cure-all for Buck's mental and emotional ills. However, it kept him occupied. How did see a change in Buck's attitude and he no longer held such concern about what damage Buck might do if not perpetually supervised. A knife in Buck's hand at one time meant nothing but trouble, now it meant that Buck was reshaping a log from the wood pile.

How noticed Katherine and Bernard with the same little girl that Scarlet had introduced to those in the lobby the other day. He watched as Bernard pointed to something in the sky and the little girl looked up, pointing along with Bernard though How couldn't see just what they were pointing at. Katherine was holding a brightly colored flower and grand smile. Buck watched through the restaurant window as he sipped at his coffee, wondering just who this little girl was and who she belonged to. Was there a guest at the Alviso that he wasn't aware of?

"Isn't she precious?" Scarlet took a seat across from How and watched through the window. "I think Katherine and Bernard are just falling in love with her too."

"Who does she belong to?" How bluntly asked, now watching Scarlet still enamoured with the sight of Gracie engaging with Katherine and Bernard.

"*Who does she belong to?*" Scarlet repeated How's question with a laugh. He made Gracie sound like a lost dog, but she understood—men just worded things differently. She answered, "She's Edward's granddaughter. The poor little thing. She lost her mother." Scarlet turned to look at How. "It's so sad, How—I mean Mick...I'm sorry."

"Go on," How pushed; he was curious.

"Her mother, Edward's daughter, was killed by a drunk driver. And, it's so ironic, sooooo ironic." Scarlet took a breath. "Her father, Gracie's father, couldn't handle it and, well, began drinking." She shook her head. "You think he would never touch the stuff but instead he drowns himself in it. Now Edward is taking care of Gracie. He's kind of old. He's really grieving himself, over his daughter. It's all so sad, Mick. It's so awful. I feel so bad for all of them."

How looked back out the window as did Scarlet and asked, "Where does Edward live?"

"Just down the road, walking distance." Scarlet kept her focus on Gracie. "She looks happy though, doesn't she?"

"Well, Katherine and Bernard sure do." It had been a couple of months since he had arrived at the Alviso and was "introduced" to Katherine and Bernard—a couple of months since being torn by guilt for keeping two seniors prisoners and forced employees in the Alviso kitchen. Now he couldn't imagine anyone looking any happier than they did as they played with Gracie in front of the Alviso.

"I'm going to see if they want lunch," Scarlet said and left the table in a joyful hurry.

How watched Scarlet jog across the parking area to the playful three. All four headed back together. Jeff was enthusiastically on kitchen duty and was happy to accommodate a lunch for four: grilled cheese for everyone and Jeff cut the bread on Gracie's sandwich to look like Mickey Mouse ears—she was thrilled. They ate their lunch at the table in the kitchen and shy little Gracie looked happy as she nibbled on Mickey's ears and listened to Bernard talk about a dog he once had.

Rosa had How take her to the hardware store, or what sufficed as a hardware store in the sprawl of this mountain town. How felt nervous; he wanted to wait in the truck. Rosa was her usual calm self. She insisted that How come into the store with her and was pleased to have someone to rely on other than Roberto: How turned out to be very reliable help—always available and happy to be so.

"Well, Rosa, you know that we don't have a large selection of paint. We have the basics, basically," Albert said, while taking repeated glances at How. He had never seen How before and having the only store in town—in the area, essentially—Albert pretty much saw everyone who stayed in the vicinity, at least once. "Let me show you." Albert walked out from behind the counter, giving How a direct gaze in hopes that would initiate a response and an introduction from How. It didn't.

Rosa followed behind Albert and How behind Rosa until Albert stopped at a freestanding wood display, a rather primitive stand that had been in the store since its opening, which was far before Albert owned it. The heavy oak stand stood as it had for over ninety years with only its offering changing. There were three rows of small cans of paint and one row of gallon cans of paint. Rosa looked up at How to ask which cans she should get. Rosa's question to How gave Albert the polite opportunity to aim his stare at How and comment outright, "I haven't met you before."

Rosa quickly introduced How as Mick, her new handyman, "Linda's boy."

Albert reached his hand out to How. "Welcome Mick; I guess I'll be seeing a lot of you from now on."

How accepted his hand, nodded and responded, "Nice to meet you." Albert's handshake, though How was sure was meant to be a welcoming gesture, felt like getting your hand stuck in a jackhammer. It was the oddest handshake How had experienced yet in life.

"Which colors?" Rosa asked again.

"This is for your mural, the wall by the register?" How asked.

"You having a mural painted, Rosa?" Albert asked and Rosa nodded still staring at the paints. Each had a dot of paint on the lid indicating the color.

"Are these new cans, Albert?" she asked due to the color dots.

"Yes, yes. Of course they're new. I'm just showing customers the color, the real color. Now they can see the color. It's easier," he answered then looked at How and asked, "So, are you the artist, Mick?" Again, Rosa answered for How.

"No, Mick's my handyman, jack-of-all-trades. He's Roberto's right-hand man."

"So who's the artist?"

"His name is Buck," Rosa answered briefly then looked back up at How to again ask for his help on what colors to buy and how much.

"What are you painting, Rosa?" Albert cut in.

"The wall in the lobby. You know the big empty wall by the register." She looked over at Albert. "I have an artist staying at Alviso and he's going to paint a mural in the lobby. I've always wanted a mural on that wall."

"That's a big space. That's gunna cost you, Rosa." Albert snickered.

"No it's not, Albert. He is staying at the Alviso in exchange for his artistic labor," she responded with satisfaction. She looked over at How and smiled. *If Albert only knew the true story*, she said with her eyes, amused. She liked having a secret from Albert. Albert was nosy, not just nosy but judgmental and a bit of a gossip which Rosa felt was due to his business. People always had a story when they came in to buy, always explaining why they were there just like with Rosa buying the paint and explaining that it was for a mural on her wall. Albert heard it all. However, it still annoyed Rosa; she didn't like people talking about her or her family or her business at the Alviso—unless it was complimentary. Everything outside of a compliment was none of anybody else's business, according to Rosa. She viewed herself as the live-and-let-live type though Scarlet would beg to differ: Scarlet saw her as critical—not honest about how she truly felt—and Scarlet often worried about what Rosa really thought of her and her station at the Alviso.

One didn't have to agree with Rosa, but one had to be agreeable with Albert to transition smoothly out of the store. "So, which colors, Mick?" Rosa continued.

"What's he painting on that wall?" Albert inquired.

"It's a garden, a path. It's an outdoor scene, wouldn't you say, Mick?

"A hacienda path," How answered.

"Yes, yes; that's what it is, that's exactly what it is." Rosa liked how he described it so perfectly and so quickly. Rosa liked so much about How, now Mick. She enjoyed his company and how he was able to say little but say a lot—not a lot of useless chatter. Roberto didn't talk much and Scarlet talked but said little of interest or consequence as far as Rosa was concerned. Mick was smart and Rosa knew he had a good heart. She was curious as to what he had done to be put in prison, but she'd let her curiosity simmer for the time being.

"Why don't you get several colors, you know—the basics, and your resident artist will know how to mix them to make whatever color he needs. Artists know how to do that stuff—that's part of being an artist, ya know what I mean?"

It made sense, but then, he didn't know Buck.

"Okay, Albert. You pick the colors, 'the basics.'" Rosa turned and headed down the aisle while Albert handed How the cans. She met them at the counter with several paintbrushes in hand.

"Albert, I need the small brushes. You know, artist brushes. Do you have them?" Rosa asked. "And stirring sticks."

"Your artist doesn't have his own brushes?" Albert asked in a way that challenged Buck's professionalism.

"Albert, do you have brushes or don't you?"

"Mountain High has everything, Rosa...you know that," Albert kidded as a way of taking back his innuendo and left to find the desired brushes, though he only had children's paint brushes.

"Mountain High?" How questioned in a low voice.

"That's the name of this store," she answered in a whisper. "You don't see a store sign because he doesn't have one. He took the sign down to repaint it and never put it back up." She smiled. "All the hippies used to come in here—-" Rosa was interrupted by her own giggle; she couldn't help herself. "They thought they'd find something other than Albert. That's how we got Jeff."

The name and the amateurishly painted picture gave an ambiguous message. What was supposed to be clouds lingering atop a series of mountains looked more like smoke spewing from brown-colored smoking pipes. Albert, who didn't have a resident artist, painted the sign himself and to Albert it was clearly a mountain scene for a general store. To the array of hitchhikers and Volkswagen buses it said rolling papers, paraphernalia and connections. They were as shocked to find Albert behind the counter as he was to have the influx of hippies visiting his store.

As they headed back to the Alviso, How mentioned that he believed that it would be a good idea for Buck to change his name then he pointed out that he doubted Buck could mix colors. But Rosa had faith in Buck's artistic abilities and confidently replied, "He'll figure it out."

And he did. It was a new challenge for the resident artist that he conquered quickly. The only problem that he was having was with proportions. What Buck (who agreed to change his name to Lucky at the suggestion of both How and Rosa) had drawn on paper and that Rosa had liked so much— a scene taken from a magazine—wasn't translating as it should on the wall: A flower head shouldn't be the same size as a stepping-stone, but Rosa believed that Buck, now Lucky, would figure it out and she'd have the mural she always wanted.

"Why Lucky?" asked Scarlet. "Though I do think it's a good idea that he changes his name." She looked at How; she wanted to observe his reaction to her next comment. "I don't think he's so bad anymore. I kind of like him around. I like how Rosa spends time with him, or he spends time with Rosa. I think it's good for her. He, well, and you, have sort of changed this place, and so fast."

How didn't show any reaction.

Scarlet continued, "Rosa seems a lot happier since you guys have come here. At least it seems that way to me. She doesn't sit so much, you know, in the lobby and read magazines and stare out the window. She always looked like she was expecting Roberto, Roberto her late husband, to come walking up." Scarlet handed How a box that she filled with the variety of stuff that had been cluttering her Trooper. "She never seemed to get that excited about anything; now she does." She paused waiting for a response from How but he still said nothing. "Well, I guess you wouldn't know the difference because you didn't know her before."

"Before we entered the place with a gun?" How commented back steeped in guilt.

"It doesn't seem to matter...not anymore. Don't you think?" Again she looked up at How.

How didn't know how to respond to Scarlet's observation. She was making him and Buck out to be awaited welcome guests. It was still confusing to How, in many ways. He still wondered daily how long this refuge was going to last. He knew that she was right about Rosa, Roberto had said the same thing to him, but it was perplexing considering how he and Buck entered the Alviso and forced themselves at gunpoint into their lives. He was more than grateful to be exactly where he was and wanted to contribute and give back to each person who so graciously allowed him the safety of Alviso. How diverted his eyes and said nothing. Scarlet dropped the subject, turning it back to Buck's new name.

"We chose Lucky because it sounds like Buck or Bucky. Roberto introduced him to the nurse and Rosa said his name at the store. Hopefully they'll think that they just heard wrong or that Rosa and Roberto got his name mixed up," How explained while he continued to help Scarlet clean out her vehicle. She had made plans to take Gracie shopping at a mall. It would be an all-day outing and Scarlet was excited. By the time she and How finished cleaning her Trooper, it was as clean and shiny as the day she purchased it.

"Where do you go shopping around here?" How wondered.

"Well, there's nowhere to go shopping around here, unless you want to shop at Mountain High," Scarlet answered. "You can go to Santa Fe or Los Alamos. I guess you could go to Albuquerque if you wanted to drive that far." She stepped back and looked at her Trooper, happy at the finished product. "Looks good, doesn't it." She had already washed the outside of the vehicle and now with the inside clean, she was quite pleased at its appearance.

"If you haven't used it in awhile, is it in good running condition?"

"I don't see why it wouldn't run fine. It started up and it ran fine the last time I used it." Her expression changed slightly, but noticeably. It hadn't entered her mind previously that there could be something wrong with it. "It's just been sitting."

"For how long?"

"Four months. Six months. Something like that." Scarlet's face crinkled, displaying her worry. "Do you know about engines and stuff?"

"Buck does." He corrected, "I mean Lucky does."

Scarlet looked up at How with trepidation.

"He's good at that stuff. I'll ask him to take a look."

"Roberto is good with engines and things but he's at Delmacio's and I don't know when he'll be home. Rosa told him to stay the night."

How smiled to himself. Not that long ago he held a gun on Roberto, held him prisoner, now Roberto was leaving Alviso in his care.

"You going today, shopping?"

"No, tomorrow. I'm taking Gracie out. I'd really like to take her to the zoo in Albuquerque but that is going to have to wait." She turned to How and added, "Now I'm afraid my car won't make it to Los Alamos."

"Lucky will check it out; he knows about car stuff. I'll go find him now so if it needs anything, needs any work, he'll have it ready for you by tomorrow. Don't worry," and How left to retrieve Lucky and his services. He didn't have to go far. Lucky was at work in the lobby on the mural. Alongside him sat Rosa, relaxing, thumbing through a magazine. Lucky was challenged enough without Rosa continually showing him other garden scenes which she liked, "a lot." He started to ignore her suggestions and began to better appreciate his own artistic flavor.

"Lucky." How tried to get his attention. *"Lucky"*

"That's you, Buck. You're Lucky," Rosa said to Buck who was forgetting his new name already. "Mick wants you." He looked over his shoulder at Rosa first then at How. They both could see that it took him a few seconds to grasp the new names.

"Ah, yeah. I'm Lucky. But hey, I *am* Lucky," he laughed. "And, you are Mick. So, what do you want, Mick?"

"Can you take a break and come check out Scarlet's Trooper, make sure it's in good driving condition for her?"

"She got tools?" he asked while dabbing his brush to fill in the stepping stone on the mural.

"Roberto has tools if you need them," Rosa answered. "Scarlet knows where they are."

"Yeah, okay, gimmee a few and I'll come out there." Lucky wanted to finish up what he was doing, to not lose his bright creative whim of foliage twisting up the walkway fence.

"I like that, Lucky," Rosa chirped. "That looks good, real good."

How shook his head: there was Buck, crazy stupid Buck, playing the artist with Rosa, his former captive, cheering him on, smiling proudly as if he were her own son. How was living in a surreal world for the time being— a world he best stay in for the time being. The Gods were smiling just a little too much on him and Buck, nonetheless, he didn't have much choice but to trust and bask in the good fortune.

"It's got, ya know, sort of worn belt," Lucky informed Scarlet.

"What belt?" She had no idea what he was referring to.

"You know, your fan belt. It's not a big deal…I mean, it's not like it's gotta cut or nothin', just wearing out," he explained. "What is that car, an eighties? How far are you going?" Before she could answer he added, "Where are you going?"

Lucky's eyes changed and Scarlet was uncomfortable. She didn't want to tell him where she was going. She instantly had visions of Lucky commandeering her Trooper, taking her and Gracie hostage.

Lucky walked off, looking back at Scarlet several times. She saw How heading down the walkway and quickly shouted his name, his old name—his wrong name. How met her halfway.

"What's up?" he asked. "You look worried."

"I'm sorry about the name, How. I mean Mick. Mick, Mick, Mick. I've got to remember."

"Is something wrong?"

"Lucky said——"she started.

"Well, you're remembering his name okay," he joked.

"Yeah, well, they sound the same: Bucky, Lucky. He said that my belt was worn."

"Your fan belt?"

"I guess. I don't know. He wanted to know where I was going, how far."

"Yeah?" It was a reasonable question for the current concern.

"Mick, I don't know. He's *scaring me.*"

"I don't understand. How is he scaring you?"

"Honestly?" she asked. She didn't want to offend.

"Yes, honestly. Tell me what you're afraid of. Did he do or say something?" Mick looked to be quite engaged in Scarlet's worry.

"I'm afraid he'll do something. I'm afraid he'll get in the car, try to take it with me and Gracie in it…he'll try to go with us and I don't know what will happen." She looked down, almost ashamed. "I'm sorry, but I guess I really *don't* trust him, How."

"Mick," he first corrected. "He's not that stupid, Scarlet" Mick said aloud while believing that he really was *that stupid.* "Would it make you more comfortable if maybe someone else went with you? Maybe Agnes or Katherine and Bernard?"

"Yeah, it would; that's a good idea. Maybe Bernard would know what to do if that belt goes or wears out." Scarlet was looking off, thinking. "Roberto can't go with me; I know that already." She paused, thinking again, then looked up at Mick. "Would you go with me and Gracie tomorrow?"

She trusted How now Mick. It was a peculiar circumstance that was both bewildering and flattering to Mick.

"I'm not sure that Roberto or Rosa would be too fond of that idea."

"No, no. I'm sure it will be fine. I'm going to talk to Rosa," and Scarlet scurried off, not waiting for Mick to respond. She didn't want anything to spoil her day trip with Gracie.

Mick agreed: Gracie did look like a little angel. Her face was an icon of innocence. Gracie's downy light brown hair was pulled back on the sides with pink barrettes that matched her checked pink jumper. A smiling pink monkey on her tiny blouse peeked over the top of the jumper. She looked up at Mick with that sweet face of purity as she trustingly offered him her small hand. Mick helped her up and into the child's car seat that was secured to the backseat of the Trooper. Mick couldn't figure out the straps of the car seat. The amused and eager Scarlet took over.

Mick had already checked the water in the radiator, inspected the fan belt and cleaned the windshield inside and out. He was belted onto the front passenger's seat while Scarlet chatted cheerfully to Gracie as they waited for Katherine and Bernard to make their appearance. He scanned his surroundings. At this juncture, luck was surely in charge. An escaped convict was enjoying not only his freedom but a pleasurable outing for the day with two seniors, a small child and a wisp of a woman—all who not only seemed to trust him, but seemed to genuinely like him. This was a bit too good to be true but Mick wasn't going to challenge it, just enjoy it while it lasted.

"Hello Gracie," Katherine said as she climbed onto the back seat. "Don't you look pretty today." She was as delighted about Gracie's company as was Scarlet. "Good morning, How."

"Mick," he answered then turned to face Katherine with a smile. "Rosa renamed me Mick."

"Oh yes. I'm sorry. I remember that. I remember you changed your name." She laughed, "Or Rosa did. It's a good idea, *Mick*. So, I'll start over. Good morning, Mick."

"Good morning, Katherine. Is Bernard coming along with us?"

"There he is. He got a coffee from Agnes," Katherine answered.

"Did Agnes want to come?" Scarlet asked. She hadn't invited her because of the lack of room in the Trooper but she didn't want to offend Agnes.

"Oh Scarlet, Agnes has found her calling," Katherine said referring to Agnes's severe attachment to her new station in life—a hostess/waitress. "You know you'll have to fire her to get rid of her. She will never quit; she'd probably pay *you* to let her waitress."

"Customers love her," Scarlet commented. She was delighted that Agnes found such gratification in doing Scarlet's job. It wasn't a job Scarlet had planned on making a career though it appeared that due to the circumstances that brought her to the Alviso, it would end up that way.

"Hello, everybody." Bernard was full of cheery enthusiasm. "Hello Gracie." His smile was huge as he moved Gracie's stuffed monkey from the seat. "Is this your monkey?" Bernard made it dance in the air.

Gracie giggled and reached for the animated monkey.

"Okay, everybody ready?" Scarlet said like a scoutmaster about to lead the pack on an awaited adventure.

"You want a sip of my coffee, How?" Bernard asked. Katherine and Scarlet were quick to respond in unison, *"Mick!"*

"Oh boy, sorry."

They were off.

It didn't take but a few miles for all but Gracie to become aware that Scarlet's driving skills were a bit worrisome. The car's speed varied in short spans with little logic behind the speeding up or the slowing down. The lighthearted chatter lessened as watching the road became priority. Mick looked over to see that she was driving with one foot on the gas pedal and one foot on the brake pedal. He took a quick glance back at the concerned faces of Katherine and Bernard along with Gracie who was as happy as could be with her monkey now in her arms.

Scarlet navigated turns as if she were driving a semi truck.

"Scarlet," Mick said hoping to not distract her too much as she maneuvered what would be, to most, an easy turn. "I'd like to replace the fan belt. It won't take long. If you see a gas station or if there is a car parts store around, I can take care of it."

Scarlet stared at the road as one stares at the tracks on a roller coaster ride, not turning her head as she answered, "Okay." Bernard was silently on the lookout for a gas station or car parts store. It felt like a considerable amount of time before signs of businesses came to view. A gas station with a "Mechanic On Duty" sign caught Bernard's attention.

"There's a place that will probably have a belt, How." Bernard corrected himself, "Um, sorry...Mick."

"Should I pull in?" Scarlet asked, grasping the steering wheel as though holding onto something that was trying to escape.

"Yeah, go ahead, pull in there," Mick quickly instructed before she got to a point where turning would be a challenge for her.

Scarlet nervously pulled between two cars and stopped just past them. Mick jumped out. It appeared that all, except innocent Gracie, wanted out of the vehicle. The ride through the mountains on the serpentine road was scary enough but now they were going to be heading into traffic.

The Mechanic on Duty sign looked to be at least fifty years old and may have been simply décor. The pumps were evidently working since a man in an older seventies truck was filling up. Mick made his way into the office and exited a few minutes later with a veritable mechanic. He took a look at the old belt, said he had one that would work and offered to put it on.

Bernard, Katherine and Mick were waiting for the mechanic and the new fan belt. Scarlet remained behind the wheel, but now turned so that she could talk to Gracie.

"This is awkward, Bernard," Mick meekly said.

"What is awkward?" Katherine was quick to respond.

"I don't have money, money to pay the mechanic," he answered.

"We do," Bernard said casually. "And, I'm sure Scarlet has money. Don't concern yourself, Mick." Bernard was pleased that he remembered How's new name. He then made a request due to everyone's concern. "Maybe you could drive, Mick. Whataya think?"

"Yeah, Mick, you think you could drive instead of Scarlet. I think her confidence is a little shaky behind the wheel."

The mechanic did his job quickly without much said. Mick walked over to Scarlet's window. "I'm sorry, Scarlet, I don't have money to pay the mechanic."

"Oh, no problem, How. I'll get it," and she immediately unbuckled her seatbelt and grabbed her purse.

"Mick, Scarlet," he reminded.

"I'll get it, by the time we get back I will have it memorized and won't make that mistake again...I promise."

Mick opened the door for Scarlet and she got out to pay the mechanic. Before she climbed back into the Trooper, Mick suggested that he drive so he could feel if the new belt was fitted and working properly. It sounded like a good idea to Scarlet. She agreed. Scarlet had no idea what to be aware of it the new fan belt was somehow incorrect. Neither did Mick, but his command behind the wheel lessened Bernard's and Katherine's worries—and his. This also allowed Scarlet to relax and she spent most of her time chatting with Gracie and Katherine, intermittently giving Mick directions to Los Alamos.

"Do they still have the Black Hole there, I wonder," Bernard half whispered aloud. He had avoided Los Alamos since selling his business.

"What's the Black Hole?"

"It was what I guess you would call a military thrift store. Great stuff. It's been so long, so long since I've been there," Bernard answered with a touch of reminiscent excitement. "Atomic Ed," he muttered with a smile.

"Since we closed the bookstore," Katherine added, "we really don't go to Los Alamos anymore." She added with a smile, "This will be fun." She turned to Bernard. "Won't it?"

"Yeah, I guess it will." There was apprehension in his voice. Owning the bookstore was one of the highlights of Bernard's life and he had mixed feelings about passing his old dream-come-true. He felt eager and agitated at the same time.

"I want to go to CB Fox," Scarlet happily added. "We can get some ice cream in town, Gracie; how about that?" Gracie nodded in excited agreement and gave Scarlet a blissful smile. Scarlet couldn't help but fix her eyes on Gracie, her face so sweet, her smile so precious. Scarlet was taken by Gracie at their first introduction. Gracie's story would tug as most hearts but it went beyond that with Scarlet. Something lighted in Scarlet the day she met Gracie. She smiled back, matching Gracie's excitement and was so pleased to show Gracie a day on the town.

"Have you been to the Fuller Lodge, Mick? Any of the atomic bomb history…."

Mick smiled. *Had Bernard forgotten the circumstances that brought Mick to the Alviso?*

Chapter 5
Where's Gracie...

"Where's Gracie," Rosa asked as she sat down across from Scarlet.

"She's back home with Edward," Scarlet answered with an obvious display of contentment. "We dropped her off. I bet she's one tired little girl now."

"You had a nice day I take it." It was easy for Rosa to tell by Scarlet's demeanor and expression.

"Oh yes, Rosa, yes. It was *such* a nice day." She took in a deep and satisfied breath. "We had a wonderful day—all of us. We got lunch and ate by the pond and went...." Scarlet gave Rosa a rundown of the day's activities. Rosa was more taken by the happiness Scarlet exuded while describing the afternoon's activities than the actual activities. They were interrupted.

"Do you know where Lucky is?"

"He wanted to see the mountains, Mick. Lucky wanted to see the mountains. He went for a hike I guess. Did you need something?" Rosa calmly responded.

Mick was nervous but tried to conceal his concern. Buck wasn't a nature lover from all he knew of him. He feared that the walk would be a trek of trouble and asked, "Which way did he go off hiking?"

"I don't know. Did you need something?" Rosa asked again.

Scarlet and Mick shared the same worried look. Neither said anything. Mick silently pondered what to do when a loud noise from the kitchen diverted his attention.

"Is Roberto home?" Scarlet asked, still looking up at Mick.

"I don't think so, but maybe," Rosa replied. "I'm going to get a cup of coffee, do you want one?" She looked at Scarlet then at Mick.

"You stay here, Rosa. I'll go get you a cup of coffee," and Scarlet got up from her chair where Mick was quick to follow. Rosa wandered over to admire her new mural in progress.

The "lid," as they were now referring to the door to Lucky's cellar room, was open and Mick dashed over.

"Lucky?"

"Yeah?" Lucky responded. "It's me. I'm getting used to my new name. Ya wanna know why?"

Mick sighed a relief. He didn't care why, he was just relieved that Buck now Lucky was back at the Alviso and their luck might hold out a bit longer.

"Ya wanna know why, *Mick*?" Lucky said as he ascended the ladder. "Hey, Scarlet." Then Lucky shared his reason for remembering his new name so readily. "I feel lucky, *Mick*," he said emphasizing How's new name. "I'm lucky and I'm Lucky—get it?" and Lucky laughed, finding his observation quite witty.

"Where'd you go?"

Scarlet handed Mick a cup of coffee before she left to give Rosa the other cup.

"Thanks." He continued, "Where'd you hike off to?"

"Out, pretty far. You should see these mountains, those cliffs and stuff. They're strange colors—nice, but have you seen red and purple cliffs before? I wanna paint them. I'm gunna paint them. I'm taking my paper and I'm gunna paint them." Lucky had never seen mountainsides like these. With his new interest and appreciation of his own artistry, he was determined to replicate the aesthetics of the majestic mountainsides he witnessed on his hike.

"Did you run into anybody?" Mick was a fraction more comfortable with Lucky's ability to play along with their new circumstances but he still held Buck as the hot-headed half-wit.

"Sort of," Lucky answered as he went for a cup of coffee.

"What do you mean 'sort of'?"

Lucky sat down at the table with his coffee. "Do you think it'd be okay if I ate this?" he asked Mick, referring to the sugary bear claw pastry sitting on the table looking rather dried out. Surprised that he even asked, Mick nodded a yes. Lucky continued. "Well, I was sittin' there, you know, staring up at those rocks n' cliffs. They sort of look like the cliffs in that Roadrunner cartoon, you know what I mean?"

Mick didn't respond.

"And I heard something, you know, moving in the weeds or whatever, those tall dried-out bushes or whatever. I'd walk some then stop to check things out, you know, what I want to paint, what I think Rosa would like—-
"

"So, was there somebody there?" Mick was impatient.

"Well, I kept hearing somethin' then it would stop."

"Come on. Get to the point."

"It was like a cow——-"

"What do you mean 'like a cow'?"

"Have you ever seen a gray cow, man?"

"So it was a cow, no person around just a cow, a gray cow?"

"Yeah, no people. Have you ever seen a gray cow? I mean gray, not brown but gray. I thought it might be a bull an' it was going to charge me or somethin' but it was a cow alright, but it was gray. Kinda weird huh?" Lucky seemed to be fascinated by this off-colored cow.

Mick put his mind at ease, relieved that he had not encountered a human, just a "gray" cow.

"Maybe it's not such a good idea to take off. We are lucky, *Lucky*." Mick lifted his eyebrows and gave an affected smile. "We have a good thing going here. We're safe for the time being. Don't get too relaxed, don't slip up, man. Don't forget you're an escaped convict—not a forgiving title."

"You took off to a city," Lucky protested.

"*Just* be careful," was all Mick was going to give to that comment. He left the kitchen back to the lobby to join Rosa and Scarlet unaware that Lucky was getting up to follow suit.

Rosa," Lucky started, "have you ever seen a gray cow?"

"You saw a gray cow?" Rosa asked and Lucky elaborated on his gray-cow encounter. He had never seen a gray cow, not even in the cartoons. As he made his way among the sage, the cacti and brush so did this gray cow, seeming as fascinated with Lucky as Lucky was with it. "It followed me, you know, like a dog sort of but at a distance but it was following me…." At first glance he thought that it was a bull and he ran to an outcropping of rocks. From atop the rocks he could see the animal watching him and he could also detect that it was not a bull. Not fearing a cow as he would a bull, Lucky climbed down from the rocks and continued his artistic survey of the area, enjoying the freedom of the trek and the colorful scenery. He wanted to paint the scene for Rosa, for Rosa to hang somewhere at the Alviso—if she liked it. Maybe she would frame it and display it prominently for customers to see since she apparently liked the work he had done so far on the wall, though she hadn't seen the carved up cellar as of yet.

He headed back to the Alviso with the gray cow following in a slow but steady pace. At one point Lucky stopped and turn to face the cow. The cow also stopped—both watching the other. Lucky made a loud "aaaaaaaaahhhhhhh" sound then ran straight for the cow fully expecting it to turn and run in fear from the approaching wild man. But it didn't. It just watched Lucky come its way. The cow didn't flinch, it just chewed and watched. It was Lucky who stopped in his tracks, hesitant to get much closer. The cow was clearly unafraid. Lucky laughed and continued on his way back to the Alviso with the gray cow following at a distance behind. At some point, and Lucky didn't know when or where, the cow stopped following Lucky and she was no longer visible to him.

"I can't say that I have seen a gray cow, Lucky," Rosa said after hearing Lucky's cow adventure.

"I wanna paint those walls, those cliffs."

Rosa had an overnight bag that could hold Lucky's paper and supplies so she offered it to him. "You can put your supplies in it, paint the scene out there. Paint it as you see it. That's what an artist would do. You take your canvas and your easel and brushes and you paint what you see, Lucky."

"Eezull?"

"It's what you put your canvas, your paper on. "Let me show you." Rosa picked up a magazine where she remembered seeing an easel in one of the ads. She loved Lucky's enthusiasm. Even though Lucky was a full-grown man, to Rosa he was like a child in a good way. With the influence of Agnes, Rosa was also beginning to believe that Lucky had a bad start in life and having some direction, like his art, might change his life as a man.

Lucky vacillated from the first night from a somewhat naïve child to an angry man with little in between. Since the beginning of the mural, which Rosa was extraordinarily pleased, she had been dealing with the rather innocent child side of Lucky. She liked calling him Lucky; it was a good new name for a possible new start in life. She hadn't asked what he had done to be put in prison; she didn't much think about it. She didn't concern herself with him being discovered or his running away. She just enjoyed Lucky and was duly impressed with his artistic ability. She believed that Lucky's talent should be encouraged and she sure had use for it. She was getting the mural she had always wanted. After Lucky left the lobby she called Pedro.

"Hello," Pedro said in his usual apathetic, moderately annoyed manner. He was never all that enthusiastic about answering the telephone. At this stage of his life, it was typically someone asking for something—not an invite, or casual conversation for conversation sake, but they wanted something from him and this call would qualify.

"Hello, Pedro. This is Rosa. How are you?" He didn't answer but waited for what it was that she wanted. "You there, Pedro?"

"I'm here. I answered the phone didn't I."

"Pedro, I want to buy your painter things. I want to buy your paints, brushes. Do you have an easel? I would like to buy an easel." Rosa knew that Pedro could be grumpy and almost always stubborn but she could handle his ways, she had for years. She knew he painted in the past and she was certain that he didn't any longer. His stuff would be old, but she knew without a doubt that Lucky would be overjoyed to have real painter's supplies.

"You painting now, Rosa?" Pedro asked, uplifted a bit since this favor would benefit him.

"So, Pedro, are you going to sell me your old paints, and an easel?" She wanted to buy them right then. She hoped to surprise Lucky by putting the supplies in the overnight bag she intended on giving him. "Well, I'm interested, Pedro, but I need them now. I would like to come by now, pay you cash. So, can I come by, Pedro?"

"You want them now, then you can have them now. Come over. How much you giving me?"

"It depends on what you have, Pedro. We'll see when I get there." Then she reprimanded, *"And open your door when I knock, Pedro."* He had a reputation of not opening his door and making no qualms that he was home while the visitor repeatedly knocked in vain.

Rosa asked Agnes to take over the front lobby desk, the counter to the world of Alviso. Rosa took cash from the register, told Agnes she'd be back in an hour or so then rushed over to Pedro's before he changed his mind. She climbed into her truck thinking how everyone has a truck, everyone in the area drove a truck of some sort. Some day she was going to get a *car!*

"Have you ever seen a gray cow, Jeff?" Lucky asked as they stacked wood against the outside wall by the kitchen door.

"A gray cow. I don't know. Maybe. Why?"

"I've never seen a gray cow. I was up those mountains and there was a gray cow, followin' me."

"What mountains?" Jeff was surprised that Lucky was off anywhere and actually came back.

"Over that way," and Lucky pointed in the direction.

"You mean by the monastery?"

"The what?"

"Did you go to the monastery?" Jeff asked, still stacking the wood. Lucky looked a bit perplexed and it dawned on Jeff that he might not know what a monastery was. "The monastery is where the monks live, like a church where they all live." He looked over at Lucky. "Did you see it?"

"I didn't see no monastery. There wasn't a church out there...but the side of those mountain was somethin' else. I'm going to paint it..." and he chatted on while the two finished stacking the wood.

"Now we need to set some of this wood in the baskets outside the rooms——"

Lucky interrupted, "Then why'd we stack em all here? Are you kiddin' me?"

"We just need to fill the baskets outside the rooms, not all of it," Jeff explained as he began placing the wood in the wheelbarrow. Lucky joined in and as they went to fill the baskets he continued on about the mysterious gray cow who stalked him in the field.

Rosa was thrilled to give Lucky Pedro's art supplies. At first Lucky was confused by this wood box Rosa was handing him. He had no idea what it was. Once she showed him that it was a collapsible easel, complete with paints, brushes, a pad of painter's paper and an old well-used wood painter's pallet, Lucky was eager to try out his gift. He kept his emotions in check but it was clear to Rosa that the easel meant more than a simple gift to Lucky—he seemed to be in his own world while he handled all that the easel entailed. He had the look of restrained excitement that was slowly giving way. He glanced up at Rosa and to Rosa, Lucky looked inspired. She was so very pleased.

The easel collapsed to what looked like a rectangular wood box, a large wood briefcase. Rosa and Lucky erected the easel and collapsed it several times like children trying out a new toy. They slid the drawer for supplies in and out, testing it and it moved smoothly in spite of its age. Everything collapsed and was easy for Lucky to carry. This is just what Lucky needed to solidify his new identity: Lucky, the artist. Not Lucky the criminal, the escapee, the bad-boy. Not Lucky the numskull, the moron, the idiot. But, Lucky, the artist.

Lucky finished the mural in the lobby, staying up late in the evening to get the project completed for Rosa. Twice Sheriff Shelton tapped on the window giving Lucky a neighborly nod and scaring the living daylights out of the Buck in Lucky. Lucky impressed not just Rosa, and everyone else who saw the new mural, but mostly himself.

This was different. He was doing something that others liked, that was pleasing to others. He was not only good at this new venture, but in the midst of the work, Lucky stepped into a place within himself that was new to him. He hadn't ever recalled feeling this way without chemical inducement. He could focus in on one thing, with reasonable peace, leaving most everything outside of his work on the periphery. In those moments the old Buck no longer existed.

Lucky was up early and gone with his easel in hand. No one stopped him, and Rosa would have prevented it if anyone tried to stop him. She admired and encouraged Lucky's talent and his new milder manner kept others from discouraging Lucky's artistic pursuits as well. He hiked back to where Jeff said there was a monastery. He saw no monastery or an indication of one. Lucky set up his easel. He didn't have a chair but he remedied that by dragging a stump over to his easel then set his folded jacket atop it.

The world around him was welcoming and his long-time natural tendency to be looking over his shoulder while on perpetual low-grade alert was at that moment sweetly fading. Lucky placed the art-paper canvas on the easel then pulled open the drawer. For a few minutes he just stared at the tubes of paint and brushes. He still wasn't sure what he was supposed to do with that odd shaped wood piece with all the paint stains and hole in it. He looked up at the cliffs, stared for a good amount of time then was ready to tackle this gift for Rosa. He began opening the paints to check out the colors, smearing them on the tips of his fingers. He was excited...then *startled*—shooting up and off the stump. A rustling in the dry brush a short distance behind him had him on alert once again—the ready-to-fight instinct was instantaneous. Where a situation would best call for one to run, Buck would rear up to fight and that instinct immediately kicked in even though, under his current circumstances, Lucky would be better off choosing to run.

There was no one to fight, just the gray cow chewing in a circular motion, staring at Lucky.

Lucky shouted at the cow, *"Damn!* Whataya want you old gray cow!"* He took his seat back on the stump before his easel. The cow remained stationary, chewing and staring at Lucky with its big steadfast eyes. Lucky continued to select his paints. He wasn't sure just where to start with this painting. He stared at the multihued cliffs for a while longer then looked at the dabs of paint on his palm. Then he glimpsed the odd shape wood piece with all the paint stains realizing that the wood piece could replace his palm. Lucky began testing the paints, dabbing and mixing them on the wood palette—doing naturally what artists do.

The cow moved a few steps closer, still chewing and staring unnoticed by Lucky who had made his first brush of color on the paper canvas. Once the first stroke of paint was placed, there wasn't much thinking about it—not that Buck had ever been big in the cerebral department. The strokes and dabs and color choices were automatic. Like Lucky would later say, "I feel like it talks to me, ya know." The cliff side spoke to Lucky and with this sense came what appeared to be an innate ability to replicate the essence of an object or a scene.

The cow (having now stepped even closer to Lucky) sneezed, announcing its new position.

"So whadaya think, old cow…old gray cow?"

The cow continued to stare, not missing a rotation as she chewed in steady rhythm.

"I don't know the name of this color, purpley color—maybe it's just purple, but I got the right colors, don't ya think?" Lucky continued to talk to the mammoth fan as he painted and this scene continued for four days. Lucky hiked out to the same area, set up his easel and the gray cow faithfully showed up. Lucky explained what he was painting and why and the gray cow was unwavering—standing close by, seeming to be paying attention to whatever Lucky was doing or saying.

Jeff couldn't have been a more polar opposite from Lucky, despite this fact, when Lucky spent much time with anyone besides Rosa, it was Jeff. Jeff had made a fire in the pit outside and the two were sitting close to the fire to keep warm as they ate their dinner: sandwiches made by Agnes. Jeff tossed a log on the fire which stirred the thought and he began talking about how he'd like to tackle making those bears out of a log with a chainsaw. Lucky hadn't seen one and didn't have a clue what he was talking about. Lucky listened to Jeff talk about his prospective roadside business for a bit before interrupting him.

"What kinda cow is a gray cow?" he asked.

"I don't know. How do you know it's a cow and not a steer?"

"What's the difference?"

"Well, if that gray cow is grazing out by the monastery then it probably is a steer, you know, what's between that bread you're eating."

Lucky swallowed his half-chewed bite and inquired, "They have gray steer?"

"What do you mean 'gray'? Like a light gray or spotted gray?"

"A dark gray. Ya know, sort of, well, sort of like a granny's gray hair. Ya know, how old ladies have that dark gray hair?" Lucky tried to explain.

"You mean blue, a blue gray?" Jeff imagined a gray associated with an old lady to be with a blue hue.

"I guess, sort of," Lucky answered. "So you think it's a steer?"

"More than likely," Jeff replied then added, "I wonder if Roberto has a chainsaw?"

Lucky thought to himself, *If it's a cow it'll get milked but if it's a steer then someone's gunna slaughter it.* It bothered him. He never thought much about cows or steers and their journey to the dinner plate before.

Lucky finished his painting of the colorful cliffs, but he wanted to do more: he wanted to paint the sky at dusk and he wanted to find this monastery that Jeff spoke of. Rosa often made the sign of the cross, so he thought maybe she was religious and would like a painting of the house where the monks lived...and, he was curious to see a real monk and where they lived.

Rosa was his biggest fan and her encouragement spurred Lucky on to continue painting, and paint for her, or at least her praise. So Lucky proceeded to help around Rancho Alviso then spent his spare time, with the permission of Rosa, out in the countryside with his easel.

This day Lucky didn't set up his easel, but hid it in the brush. He stood around waiting for Granny, the name he had given the gray cow, to show up. Lucky was genuinely enjoying his new bovine buddy from the brush. Granny had been standing there all along, Lucky hadn't noticed her between the sage and short trees.

"Come on, girl...we're gunna go hunt down some monks."

Granny followed a distance behind as Lucky trekked farther into the canyon. The sound of water drew him to a large creek with a wide spread of water in the middle.

"Is this where you drink, Granny?"

Granny stared, per usual, at Lucky as he spoke.

He continued on.

"Come on, Granny, hurry it up old girl," he shouted back at Granny. She wasn't keeping pace and Lucky was eager to find this monk house. He quickened his gait but Granny stopped, chewed and watched Lucky until she could see him no more then Granny sauntered off on her own mission.

"Damn," Lucky exclaimed aloud. He stared up at the steeple supporting a cross. It was a similar pink and beige as the face of the sandy rock cliff behind it. If it weren't for the cross atop it, he may have missed it altogether. Lucky turned right, heading toward the structure, excited and a little nervous. The building that came into view looked like a church. He stopped to look for Granny, unsure if a cow would be acceptable company. She was nowhere to be seen. Lucky continued up the road that narrowed to a driveway. There were paths leading off in different directions and he was unsure which to take, unsure if he should take any of them...but his curiosity urged him onto a narrow dirt path snaking through groomed bushes. He was apprehensive: would he be trespassing and if caught bring on trouble he couldn't afford.

The path led to an expanded area where a tall wood cross stood erect from the rock covered ground. Stones encircled the cross for several feet. A small cross was carved out at the top allowing the bright blue cloud-filled sky to shine through it. Something was written in a language not familiar to Lucky on a piece of wood near the base of the cross. He continued up the path. It seemed to be leading to the building that, to Lucky, looked like a church. Everything was of nature however groomed, neat—a work of God and man. A short distance from the first cross was another, again planted into the ground and surrounded by rocks with writing he couldn't understand. Lucky continued to walk on the winding path to another tall wood cross. This cross had a wood bench positioned across from it. He sat down. This was a peaceful place and he was certain that he had found the monastery Jeff was talking about.

Walking so quietly that he was almost silent, a man wearing a robe walked past Lucky, not saying a word, only a slight nod and a slight smile. Lucky watched him proceed up the path between the well-groomed trees and believed that he just saw a monk and the monk didn't appear to be alarmed or bothered by Lucky's presence.

Lucky followed up the same path, passing several large wood crosses on his way. He came to an open area with crosses scattered about like flowers in a garden. He looked around but didn't see the monk. Lucky crossed the low stone fencing to take a closer look. He quickly realized that he was stepping onto a graveyard and backed over the fence. What looked like a church blending into the side of the cliff towered above him and he dared to pursue his curiosity.

He saw no one. He stood stationary, looking about and waiting for someone to appear—someone to ask him who he was and what he was doing there. But no one did. Lucky walked up to the two ornately-carved wood doors, placed his hand on the handle and pulled fully expecting the doors to be locked, but they weren't. He looked around again for a roaming monk or for any person but saw no one. Lucky stepped into the church. It was small with tall ceilings. There was an enormous multi-pane window that peaked up to the ceiling displaying the pastel cliff behind it and giving light to the church. To the left and right of the church were several rows of dark wood pews with an open circular space between them.

Again, Lucky waited for someone to make an appearance and to question his uninvited presence in the church, but no one appeared. He noticed rows of small candles in red glass holders. Each lighted. He looked around the church again, expecting someone. The silence was different and Lucky remained still until the old metal stand tiered with lighted candles beckoned him, or so it felt. They flickered as he stood before them and the spattering of light danced across the wall and onto the feet of Christ. It was mesmerizing. The large hand-carved, hand-painted figure of Christ on the cross above looked as though He was smiling at Lucky. The Christ's eyes appeared to be staring right into his. Lucky was still, staring back, though not smiling. His chest began to feel light, then his shoulders as if the feeling were creeping up his body. Lucky quickly shook his head and looked away.

Tall slivers of headless matches stuck up from a four by three inch metal container of sand. He pulled one up, examined it and as he stuck it back into the sand he noticed a slot in the metal to his left. Curious, he placed his hand beneath it and with only the slightest touch the metal box fell from the stand spilling coins and bills onto the floor and breaking the silence of the church and the calm in Lucky. Money lay before him, something he had none of. Not just coins but dollar and five-dollar bills.

Lucky didn't hear anybody come into the church but he felt something and turned to see a man in a robe, not the same man in a robe that was on the path. Lucky panicked; though he had instantly thought of taking the money, he hadn't—yet—but was certain now that he was going to be accused of trying to steal money. The Buck in him said *grab it, appear threatening and get the fuck outta there.*

The monk, with his robe and belted cross swaying rhythmically, quietly approached Lucky in an unhurried pace while Lucky remained crouched, waiting...thinking as best he could. Buck typically didn't think in such situations but reacted, sometimes thinking later...but often not.

"We need to fix that," Brother John commented in a hushed tone. "I thought I had that fixed." He gave Lucky a gentle smile. "I guess not." He bent down and reached for the metal box then began retrieving the scatter coins.

Lucky grabbed the bills from the floor. The monk looked his way, held up the box and Lucky complied, placing the bills into the box.

Once full, he emptied the metal collection box into the pocket of his robe.

Lucky bent down and craned his neck to look at the empty space where the box had been attached.

"I can fix this, easy, Mr....ah, Mr. Monk," Lucky offered, a bit nervous, anticipating some kind of inquiry as to who he was and what he was doing there. "I just need a screwdriver and a couple a screws."

The monk responded, "I don't know where Brother Charles keeps his tools. I do appreciate your offer," he paused, waiting for Lucky to offer up his name but Lucky didn't catch the hint—he just stared at "Mr. Monk." "We'll get this taken care of." He smiled at Lucky, set the small metal collection box atop the slot and exited the same way he entered leaving Lucky dumbfound that his presence was not questioned and even more so that he had not been accused of attempting to steal the money from the fallen box.

Lucky looked up at Jesus who was still staring back down at Lucky.

"I wasn't stealing any of the damn money," he proclaimed in a whisper.

Lucky almost tiptoed toward the door, looking back and up at Jesus as Jesus's gentle gaze followed him to the door. Slowly, and gently, he shut the door behind him. He followed the path he took to find the church back down the hill and in a jog made his way to his hidden easel passing Granny along the way. She was by the water, by herself. "Hey Granny," Lucky shouted as he passed. Granny chewed and stared, keeping her big brown eyes on Lucky until he was out of view.

Once back at Rancho Alviso, Lucky went immediately to his artist den, or rabbit hole as Jeff called it. He was in for the night, only coming up to make a cheese sandwich (due to Granny, eating beef was starting to bother him) and to use the bathroom. Other than Rosa, no one seemed to be too concerned about what Lucky was doing anymore and Rosa was preoccupied.

Roberto asked Rosa and Scarlet to come to the front, to the bench outside the lobby doors. He looked very stern, very serious and a bit nervous. He had something to tell them. Scarlet and Rosa sat on the bench, waiting and puzzled, while Roberto stood before them.

"I'm going to be gone for a week or so," he informed in a statement rather than seeking permission or acceptance. He was determined and resolute about this trip and he wanted to relay that from the get-go. Rosa looked unaffected by the news while Scarlet looked troubled. He continued, "Delmacio needs my help moving a statue to Saint Francis Cathedral so I'm going to go with him, to help him."

"That's nice." Rosa smiled.

"Why would that take a week or so to move a statue?" Scarlet asked, perplexed by the news.

"Because the statue is in Mexico and we have to bring it back to Santa Fe. It's some special statue; it's a big undertaking and it might take more than a week," Roberto explained in a tone Rosa recognized. She knew if either or both objected to his absence a change in his plans was not very likely. "Look," he said staring directly at Scarlet, "Delmacio needs my help and this place will run fine with me gone for a while. Ya got Mick and Jeff, and Agnes. With their help everything is going to be fine. Nothing is going to go——"

Rosa interrupted, "Nothing is going to go wrong. We'll be just fine. You go help Delmacio and the church." She turned to Scarlet, placed her hand on her arm. "We'll be just fine, won't we Scarlet?"

"But it's nearing tourist season," Scarlet reminded.

Rosa looked up at Roberto. "When do you leave?"

"Well, I really should go right away. Some guy couldn't make it and they needed one more and they're leaving. I really should go talk to Jeff and the others," he answered, insistent and hurried.

Scarlet looked to Rosa, taken aback by the suddenness of his departure. Rosa gave her a reassuring pat with a satisfied smile. She was pleased to finally see Roberto get away from the Alviso. She knew that he had not only wanted to get away for some time but that he needed to get away.

"We'll be just fine, Scarlet, just fine. We have pretty good help here now, don't ya think?" Rosa was sympathetic yet unyielding.

Scarlet felt obligated to respond with a grin, forced as it was. She knew Rosa was right. Everything would run just fine; this was only another change Scarlet would have to accept.

They sat on the bench and talked, talked about the changes at the Alviso: one being the new inventory for the lobby. Impressed with the sales of the old blankets and the faded post cards, Rosa wanted to fill the lobby with gift items. She asked Scarlet for suggestions which engaged Scarlet to the degree that it appeared her anxiety over Roberto leaving had diminished. They were still engaged in conversation on the bench when Roberto's truck raced out of the parking lot onto the road that would take him away from the Alviso. He wanted to leave immediately, before anything could possibly hinder his departure.

It was early morning. Jeff, Agnes, Katherine and Bernard were chatting about Pedro's eternal Christmas display as they readied the kitchen for breakfast orders. The lid opened on Lucky's lair, surprising the kitchen crew due to the early hour. Lucky emerged with easel in hand. The drawer designated for brushes now held a handful of screws, a screwdriver and a small hammer—the tools he needed to fix the metal collection box. Without a word, he rushed out the kitchen door.

The cool air, the array of nature's scents embraced Bucks's new position in life. He was Lucky, free to come and go as he chose. He was an artist, and the people at the Alviso seemed to like him. He felt wanted—for himself instead of a crime. Unlike How who would analyze his predicament each day, each situation, Buck just accepted that he now had a life as Lucky, the artist.

"What the hell?" The words fell out of Lucky's dropped jaw. His eyes set like steel on the ridge above him. Frances, the old nurse who had cared for his cut hand, was walking with an animal on the dirt path. It wasn't a dog, not a dog like he'd ever seen before.

"Hey," Lucky shouted. When she didn't respond, he jogged through the brush to get closer. "*Hey!*" he yelled again but this time even louder. Frances kept on walking but her trail companion stopped, turned its head to search the origin of the sound. Though Lucky was somewhat hidden in the brush, the animal's eyes fixed directly on him—its head crouched, teeth exposed from its long naked snout. The animal's shoulders were hunched up as though it was prepared to attack.

"What the fuck?" Lucky was afraid to move.

Frances stopped once she noticed that her companion was no longer trotting alongside her. She craned her neck trying to see what he was watching but saw nothing out of the ordinary and did not see Lucky. She waited a few seconds before calling, "Chupi. Chupi, come on." Chupi was focused on Lucky while Lucky stood frightened, motionless, wishing he had kept his mouth shut. "Come on, *Chupi!*" Frances commanded. For fear that Chupi had spotted prey and would take off in pursuit, Frances hurried over to clip on his leash. They needed to get home while it was still early. "Let's go, Chupi, my good boy." Chupi looked over his shoulder in Lucky's direction several times before he and Frances disappeared into the woods. Once out of sight, Lucky could breathe again, relieved that the four-legged whatever-it-was was gone.

He hardly had time to settle his nerves when a sound from the brush had him frightened once again. He spun around, fell over his easel and landed on the ground face up. Visions of that "thing" with Frances attacking him from the brush flashed through his mind, only to see Granny with her perpetually rotating jaw standing before him. She was a welcome sight, for many reasons.

He gathered himself, and his easel, to continue his trek to the monastery. As he looked at Granny, he wondered if he could get close enough to pet her. He'd give it a try.

"Goooood morning, Granny," Lucky said in a soft soothing voice as he slowly approached, his arm extended, his fingers wiggling. Granny just stared; she didn't budge. He bent forward and cautiously put his hand up to her wide wet nose. She reached her head forward and sniffed his offered hand then promptly sneezed, spraying Lucky's hand like an atomizer.

"Aaaaaaah, Granny. Shit." Lucky wiped the wet off his hand onto his pants and continued on his way. When he glanced back at Granny, she appeared to be smiling. Maybe something was caught in her mouth and she lifted the corner of her mouth to maneuver the stuck wad, but whatever she was doing, she looked as though she were smiling at Lucky which gave him a good laugh. He loved that cow.

It didn't take Lucky but ten minutes to reattach the collection box to the votive candle stand. He spent most of his time moving from place to place within the church, watching the eyes of the carved image of Jesus watching him. His eyes seemed to follow Lucky, tracking his every move. Lucky tried to find a spot in the church where Jesus couldn't see him but other then moving around the corner, or leaving, he couldn't get away from His penetrating stare. Even if Lucky moved swiftly, Jesus's eyes were just as swift. Lucky decided to move on and out of the church.

Chapter 6
Katherine Needed To...

Katherine needed to find Rosa. She was watching the front desk and fully anticipated spending her time thumbing through one of Rosa's magazines until Rosa got back. Katherine wasn't prepared when a woman walked into the lobby wanting a room. And she had a dog. Katherine not only didn't know if there were any rooms available but she wasn't sure what Rosa charged on each room and if Rosa accepted a pet. Katherine was flustered as she stood behind the grand wood counter before the waiting woman whose dog was hanging out of the window of her still-running car.

"Oh, uhm, let's see here," Katherine fumbled along. "I'll be right back." She attempted to look confident as she left the lobby to the kitchen looking for Agnes.

"What's wrong?" Agnes set her pastry down.

"Oh, I feel so stupid, Agnes." Katherine shook her head. "There's a young lady wanting a room. I'm supposed to be watching the front, and I don't know a thing."

"Well, there's a room available," Agnes informed.

"But how much is a room for one person? Are the rooms different? And, she's got a dog...and her car's running. She's standing in the lobby." Katherine, the typically calm Katherine, was on the mild side of frantic.

"You'll do fine, Katherine," Agnes reassured. "The prices are listed in the drawer but I don't know if Rosa allows a dog. Why don't you go out and give the young lady the room rates and I'll go find Rosa, see if she accepts a dog."

"Yeah, she'll accept a dog," Jeff called out from the other side of the kitchen. "Ask her if she wants lunch. Try to get her to have lunch at the restaurant. Tell her we're having a special."

"What special?" Agnes had posted the day's menu and there was no special on the board.

"I don't know...tell her quesadillas are on special." Jeff believed that a quesadilla could and should be a meal, not an appetizer. And, he knew it was a good way to move the leftovers.

Feeling a slight more confident, Katherine stepped back through the door to the lobby with a smile. She found a sheet of laminated paper with a hand-drawn rendition of Rancho Alviso in the drawer. There was a different price for each room. The sheet also noted the size of the beds and how many.

"Thank you for waiting," she said with a customer-service sort of smile. "Yes, we do accept a pet. One bed? A twin? Or," she hesitated as she read to herself *Bigger than a twin*. She didn't want to say "bigger than a twin" as an option. As she looked back up at the waiting woman, Katherine realized that she may now know the price of each room but she didn't know which room or rooms were available. "Can you excuse me again for one minute, please?"

"Of course," the woman answered seeming to be in no hurry. "I'm going to go turn off my car; I'll be right back."

Katherine rushed back into the kitchen.

"Agnes, which rooms are available and what is a 'bigger than a twin' suppose to mean?" She was hurried, and a bit annoyed.

Agnes took a few seconds to think. She was trying to remember which rooms were empty. Again, Jeff ended the dilemma.

"The room facing to the west, at the end, that's available and bigger than a twin means just that: bigger than a twin bed."

"I don't want to say 'bigger than a twin,'" Katherine mumbled to Agnes.

"Just give her the room on the end...I think it's the only room available anyway. If she has a dog then that's a good room—she can let the dog out to that open area right outside the door. Give her that room."

"What number is it?" she asked, sounding and looking a bit like Buck his first night as a waiter.

"They're letters, Katherine. Remember? Your room has a letter not a number," Jeff answered a bit amused by Katherine's anxiety over the minor matter.

She rushed back out to the lobby reaching the counter as the young woman came through the doors.

With the room, price and bed size approved, Katherine felt a sense of relief and competency—until the woman handed her a credit card, which set Katherine right back into a panic.

"Oh, let's see. Ummm, let's see. Well…oh, I'm sorry. What is your name?" Katherine asked.

"Lena," she answered. "Do you need me to fill out a registration form?"

"Well, Lena, I have never done this before. I apologize. I was watching the front desk here for Rosa—she owns this place; she should be back any minute. I don't know how to do, process, a credit card. I don't even see one of those credit card things. Oh," she audibly exhaled, "Bernard would know how to do this but he went for a walk."

"Would you like me to pay you in cash? Would that make it easier?"

"Oh, could you? Yes. Now that I can do, open the cash register…I think." Katherine looked befuddled as she glanced over the cash register. She had opened it before but now her mind was going blank. With the customer watching and waiting, it was near impossible for Katherine to think clearly. "I should get somebody. Can you wait again? I'm so sorry."

"No problem," Lena responded with amused understanding.

Katherine disappeared into the kitchen while Mick entered the lobby.

"Can I help you?" he asked the waiting woman.

"I've been helped, but I think the woman helping me is having a problem checking me in. I think she said this is her first time checking someone in."

Mick stepped behind the counter. "One room for one?" he asked.

"Yes, and my dog. She already assigned me room "M" but I haven't signed any registration form or paid yet."

Mick pulled out a form and handed it to her along with a pen. He opened the drawer to retrieve the key for the room and grabbed a pamphlet that is given to each patron staying at the Alviso describing their services, such as the restaurant, long term rates and hours plus what businesses were in town and a description of the natural wonders surrounding the Alviso. Roberto Sr. wanted to include some of the history of Rancho Alviso but Rosa and Roberto Jr. talked him out of it since much of it was in dispute and some was of a morbid nature.

Katherine and Jeff were soon by Mick's side.

"Do you know how to do a credit card, Mick?"

Jeff reached under the counter and pulled out a manual credit card machine that took everyone aback. It was huge and looked like an oversized stapler.

"That's the credit card machine?" Mick asked in serious doubt.

Lena smiled.

Jeff dropped the heavy apparatus on the counter, which if the counter-top had been glass may have broken it. He reached his hand out for Lena's card, while Mick's doubting eyes watched Lena hand it over with a smile verging on a laugh, but Jeff knew what he was doing. Katherine handed him the registration form where he added the room letter, amount and tax. He placed a carbon copy credit card slip under the heavy arm of the machine and slammed it down.

"There ya go," Jeff said and handed Lena her copy, while Katherine checked out the information on the registration.

"Lena Shelton?" she inquired.

"Yes."

"Our sheriff's name is Shelton. Could you be related? Are you from around here?" Katherine inquired.

"No, I'm not from around here but there's always a chance we could be related somehow," Lena answered, a bit in a hurry to get to her room.

"I'll show you to your room. If you want to park in front of the room, just follow me," Mick instructed as he held up the key and headed out the door. Lena followed him out the door then veered over to her car. She pulled up with Pepper panting out the window to where Mick stood waiting.

"You have a dog," Mick commented.

"I was told that you accepted a dog, is that wrong?"

"I'm sure it's fine." He put the key in the door to open it for Lena then handed it to her. Before leaving he praised Alviso's restaurant and extended an invite adding that the chef was open to culinary challenges if she has any. When Roberto allowed, Jeff replicated dishes seen in Rosa's magazines and he did it quite well. He had a knack at reproducing the visual appeal of a dish as well as the flavor palette. In cooking, Jeff had awakened a sleeping talent.

When Rosa returned, Katherine gave her a blow by blow of the just occurred events. Rosa was pleased at how each contributed to get the process moving but she wasn't all that happy about the dog.

"What kind of dog is it? Large or small?" she asked Katherine.

"Jeff said you accepted dogs, Rosa. And, ah, I think it would be considered a medium dog. She was a nice young lady and her dog seemed well-behaved."

"She brought the dog inside with her?"

"Oh no, Rosa, her dog stayed in the car but the window was open and the dog stayed in the car like it was supposed to. It wasn't a wild dog, you know, like jumping out the window. It seemed well-behaved. Oh, don't tell me that you don't allow dogs." Katherine gave the exhale of failure. She saw the woman walking her dog and immediately pointed them out to Rosa.

Rosa walked over to the window to take a better look. She commented no further and relieved Katherine of front counter duty.

It wasn't long before the new patron was in the lobby on her way to grab a bite to eat at the recommended restaurant. Rosa was in the kitchen and no one was attending the counter so Lena walked on through the lobby to the restaurant and seated herself. It didn't take long for Agnes to appear, spry and courteous and happy to have a customer to serve. They chatted a bit about the day and the weather then Agnes did as Jeff desired: she recommended, or rather pushed, the quesadilla. She hailed the quesadilla as a guaranteed palate pleaser. Lena took the bait, particularly since she could dictate the type of ingredients she wanted: vegetarian with lots of cheese. She also agreed to a salad with Jeff's homemade green chili ranch dressing.

"So, what kind of dog is that you have?" Rosa appeared at the table.

"He's a Shar Pei/Foxhound mix," Lena responded, proud of her faithful companion.

"I haven't had a dog in so many years. It's so far back that I can't remember the dog's name," Rosa commented, staring out the window in thought.

"I don't know what I'd do without him," Lena replied. "My name is Lena, and yours?"

"Rosa."

"Would you like to sit down: I'd love the company," Lena offered. "Can I buy you a cup of coffee?"

Rosa gave a slight laugh then answered, "Yes, I think I would like to sit down."

Agnes approached the table with Lena's salad and a glass of water.

"Would you like a cup of coffee?" Lena asked once more. "It's on me."

"Would you like a glass of sangria, young lady?" Rosa replied, but before Lena had a chance to respond she looked up at Agnes and said, "Get us two sangrias."

Lena smiled and added, "Then the sangrias are on me."

Maybe it was because Lena was just passing through, or maybe it was her friendly spontaneous invitation but for some reason Rosa opened up to Lena like she was an old friend. They talked and laughed and what Lena had expected would be a quick lunch turned into over an hour. Lena still had no idea that Rosa owned Rancho Alviso.

"So, just where are you heading to? And you come all the way from California? You have family here?" Rosa was curious.

"Well, sort of. I'm headed to Pista to visit some friends who, really, are more like family. I haven't seen them in years." She paused for a few seconds. "I think it's gunna be pretty emotional seeing them, but I can't wait to see them. And what brought you to this place?"

"I own it." The tipsy Rosa grinned.

After bringing Rosa three sangrias and Lena two, Agnes watched them from the kitchen door. She was surprised and amazed to see Rosa so animated, and tipsy. This was a side of Rosa she had yet to experience.

Rosa told Lena about wanting to revamp the lobby. She asked, as a customer and traveler, what variety of items would appeal to her and what did she think people passing through would want to buy.

"Turquoise jewelry," Lena answered right off.

"And what else?"

"Post cards. Probably salsa or something like that, you know the type of things the southwest is known for—the kind of things people like to bring home as gifts. Probably anything chili related; you know what I mean?"

"Well, young lady with a dog, I gotta get to that market in Santa Fe..." and it wasn't long before Lena offered to drive Rosa to Santa Fe and to assist her in finding all the touristy things to fill up the lobby.

Rosa needed a bit of assistance due to the several sangrias she socially finished off and they left the table arm in arm. They walked out to the front and sat on the bench. Lena was sitting with a new friend enjoying the New Mexico sunset just like back at Broken Arrow. They both sat quiet, both engulfed in separate moments from their pasts. Rosa feeling the effect of the sangrias—something she hadn't experienced in many years—and thinking of her late husband while Lena stared at the sunset and thought about her time back at Broken Arrow.

"I better go check on Pepper," Lena softly commented, not wanting to interrupt Rosa's pensive state.

Rosa looked up at Lena, who was now standing, her face having an expression Lena didn't know how to interpret. Rosa looked as though she was on the verge of tears, but it could have been the sangrias, Lena didn't know. She smiled at Rosa and Rosa turned away.

Rosa didn't return to the lobby that evening nor did she stop in at the kitchen for dinner. However, Lena did return for dinner, much to the delight of Jeff. She had made a point of letting him know how much she loved the quesadilla and he was happy to see her back. The dining room was busy. It was a Friday night and from spring through fall Friday through Sunday was the restaurant's busiest time. Bernard was enthusiastically working the lobby since Katherine preferred to help in the kitchen, avoiding a repeat of the afternoon's embarrassment. Strangers made Katherine a bit nervous but Bernard liked to chat. His station in the lobby suited him just fine. Besides, being behind a cash register reminded Bernard of being back at his bookstore and he rather enjoyed the feeling.

With Rosa squeezed into the little car and Pepper left in the confines of the cottage yard, Lena turned onto the winding road heading away from Rancho Alviso and towards Santa Fe. Rosa wasn't as upbeat as she had been the previous day. She had a bit of a headache, so she said.

"Would you like to put on some music instead of talking?" Lena asked.

Rosa took a deep breath.

"Would you like me to put the top down?"

"Do whatever you like. Just ignore me for a bit," Rosa responded in a lazy voice, as if she were still half asleep.

"Coffee?" Lena offered.

"Santa Fe," Rosa answered.

They passed a waving Albert as they sped by the Mountain High hardware store. Rosa gave him a glance but she didn't wave back; she didn't have the energy at the moment.

Lena listened to the radio and repeatedly searched for a more agreeable station. The closer they got to Santa Fe the more animated Rosa became and by the time they reached the turn off to the Santa Fe flea market her vitality and enthusiasm were in full gear. With Rosa's age and stature, getting in and out of the little Karmann Ghia was a bit of a challenge. She squeezed out as fast as she was able, grasping the car door for balance. The two were off to make the lobby of Rancho Alviso the proper tourist gift shop.

Scarlet was showing Jeff how Roberto makes his nopales cactus salad while Mick sat at the table eating Jeff's quesadilla screw-up. Lucky was off on his own again, but this time without his easel. He'd finished the mural in the lobby and Rosa hadn't given him another assignment. No one was quite sure what he was doing. A Fourplay CD was playing in the background—nothing out of the ordinary, until Sheriff Shelton came through the back kitchen door.

"Hey," he hollered.

Everyone stopped what they were doing. The sheriff had their full attention.

"Well, guys, you know Albert, over at the Mountain High hardware store," he shook his head, "well, he got robbed."

"When?" Agnes asked, a bit shaken. "And by who? Do you know who did it, who robbed him?"

Mick and Scarlet exchanged a worried glance. That was Buck's forte. *Where was Lucky?* Mick's heart began to race as the sheriff looked his way.

"Well, it was a white guy," he answered. "Albert didn't recognize him. Anybody new come by here?" he asked and looked to each person in the kitchen.

"I'll go ask Bernard. He's in the lobby; he might have seen someone," Katherine offered and rushed out the kitchen door to the lobby.

"Yeah, Albert said the guy came in, looked like he was looking for something then surprised him at the counter with a knife," Sheriff Shelton explained, not looking as concerned as Agnes believe he should be. Lucky never entered Agnes's mind as being the possible culprit. However, Jeff, Scarlet and Mick were silent in worry that Lucky had reverted back to Buck—and the silence would have been the eight-hundred pound gorilla in the kitchen if Agnes didn't cover with her chatter.

Bernard entered the kitchen. He first made eye contact with Mick before informing, "I didn't see anything unusual, Sheriff Shelton. A few came in to eat and a couple came in for directions, but nothing unusual...is Albert okay?"

Jeff also wanted to know if Albert was okay.

"He's fine. Shook up a bit and a couple hundred dollars poorer, but he'll survive." He gave a bit of a smile which puzzled Scarlet. *Was this some kind of joke?*

"Now, Jack, why would you be smiling," Scarlet asked. "Are you joking with us? Did Albert really get robbed?"

"No, no joking, Scarlet, in fact, I came to warn you guys. Albert thinks the guy was on foot so he couldn't have gotten too far, or maybe he's hiding somewhere around town."

"Then why are you smiling?"

"Albert, just Albert; have you ever seen Albert get upset?" he asked trying to hold back a laugh.

"What do you mean?" Agnes was now curious.

"He's a hoot. I listened to twenty minutes of I-shuddas. He thinks he's Chuck Norris," then the Sheriff couldn't help himself and laughed aloud. "Aaaah, sorry. I know, being robbed isn't funny but, hell, Albert is." Again he laughed.

"Well, I wanted to warn you guys, find out if ya saw anything, or anyone, suspicious around here or around town. I'm gunna get on the horn and get the warning out. We'll probably pick the guy up on the road before dinner's over." He headed for the door adding, "You all be on the alert now. I'll keep you posted. By the way, when does Roberto get back?"

"Probably next week. He's doing a good deed, Sheriff, moving a statue from Mexico to Saint Francis Cathedral—gettin' points upstairs," Jeff answered. He was in no hurry for Roberto to come back. He liked his new position at the Alviso.

As Sheriff Shelton stepped out the door he suggested that they lock the back door behind him for the time being, and Agnes promptly did just that.

"I don't think so, Mick," Scarlet tried to relieve Mick's obvious anxiety. "Really, he's changed." She sat down in the chair next to him. "You don't really think Lucky robbed the hardware store, do you?"

In a whisper Mick responded, "I don't know; but...I think I need to get away from here."

"Why?"

"I don't know that it wasn't Buck. Where is he, you know...no one has seen him. A knife? He could have done it." Mick took a deep and shaky breath. He looked around the kitchen then abruptly got up and left the table. He lifted the door to Lucky's cellar room and quickly disappeared down the ladder. Once he found the light, Mick did a quick inventory then climbed back out to a waiting and anxious Scarlet.

"His easel is there so he's not out being the hillside artist." He looked Scarlet directly into her eyes. "I need to get out of here."

A strained silence sat between them, with Mick nervously looking around the kitchen, trying to figure his next move. Scarlet spoke up.

"You can't go walking down the road, I mean, that's what they're looking for—some guy on foot."

"I have the truck."

"No you don't. Remember?"

He had forgotten. Roberto took his truck to hide it. He didn't know where Roberto took the truck, and neither did Scarlet.

"I'll ask Bernard for a ride," he said, getting more anxious by the minute. "I'll fucking kill Buck if he did this," Mick added through his clenched teeth.

"No you won't," Scarlet responded in a whisper. "Stay here, Mick. I'll go ask Bernard." As she made her way to the door she suddenly stopped, turned and hurried back to the table. "I have an idea," she said with conviction. "I want to take Gracie to the Rio Grande Zoo in Albuquerque. I've wanted to take her there so badly and she really wants to go. You go with us."

"I have to get out of here now." Mick began shifting in his chair.

"We'll go now. I'm going to call Edward, Gracie's grandfather. You get your things, okay? Just grab your things and put them in the Trooper." Scarlet left the kitchen.

"Where's she going?" Agnes called out to Mick but he was preoccupied and on his way out the back door. She turned to Jeff. "Where are they going?"

"I don't know but are you going to be my sous chef tonight or is Katherine?"

"Oh thank you, Edward, and I do apologize for the short notice. I promise, Gracie will have so much fun." Scarlet was responsible and reliable.

Edward trusted her completely and put Gracie on the phone where Scarlet told her of their surprise trip to the zoo. And, as Scarlet was confident she would be, Gracie was overjoyed. She kept yelling to Edward, "Grandpa, I'm going to the zoo, Grandpa. Monkeys, Grandpa…."

Scarlet pulled Jeff to the side so that she could speak to him in private. She explained her plan to take Gracie for a fun weekend at the zoo and to bring along Mick to get him away from the Alviso. She asked him to explain the situation to Rosa in private and to pretend to the others, Sheriff Shelton included, that he didn't know where they went. They talked a bit about Lucky then Scarlet let Jeff know that she would call from Albuquerque but hoped to only speak with either Rosa or him. Scarlet rushed out the back kitchen door to pack for the trip, and there was Mick, sitting on the boulder, ready and eager to leave.

The words rushed out of her mouth as she raced by, "I'll be ten minutes. No, maybe fifteen minutes. I'll hurry, I promise."

Scarlet kept her word and took no longer than fifteen minutes before she was out the door waving Mick to the Trooper. Once at Edward's, Mick decided to slump down on the passenger's seat while Scarlet retrieve little Gracie. Edward was delighted about Gracie's excursion to the zoo and Gracie was eager and ready to go with her little Teletubby suitcase on travel wheels grasped tightly in her tiny hand. While Scarlet gave Edward her expected itinerary, the impatient Gracie was making her way to the Trooper with her little suitcase bumping along behind her.

"I'll call you when we get there, Edward," Scarlet promised as she rushed to catch up to Gracie.

Gracie spotted Mick while Scarlet secured her into her car seat and smiled to a giggle. Mick put his finger up to his lips with a quiet "shhhhh" as though his presence in the car would be a surprise for Scarlet. Scarlet hopped onto the driver's seat and she was off, paying no attention to Mick as she carried on about all the animals Gracie would see at the zoo. This only contributed to Mick's game of pretending that he was hidden to Scarlet.

Once they were on the road, Mick popped up and mock shouted, "*Surprise!*"

Scarlet instinctively and aptly reacted, "*It's Mick, Gracie!*"

Gracie repeated, "It's Mick."

Scarlet's driving skills hadn't improved from the last trip to Los Alamos.

"Scarlet, why don't you let me drive; you and Gracie can make plans, and talk."

That sounded like a great idea to Scarlet. She pulled over, switched seats with Mick then turned to face Gracie in the backseat where the majority of her attention was spent for remainder of the ride to Albuquerque.

"Well, are you happy with all your purchases?" Lena asked a satisfied looking Rosa. The backseat and trunk were filled to capacity.

"I think we did good, Lena. I think the lobby's going to have a proper gift store now.

So, Lena, are you going to help me set up, put all these things in the lobby?" Before Lena answered she added, "You know, I don't have shelves or, you know, those display cases." Rosa turned to look at Lena. "Will you help me?"

"Aaaah, yes, of course, but Rosa I was planning on leaving this evening...grab a bite to eat then hit the road."

"Free couple a nights...rest up for your trip to Pista?" Rosa coaxed and Lena went from a big smile to a head tossing laugh.

"What? I didn't say anything funny," Rosa was quick to respond to her boisterous unaccounted-for laugh.

"That's how I ended up in Pista so long." She was grinning from ear to ear. "I stopped to rest before finishing my trip to California and I ended up staying on like I lived there."

"You like small towns, you know, like Pista?" Rosa asked, thinking that it was the appeal of a small town that kept Lena in Pista.

"Well," she had to think, "I love where I live in Monterey but I fell in love with Broken Arrow, the place I stayed in Pista."

"Small towns can be unfriendly. People have their ways. They don't want to change and don't want people coming in and changing things. Territorial, I guess." Rosa lived in a small town, grew up in a small town and figured she would die in a small town but a big part of Rosa wished to be in another place.

"I guess I was lucky, Rosa. Everyone was pretty nice to me right off, and nice to Pepper, my dog. But then, I was staying at Broken Arrow Campground so everyone was from somewhere else, well almost everyone."

"That makes a difference, Lena. At the Alviso, same thing, and everyone is friendly. But in town, you know if you were to buy a place or open a business, I don't think it would be easy. People don't like change. Don't trust strangers."

"So how 'bout you, Rosa, do you like living in a small town or would you prefer to live in a more metropolitan area?"

"Me? You mean a city?" Lena nodded a yes and Rosa continued, "Lena, I love my Alviso, but Roberto, Roberto my husband, he is the one who was in love with the place. I think I'd like to go to somewhere where there is more going on: lots of stores, restaurants, things to do...."

The two talked on about the pros and cons of a small town versus a city. They matched the odd characters typically found in both. For every character Rosa could come up with, Lena had one on par to describe and make Rosa laugh.

"Aaaaah, how we love our weirdos," Lena chuckled.

"And someone is probably describing us right now saying the same thing," Rosa added with a chuckle herself.

With the top down on the little car and a beautiful day behind and before them, they chatted and laughed as they wound their way up the road to the Alviso. Once there, they were met in the parking lot by a harried Agnes. In what seemed like one long breath she told of the robber on the loose.

Rosa laughed in response, confusing both Agnes and Lena who gave each other a quick, quizzical glance.

"That's probably why Albert was waving at us; he was waving us down," she said still laughing. "He'd just been robbed." Like Sheriff Shelton, the scenario struck Rosa as humorous.

Once inside, Jeff pulled Rosa aside for privacy. He explained all that had transpired while she was gone and Rosa's first concern was if Lucky had been the robber, just as everyone initially suspected, everyone but Agnes. Jeff reassured her that it wasn't Lucky. He had been at the monastery helping the monks. Lucky had told the monks that he was a painter. Of course, Lucky was referring to his artistic abilities where they assumed he was a painter of houses and the like. Lucky didn't correct them, only offered his talents with a wider brush.

Chapter 7
Mick Had Some Cash...

Mick had some cash, cash he kept private; it was the cash he would need in his getaway. Rosa had offered him money for his work at the Alviso, but Mick couldn't bring himself to accept it—not after what he had put Rosa and everyone at the Alviso through. It was in gratitude and obligation that Mick did the work. Roberto Sr.'s old workshop was his room and Mick ate at the kitchen—this was compensation enough, though he felt that he was the one who needed to do the compensating.

Mick needed to keep what money he had but standing at the hotel counter watching Scarlet hand the clerk her credit card made him feel ashamed.

"Are the rooms side by side?" Scarlet asked the rather indifferent clerk.

"I thought that's what you'd want," he answered with no expression then added, "There's a door connecting the rooms you can unlock and use if you want." He stood looking at Scarlet, then at Mick.

"That's fine; thank you." Scarlet reached for Gracie's little hand and the three left the office for their rooms.

"So Sheriff," Rosa started as soon as Sheriff Shelton entered the door, "did you find the robber?" She smiled and added, "Is Albert alright?"

Sheriff Shelton smiled back, acknowledging the glint in her eyes holding back laughter, a laughter he found easy to reciprocate. "Yeah, we found him right away. Found him asleep by the side of the road. Albert identified him. You know, robbing some store owner in the middle of the day with a little knife then heading down the road to take a nap, not the brightest light on the Christmas tree, ya know?"

"Little knife?" she questioned.

"What'd Albert tell you, it was a machete?" He now let out a half-laugh.

"I haven't talked to him...oh, Sheriff, let me introduce you." Rosa turned to Lena. "Lena, meet our sheriff, Sheriff Shelton. You're long lost cousin."

Lena got up from the floor where she was emptying boxes of items Rosa purchased for the lobby's new gift shop makeover.

"Hi." Lena extended her hand. "I'm Lena Shelton. Could we be related?" she asked in jest.

"Well, hell. We might be. Where you from?"

"Northern California. And you?"

"I guess I'd say I'm from these parts. Don't think I have anyone in California, might...but I do have some relations across the Pacific in Hawaii."

"Wow," Lena was taken aback. "So do I. Oh my God, we may actually be related. Small world."

"Hey cousin," Sheriff Shelton exclaimed with a grin then turned his attention back to Rosa. "So what are you doing in here, Rosa?" Lena remained standing, stretching a bit while Rosa explained how she was making the lobby into a lobby-gift shop. "All these changes, Rosa, you going through a midlife change, you know, midlife thing?"

"Midlife, come on Sheriff; that passed me long ago. I'm making changes, improving the place. Now that I have extra help," she paused to look at Lena. "I'm making improvements.

"Now, Sheriff, you never commented on my mural."

Both Sheriff Shelton and Lena Shelton turned to examine Lucky's work of art on the lobby wall.

"You do that?" he asked.

"No, I can't draw. Like I told you, Sheriff, I have good help, an artist. I can make changes, spruce things up with the extra help." Rosa turned to face the sheriff displaying the grin of a winner before getting back to work.

"Nice to meet you, Sheriff Shelton," Lena said as she too went back to helping set up the gift shop appearance of the lobby.

"Yeah, nice meeting you cous.

"Well you gals get back to work. I just dropped by to let you know, Rosa, that we caught the crook, didn't want ya worrying, ya know. Is Jeff in the kitchen?"

"He should be, seems to be in there all the time now. He's even getting Pedro to stop by for a bite, and pay for it."

"You think Pedro will ever take those Christmas lights and crap down?" Sheriff Shelton asked the never-ending question.

"No," Rosa snapped. She knew Pedro a lot longer than Sheriff Shelton and knew his stubborn side well. She continued on about Jeff. "Jeff's been the chef while Roberto's away but I don't think he's going to give up his job easy when Roberto gets back. Go in there and get him to make you a burrito. He's getting good at 'em," Rosa insisted and he took her up on the offer.

"Christmas lights this time of year?" Lena questioned.

"All year," Rosa answered, not going into detail.

Pedro put up enough Christmas lights to cause a black out, according to Albert, and lawn decorations combining religion with Santa Claus and his crew of reindeer. It was quite gaudy, if not humorous. When he was slow to remove the Christmas blight and comments came his way—in typical Pedro fashion—he then refused to remove them altogether. It amused Rosa; she believed people should have known that would be his response to their chastising. Pedro was a grump and stubborn—push and he'll push back with everything he's got, even if it's not much. Sheriff Shelton could find no law against his year-round garish décor so there they still sit—faded, some broken and all an eyesore. He rarely turned the lights on, which were actually kind of pretty: he basked in the irritation of his large, faded (what was meant to be temporary) statuary.

Lena helped out for a bit more then left to walk and feed Pepper. She returned at Rosa's request to have dinner with Rosa and finish with the lobby.

Lucky was again at the monastery and this evening he was sharing a meal with the monks, a vegetarian meal. Lucky often got up early, leaving his easel behind and headed for the monastery encountering Granny on his way—and if it was early enough, he'd see Frances with her odd looking companion. If he left the monastery at sunset, he wouldn't see Granny but he'd often see Frances and her four-legged friend. They were always a distance away. He was certain that Frances didn't know he was there, however, he was convinced that that *thing* was aware of his presence. Frances looked forward along her chosen discreet path while her companion repeatedly stopped to look back in Lucky's direction. He would have hollered a hello to the nurse who successfully treated his hand, but Lucky was truly afraid of her scrappy-looking companion.

"I think this looks great, Rosa," Lena commented, standing back to proudly view their work, mostly her work since Rosa spent most of the time watching. Rosa had old shelving she felt best tossed away or burned but Lena found to be classic and perfect for the ambiance of the new gift shop. They found a display case of sorts in Roberto's old workshop which Lena convinced Rosa to also add to the new gift shop. "You're gunna sell a lot, particularly the jewelry, Rosa—just watch."

"If they can see it through that old glass," Rosa worried.

"No, that glass is perfect—old and wavy. I love it, but if you don't like it it's easy to replace, but personally, I would leave it; it has character. You might want to put a light in the case but keep the old glass. I think it's great." Each described the look they thought best for the lobby. Rosa wanted it to match her new mural and Lena thought the more old Southwest the better.

Katherine and Agnes were thrilled with the revamped lobby. While they acted like tourists shopping in the new gift shop, Rosa join Lena on her walk back to her room. Lena was still thinking about leaving that evening and Rosa tried to convince her to get some rest then leave in the morning after breakfast, where she would gladly join her. However, Lena was wide awake and a bit antsy to be on her way. She hadn't seen those she loved and missed at Broken Arrow for years and she was eager to make her way back.

"Is Shelton a common name?" Rosa asked.

"I didn't think so. Are there a lot of Shelton's in this area?"

"I don't think so. I think he has a brother. He's not married. You think you could be related?" Rosa wasn't truly curious about the common last name, she just wanted Lena to spend more time with her. She was comfortable with Lena. Rosa brazenly engaged her sarcastic sense of humor when with her without worry of judgment. She could let down her guard along with her matriarchal position, and she was in no hurry to see Lena leave.

"The fact that he has relatives in Hawaii and so do I, well, that might be more than a coincidence." She hushed when she heard someone a short distance away. Someone was walking out of the wooded area past her room. "Who is that?"

Rosa squinted, walked a few yards closer to the lineup of trees. The noise and the man got closer. Rosa calmly said, "Oh, that's Lucky, our resident artist. He did the mural in the lobby—very talented." She sauntered back to where Lena was standing outside her room while Lucky passed by as though he hadn't seen them.

"Can I give you a hug, Rosa?"

"Why don't you leave in the morning?"

"Can I give you a hug?" she asked again with an appreciative smile. She liked Rosa, enjoyed the time she had spent with her but she wanted to be on her way.

Rosa leaned forward giving and allowing a fond embrace. Rosa was not the hugging kind; she was not the touchy type and everyone knew that and no one bothered Rosa with hugs—but Lena didn't know that.

"You coming back this way on your way home?" Rosa asked as though an invite.

"I can," Lena accepted. "You know, you are always welcome to come visit me out in Monterey, out in California. Here, let me write down my home address and phone number." Lena reached into her purse for a pen and paper.

"You know I might do it," Rosa commented almost sounding like a dare accepted.

"I wish you would. I really do…."

The two talked for a while longer then Lena entered her room to retrieve her things and Rosa headed back to the lobby.

Gracie watched Scarlet place her suitcase on the bed and tried to pull her Teletubbies suitcase on wheels up onto her bed in the same fashion.

"Let me help you." Scarlet stepped over to lift the suitcase in a way that made it appear Gracie had done the heavy lifting. "Let's unpack your things." She unzipped the little suitcase and together they began pulling out the items of clothing, placing them across the bed. Scarlet's eyebrows began to rise. It was a mishmash of colors and patterns, none of them matching.

"Who packed your suitcase, Gracie?" She attentively asked, observing the odd combination of clothing.

"Grandpa," Gracie answered as she patted flat the clothing scattered across the bed.

Mick lightly knocked on their adjoining door and Gracie ran to answer with Scarlet following behind to unlock it.

Both Mick and Gracie donned the same happy grin.

"You guys hungry?"

Gracie turned to Scarlet as if to ask *Are we hungry?*

Amused and delighted, Scarlet responded, "Yes, I think we might be hungry after that long ride; don't you think?"

Gracie shook her head multiple times to say yes then ran to the window where she could see the busy street below. It was all so exciting, and she couldn't wait for whatever was next…*and* for the next morning when they would be off to the zoo.

"Would you mind, Mick, if we went to the mall. Maybe they have a place there we could get something to eat and then I can pick up some things for Gracie to wear."

"Doesn't she have clothes?" Mick was perplexed.

"Edward packed her clothes. Nothing matches…well, look on the bed." She stepped aside.

Mick took a few steps farther into the room to take a look at the clothing neatly strewn across the bed. He didn't see the display of clothing as Scarlet saw them. They looked fine to him. He headed back to his room saying, "Whatever you want to do. Just knock on the door when you're ready. You know tomorrow Gracie'll probably like getting a shirt or something at the zoo."

Buying clothing for Gracie touched something in Scarlet, something she didn't recall ever feeling before. She enjoyed and cherished every part of the process. It felt indescribably better than ever shopping for herself—from the gamut of clothing to choose from to Gracie's smiling, approving face to being handed the bag containing the pint-sized outfits by the clerk. She held Gracie's one hand while Mick held the other with a blissful energy passing through them as they exited the last store.

They decided on Chili's Restaurant for dinner. It was just across from the shopping center and neither Mick nor Gracie had been there before.

Gracie looked at the pictures on the menu and pointed to what looked good, as did Mick.

"Why don't we get several things and share," Scarlet suggested, feeding off the happy energy. She felt so alive, so in her own moment—not helping to satisfy someone else's moment or purpose.

"A deal, Scarlet. Whataya think there, Gracie?" Mick put down his menu. "You think you can eat all that grown-up food?"

"Yessssss...I can eat that, an' that..." she squeaked in her sweet high-pitched little girl's excited voice while pointing to most every picture on the multi-paged glossy and oversized menu.

"Can I get you all something to drink?" asked the young waitress with a row of silver earrings dangling from one ear.

"Yes, I'll have a coffee with cream," Scarlet answered then looked at Mick.

"I'll have a margarita."

"And your little girl?" The waitress exaggerated her smile at Gracie.

Those words rushed through Scarlet. She felt a sense of pride and elation...this sense of being exactly and perfectly where she should be. This is how life felt at its best and Scarlet was gratefully taking it all in.

"You want a Coke, Gracie," Mick asked but his suggestion was immediately overruled by Scarlet's request for apple juice.

"Are you ready to order or would you like me to come back?"

"Are you ready, Mick?"

"Yes, we're ready. Okay," he said picking the menu back up, "we're going to share several dishes..." and Mick ordered just that, several dishes—feeling at ease since he would insist on paying. Scarlet didn't care whether he paid or not, but Mick did. He'd find some means to replenish his stash of escape money; he was not going to endure the weekend feeling like a polite parasite. "And can you bring a dish or two in a hurry? My girls are hungry," Mick playfully requested.

"I sure can."

And she did.

"Scarwet," Gracie said, "is today my birfday?"

"What day is your birthday, Gracie?" Mick asked, and Gracie just shrugged her shoulders, but it felt like it was her birthday.

"Well, we can celebrate your birthday today. In fact, we can make this your birthday weekend," Scarlet offered. "Would you like that?"

Gracie nodded with enthusiasm while she stuffed a piece of potato skin dripping with cheese into her mouth. Her raw pleasure made Scarlet and Mick grin.

The food, conversation and the laughs were plentiful. Midway through their meal Mick excused himself from the table. Scarlet naturally assumed he was leaving to use the restroom, but he wasn't; he was arranging for a piece of cake with a candle to be brought to the table for Gracie.

The table was cleared and not just their waitress approached with the glowing piece of chocolate cake but a crew of five waitpersons arrived surrounding the table singing a loud and lively "Happy Birthday" and ending with a "happy birthday, sweet Gracie, happy birthday to you." Gracie was jubilant. She laughed and clapped her little hands. Her joy was contagious and the surrounding tables joined in on the celebration with a hearty round of applause.

"Are you praying, Lucky?" Brother Chinh softly asked.

"Ah, ah. Nope. I was just looking." Lucky pointed up at the Jesus figure on the cross. "He looks like he's looking at you all the time."

"He is, my friend. He is." A slow smile reached across Brother Chinh's face. He placed his hand on Lucky's shoulder for a brief moment then left Lucky alone in the church. For the umpteenth time, Lucky wandered the confines of the church, watching to see if His eyes were still upon him—and they were.

Lucky was a true jack-of-all-trades and they were as grateful to have him there as he had become grateful to be there. He was a decent mechanic, something the monks desperately needed since none were mechanically inclined. A few could do minor repairs but they depended upon the kindness and generosity of others for the more significant tasks. Lucky wouldn't talk much when he was with the monks volunteering his services, he would mostly listen. He wasn't just hearing the monks talk, he was taking in what they had to say. It was like reading a book, but he didn't have to do the reading and he was beginning to believe Brother Chinh's words, along with the teachings of the other monks.

Proud of his newly discovered talent, Lucky offered to paint a mural on the large canvas of the blank wall inside the building housing the monastery offices and a small gift shop. His offer created a buzz at the monastery, one that Lucky was thrilled to accommodate.

"Well, we don't see much of you lately," Rosa commented as Lucky entered the kitchen. "You have any new paintings?"

"I started a painting for you, but, um, well I'm doing a painting for those monks. Ya know, like on the wall, like painting on the wall like I did here," he answered almost in an apology.

"A mural," Jeff shouted over.

"Yeah, a mural. I'm doing a mural for the monks."

"That's wonderful, Lucky. What are you painting?" Rosa was truly impressed, even honored that someone from the Alviso would be doing such work for the monastery.

"Ah, well, some saint, some saint who lived in a cave or something. I'm not sure. They gave me a picture to copy."

"Saint Benedict," Jeff interjected.

"Yeah, I think that's it."

"Would you like something to eat, Lucky?" Agnes asked. "I'm having a hamburger, would you like one also?"

"No, no thanks. I don't wanna eat meat——"

Before he could go further Jeff offered him a vegetarian quesadilla.

"Okay. I'll be right back." Lucky opened the lid to his room and descended down the wood ladder while Rosa, Jeff and Agnes exchanged glances, perplexed by Lucky's desire to be a vegetarian.

"What?" Katherine entered the kitchen amidst the bemused expressions.

"Lucky's a vegetarian now," Jeff informed.

Katherine didn't find such a decision to be out of the ordinary, even if it was Lucky and looked bewildered herself by their reaction to Lucky's decision to not eat meat.

"I bet it's the monks," Jeff speculated.

"Are they vegetarians?" Rosa was sure they were not vegetarians, otherwise someone surely would have said something when she sent over dishes containing meat at Christmas.

"I think they are, Rosa."

"Hey Lucky, quesadilla's ready," Jeff shouted towards the open lid to Lucky's room and it only took a minute or two for Lucky to appear.

As Jeff handed Lucky the dish he asked why he wasn't eating meat, positive that Lucky would attribute this change to the monks.

"I don't wanna eat Granny," Lucky calmly answered.

Now everyone, including Katherine, was exchanging befuddled glances.

"*Granny?*" Rosa questioned. "Why would you be eating...Granny?"

"Now, who is Granny?" Agnes asked in her gentle voice, like one would ask when digging for an answer from a small child.

Jeff laughed. He knew Granny was the gray cow Lucky seemed to be so intrigued by.

"Go ahead and laugh; I don't care." Lucky swallowed his bite of the quesadilla. "This is really good, man. Is that shrimp?"

"Thanks. Yeah, pink shrimp." Jeff smiled. He had made it his mission to make a quesadilla a real meal, to make them with every kind of ingredient imaginable and in various food styles—from southwest to Asian. He was on to perfecting the dessert quesadilla.

"Where'd you get the shrimp, Jeff?" Rosa hadn't purchased shrimp for the restaurant.

"We're expanding the menu, Rosa. Roberto called. He said go for it."

"So who's Granny?" Agnes persisted.

"A gray cow?" Jeff hinted.

"A gray cow?" Rosa added.

"Tell em, Lucky," Jeff pushed. "Tell them about that cow."

And he did. He told of how she greeted him when he spent time painting by the cliffs; how she followed him like a companion dog. And when he talked to her, she really did listen. He didn't say that he loved her, but he did, and the thought of eating a Granny now was not acceptable. He hadn't tied in the leather factor as of yet.

Katherine chuckled. "That's an odd companion, don't you think?"

"Not as odd as that old nurse's," Lucky shot back rather defensively.

"Now what are you talking about?" Agnes was truly confused. "What old nurse. Now I am really confused, Lucky."

"Frances, Lucky. Her name is Frances."

"Yeah, the nurse who fixed my hand; you should see what she has as a companion." Lucky shook his head.

Jeff had encountered Frances and her cherished pet, whom she loved like nothing else left on this earth and whom she kept private and well-guarded. Jeff respected not only Frances but her wishes and her wish was to keep her beloved Chupi her secret.

"What pet does the nurse have?" Agnes inquired and Jeff jumped right in. He wanted the topic of Frances's pet ended as quickly as possible.

"She has an old scrawny dog who isn't very friendly."

"So, Lucky, you a strict vegetarian or only not eat cows now?" he asked to veer the topic off of Frances's companion. And it worked. Agnes chimed right in about reports stating that refraining from eating red meat was a heart-healthy thing to do which led the conversation down a path of food topics and Frances's odd companion was soon forgotten.

Gracie was tucked into bed, cozy in her new pajamas. She picked them out herself. They were pink with the smiling faces of her favorite critter of all, monkeys. Scarlet sat in a chair next to the bed and read to Gracie. She worried that Gracie might become frightened being so far away from home. But, she wasn't. She was comfortable, and fell right to sleep. Scarlet continued to read until interrupted by a soft knock on the adjoining door.

"Hi," Mick whispered. "Is she asleep?"

"Yes." Scarlet whispered looking at Gracie. "She looks like a little angel."

"I was thinking that maybe one of us should call Alviso and see what's going on, ya know...see what's up with the robbery, and Lucky?"

"Yeah, that's a good idea.

"I don't want to wake Gracie," she looked over her shoulder at Mick.

"Use the phone in my room," he suggested. He wanted Scarlet to call instead of himself.

"What if she wakes up...and she's alone in the room. It might frighten her," Scarlet worried.

"I can sit in here, or just leave the door open; she'll be fine, Scarlet." Mick could see in everything Scarlet said and did that she loved this little girl as though she were her own. "She had a big evening; she's tuckered out... probably dreaming about the zoo, monkeys at the zoo." Mick smiled and Scarlet agreed.

Mick sat on the corner of the bed where he could see into the other room while Scarlet made her call. She spoke with Rosa. The conversation was short. She then called Edward to let him know about Gracie's day and about their plans for the next day, but mostly to assure him that all was well. Mick listened while glancing over at the still and sleeping Gracie.

"Well?" Mick was a bit anxious.

"Edward seems really happy that we brought Gracie to Albuquerque. I don't think he can do the drive himself. He was really pleased. I know, you want to know what Rosa said." Scarlet's smile relieved his anxiety. "Rosa said that they are doing just fine without us, 'have fun' and stay a couple of days if we want."

Mick's eyes widened. She wasn't relaying the information he was restless to hear.

"Oh, everything is fine, Mick. Lucky," she laughed before continuing, "is innocent. He was at the monastery and they caught that robber. Rosa said he was by the side of the road sleeping when they caught him."

"Oh...man, what a relief." Mick brushed the back of his hand across his forehead as if to wipe off sweat from worry.

"I didn't think Lucky had done that. Did you, really?"

"Yeah, I did. Well, I thought it was a huge possibility. Buck has always been a pretty self-serving asshole, to be honest. I didn't choose to have him with me." He hesitated a few seconds. "It just turned out that way, unfortunately."

Scarlet was curious just what Mick had done to put him in prison, and what Lucky had done also, but was too uncomfortable about the topic to ask.

"But Lucky is different; I think he's changed, don't you? I mean really changed." Scarlet, who had feared Buck the most, had grown to trust and like Lucky.

"Maybe." How knew Buck's past too well. His new identity as Mick hadn't made him a changed person and he hardly believed that the new Lucky could have made such a drastic transformation in such a relatively short time. "I'm not convinced."

"Rosa is a very good, veeeery good judge of character and she trusts and believes in Lucky. You remember, she wasn't afraid of you from the beginning. Sometimes I think Rosa is actually psychic. She just seems to just know things. Not much ever surprises her. It's like she already knows what's going to happen so she's never surprised, or something." Scarlet loved and admired Rosa though she never felt particularly loved by Rosa and would not claim to be close to her mother-in-law, not any closer than anyone else from town who knew Rosa.

They sat on the bed and talked for a while then Mick offered to go to Old Town for coffee.

"You can take the Trooper," Scarlet offered.

"I can walk." Mick didn't want to take any chances getting stopped in the Trooper. He wasn't sure about the streets and parking, and he didn't want anything to ruin this weekend for Gracie, or for Scarlet——or himself.

Crossing Central Avenue was daunting. Cars appeared to be aiming for Mick. No one slowed down. No one seemed to acknowledge his presence as they sped down the road as though racing desperate to some destination and anything crossing their path was potential road kill.

Mick strolled back across the busy plaza with two coffees in hand. He was like anyone else there, weaving through the crowds, exchanging smiles with strangers and feeling the upbeat energy of tourist on vacation. He not only felt happy, but felt the soar of freedom. No locked gates, no escort, no one monitoring his interactions with those not sentenced to spend years behind bars. Mick could turn left or right, he could sit or run, without permission. He listened to the sounds of life as a free man all around him. People were laughing, yelling out to each other. They wandered from shop to shop, sat at tables on the restaurant patios, sat on benches resting in silence. As he headed back to the hotel, Mick wondered if sticking around New Mexico, the Alviso, staying in one place, wasn't jeopardizing this newfound freedom.

A Mariachi band blared from the gazebo. Mick stopped for a moment to listen then followed the sidewalk to the alley that opened up to the parking lot and to where he needed to cross to the hotel. Mick watched those around him carrying on with their free and busy lives. He could easily put down one of the coffees and put out his thumb. Mick could disappear by way of the celebrated Route 66 with cars coming and going at a steady pace. The freeway wasn't far. He paused at the bus stop. Life put him in the perfect place at just the right time; the bus was on its way.

Mick set the one coffee down on the bus stop bench then stood in front of it. The bus was green and looked like a giant caterpillar careening down to swoop him up, and he was ready, ready to hold onto a chance at permanent freedom.

It was warm with a slight breeze and Scarlet stood outside the open door to take advantage of this perfect evening. Scarlet leaned against the railing, pushing her dark hair back off her face and savoring the night air. She spotted Mick balancing the two coffees in his hands as he maneuvered through the crowded sidewalk then she lost sight of him. The bus squealed to a long lagging stop. Mick knew Scarlet would understand. She would know why he had to take this opportunity—she was a kind and understanding woman.

Chapter 8
Where's Bernard...

"Where's Bernard, Katherine?" Rosa hadn't seen much of him and he usually was within sight throughout the typical day.

"He's helping Albert at his store," Katherine answered, stopping to take this opportunity to visit with Rosa, if Rosa was willing. Rosa could be somewhat offish and seemingly moody, in Katherine's opinion, so she wasn't certain when imposing her company on Rosa was acceptable.

"Why is he helping Albert, isn't there enough for him to do around here?"

Katherine worried that Rosa might be upset that Bernard was doing work at Mountain High instead of at Rancho Alviso, after all, she was giving them free rooming in exchange for their help (and, Katherine believed, to safeguard their secreted convicts). It was hard to tell when Rosa was truly annoyed since her usual expression was tainted with indifference.

"Oh, Rosa, he is just helping out a bit, socializing mostly. To be honest, I think he really misses having his own store. I think Bernard regrets selling the bookstore; well, I know he regrets selling the bookstore." She thought for a second then made the suggestion, "Maybe Bernard could run your gift shop, here. I know——"

Rosa quickly cut her off. "He's going to have to get his own store, Katherine. This one's mine." She lifted her upper lip in a dubious smile then, without excusing herself, left for the kitchen to have Jeff make her lunch. She was enjoying his culinary creativity, and with Roberto's approval, she wanted Jeff to create a whole new menu. Their menu was "traditional," which was a more inviting way of saying *same old menu.* Roberto would add a special here and there but the Alviso menu didn't look much different from thirty years ago.

Katherine stood there, not knowing whether she was supposed to take over the counter for Rosa or, with Rosa's proud ownership of the new gift shop, if in doing so she would irritate Rosa. Katherine compromised by staying in the lobby on the customers' side of the counter so she could look after the gift shop without appearing to takeover Rosa's position.

When Bernard strolled through the lobby door, there to help out in the kitchen if needed, Katherine confronted him in a semi-panic. Her expression denoted something was up and before she could get a word out Bernard asked a carping, "What?"

"Bernard, I think Rosa is mad that you're helping Albert out at the store when you're supposed to be helping out here."

"There's nothing to do here," he exclaimed in a low voice and a scrunched-brow. "Come on, this place isn't that busy, Katherine. Albert needed some help, good God…" and he listed the tasks that he helped Albert with at the store. Katherine could see that Bernard missed running a store, that working in a kitchen was not his cup of tea. "I'll go talk to her, good God. Where is she?"

"Now don't go in there with an attitude, Bernard. She's been very good to us." Katherine paused, waiting for Bernard to respond. He didn't, so she continued, "She's in the kitchen having lunch with Jeff. Now be polite, Bernard."

As he placed his hand on the door, he turned back to Katherine. "You know the nurse, the one who helped Lucky?"

"Frances?"

"Yeah, Frances; well, someone came into the store and said that she was in the hospital in Los Alamos."

"What happened?"

"I don't know. Should I tell Rosa what I heard?" he asked, not sure if this was a good time if Rosa was annoyed with him or in a bad mood.

"Yes, of course. Yes, tell her; she may not know."

Bernard nodded and continued into the kitchen. Rosa and Jeff were sitting at the table, Rosa eating and Jeff reading; neither looked up. The lid on Lucky's artist den, as they had all come to call it, was up. Bernard grabbed a cup of coffee then opened conversation inquiring about Lucky. "Is the artist at work?"

"Not sure what he's doing, Bernard," Jeff answered. "He leaves in the morning to that monastery and is gone all day. He came back to get something and left again. Guess he left his lid up." Jeff looked up at Bernard then added, "Ya hungry?"

"Coffee's fine, thanks Jeff." It dawned on Bernard that Roberto was gone, Mick and Scarlet left town, Lucky was away from the Alviso most of the time and now he was gone helping his new friend, Albert, at the hardware store. Maybe Rosa was feeling abandoned—whether the establishment was busy or not, half her staff was nowhere around. Bernard intended on talking to Rosa about his continuing to help Albert out but now he felt uncomfortable about the request so he decided to just pass on the information, what little he had, about Frances.

Rosa looked up from her plate and demanded, "What's wrong with her?"

"I'm not sure."

"So who took her to the hospital?" Jeff asked, just as intently as Rosa had posed her question. Again, Bernard didn't know. "Is someone at her place?" Jeff wanted to know.

"I don't know that either," Bernard uttered, sounding apologetic for presenting such critical news void of essential details. "I'll go call Albert; I'm sure he has the answers," and he left for the lobby.

Rosa and Jeff exchange a silent and knowing stare. The fact that Frances had an issue that required her to be in the hospital was not shocking news, not at her age, but there was another issue of deep concern.

"I'll go over there," Jeff offered and Rosa nodded her endorsement. "Now?" and Rosa nodded again—*now* would be a very good time.

Jeff retrieved some meat and a couple of hardboiled eggs from the refrigerator, put them in a paper bag then rushed out the kitchen back door, passing Lucky as he dashed across the parking lot.

"What's your hurry?" Lucky shouted over but Jeff didn't acknowledge him. He didn't want to engage him, have to explain where he was going or what he was doing or chance Lucky insisting on going along. It was just easier to ignore him, pretend that he didn't hear him.

Once at Frances's house, Jeff stood at the front gate, listening for any noise coming from the front yard. He tapped on the gate and waited for a reaction. Nothing. He slowly opened the gate, leaned in and scanned the area. Nothing. He cautiously stepped into the yard closing the gate behind him. Jeff slowly walked to the front porch and peeked through the window, then tapped on it. Nothing. He checked if the door was locked, not that he would have entered if it had been unlocked, then walked around to the backyard fence. Jeff tapped on the locked gate. This time he got a response, a shallow and guttural growl.

Using his most submissive tone Jeff muttered, "Okay, Chupi. It's okay; I'm just here to feed you, boy." Jeff got down on his knees at eye level with the gap in the wood that shielded the chain link fence. He had always wanted to get a look at Chupi up close and this was his opportunity. Jeff slowly turned his head, pressing his cheek against the fence where his eye could see between the slats. Chupi knew just where his face would be and met him there before Jeff's eye could focus. Jeff tossed the bag of meat and eggs over the fence and ran, ran across the front yard, out the gate, with his heart beating to match his adrenaline.

"Good afternoon, Lucky, "Rosa said, looking up at her scarcely seen worker.

"Hi," Lucky replied so unruffled, so calm, so unlike the Buck of the recent past.

"At the monastery?" she asked, curious as to just what he did there on a regular basis.

"Yeah," is all Lucky had as an answer before descending into his artist den. Lucky had been a volunteer handyman of sorts at the monastery but more than that, Lucky had been learning from the monks, learning to pray, to talk to God and to meditate where he would learn to listen to God. And, since the Jesus in the church couldn't keep His eyes off of Lucky, Lucky began to respond to the mystifying carving on the cross. He talked to it, and ultimately, it talked back—not an audible voice but a voice Lucky swears he heard from within. At first he was not just hesitant to expose this experience but fearful, fearful of ridicule and rejection from the monk he chose to confide in. Just the opposite happened. The monk embraced Lucky's experience as sacred. He confirmed and validated its authenticity praising Lucky for opening his heart and soul so that he might hear "our Lord" speak to him. Lucky shut the lid to his den leaving Rosa to remain curious.

Scarlet watched, waiting for the bus to continue on its way and for Mick to continue on his way back to the hotel. She strained to see past the semi blocking her view. It finally moved along with the traffic but there was no Mick waiting to cross the busy road. She searched the area within her view but Mick was nowhere in sight. Scarlet stepped the few feet back into the hotel room to check on Gracie. It was nothing but pure joy to witness the hallmark of innocence peacefully sleeping. Gracie was everything that was good about life to Scarlet and made her feel the benefit of living like no one else. If this is what it felt like to be a mother, then Scarlet had no doubt that is what she wanted to be.

"Cream and sugar, and lukewarm," Mick said raising the cups of coffee. He'd make his escape some other time, some other place. This was Gracie's birthday weekend.

The next morning they were among the first of eager visitors to arrive at the zoo. Gracie was too excited to sit down for breakfast. With her new pink shirt donning the exaggerated face of a smiling monkey and her excited wide eyes, Gracie was fixated on the front gate, peering through the bars like a caged bird waiting to be set free.

The gates opened and everyone rushed through. The first exhibit was flamingos lined up on one leg like a pink welcoming committee. "They're pink," Gracie exclaimed; she was also wearing pink and the connection was not lost on Gracie. She beamed.

Mick held open the map with directions to the array of animal exhibits. "Monkeys?" he asked Gracie, eyebrows raised with a knowing smile. "That way." Mick took her little hand and up the pathway they rushed, but not fast enough for Gracie. Midway, where the large wall enclosed the exhibit, Gracie pulled her hand free from Mick and ran ahead. Scarlet raced off to catch up to her. Gracie rounded the corner to a large Plexiglas window with a gorilla sitting on the other side. She stopped, speechless, but only for a few seconds, then Gracie raced to the gorilla with a joyful scream. Her expression was priceless and Scarlet didn't have a camera.

"Oh God, Mick; we don't have a camera." Scarlet's voice was anguished.

"Yes we do; I'll be right back." And Mick jogged off to the zoo's gift shop. They sold disposable single-use cameras. He grabbed several of them. As he waited to pay, a stuffed monkey hanging from straps off an artificial tree caught his attention. "Is that a kid's backpack?" he asked as he paid for the cameras. The clerk took it down to show him and Mick added it to his purchases.

"No, I don't need a bag but can you cut off the tags on the backpack, please?"

Mick placed a camera inside the monkey backpack and sprinted back to the gorilla exhibit where he found Gracie sitting on the ground in front of the plexiglass window, her hand pressed up against the gorilla's hand, and Scarlet admiring Gracie's every move. Mick immediately handed Scarlet one of the cameras.

They went from exhibit to exhibit with the excitement never waning. One exhibit consisted of nothing but parakeets—the rare parakeet. Mick and Scarlet were amused while Gracie was in awe of the colorful and noisy flock. Peacocks strolled pass displaying their beautiful feathers like evening gowns as they enjoyed lunch at the outdoor cafe. She fed the ducks and fish and with each exhibit, each activity, she only grew more invigorated; she showed no signs of wearing out, unlike Mick and Scarlet.

Near the end of the day, the old lion roared to wake the dead which only seemed to thrill and energize Gracie even more. The entire day at the zoo was magical and they stayed till closing. Gracie hadn't lost her exhilaration from the excitement of the day and was still full of energy. However, Mick and Scarlet were exhausted. It would be another night at the hotel in Albuquerque where they planned to leave the next day.

What they didn't plan on, as they left the city, was coming upon an open market where not only did they have fresh produce, displays of local art and homemade goods, but there was a pony ride—bored ponies tethered to a hub walking in a large circle with small saddles and small humans upon them. Gracie hollered out in excitement and they were immediately pulling in to find a parking space.

They couldn't get to the pony ride fast enough for Gracie. Scarlet handed the exaggerated cowboy a ticket and he hoisted Gracie onto the jaded pony. In short, the ponies were going round and round at a slug's pace in their designated circle. When the ride was over and the cowboy man came to unstrap and lift Gracie off the pony, her look of longing to stay on for another round had Scarlet purchasing another ticket and Gracie blissful again.

Scarlet delighted in purchasing handmade soap and body lotion. She bought some vegetables and two pies: pumpkin and apple. There was a man sculpting log stumps into bears with a chainsaw, just like Jeff wanted to do to sell at the side of the road by the Alviso, and it made both Mick and Scarlet laugh. It took a sure hand and a definite degree of muscle and skill to safely accomplish this art which they both knew Jeff did not have. The sole musical entertainment was a man playing flamenco-style guitar. Mick reminisced as he listened, stirring his desire to pick up a guitar again. This wasn't a day that neither Scarlet nor Mick wanted to give up easily and just like at the zoo, they stayed until closing.

The ride back to the Alviso was even more lively and enjoyable than the ride to Albuquerque. They had so much to talk about which included some sharing of their pasts. Mick was focused not only on the conversations but the desire for a guitar. The acoustic sounds from the market were still resonating within him.

It was dark by the time they entered town. Mick was driving, feeling that it was safer for him to drive on the back roads which allowed Scarlet to more easily interact with Gracie. He thought that he remembered the way to Edward's house but he took the wrong road and Scarlet, engaged with Gracie, didn't notice.

"Chwismus!" Gracie almost screamed. *"Look, Scawlet, Chwismus!"* Her eyes lit up, her face lit up. All of Gracie lit up just like Pedro's offensive front yard Christmas display. What was hideous to most in the town was magnificent to Gracie, who due to the most unfortunate of circumstances, was not able to celebrate last year's Christmas.

"Mick, pull over," Scarlet said in a hurry. And Mick did just that. He pulled up to the front of Pedro's phosphorescent front yard. All three got out to stand before the discolored glow illuminating through the faded plastic figures. To Mick it looked a shambles but both Scarlet and Gracie were staring at the weathered décor with delectation, not paying mind to the poor condition of the Christmas display.

Pedro peeped through the curtains and was immediately irked by the uninvited guests. He watched, waiting for them to bother him further by knocking on his door. But, the longer he watched, the more Pedro was taken by the joy in Gracie's face as she delighted in his Christmas decor. Pedro quietly opened the side door, sneaked to the side of the house and plugged in his biggest electricity eating and neighbor irritating display: Santa Claus with a full set of reindeer riding across his roof. He then plugged in the second set of lights adorning his house. Pedro didn't stop with the lights. Pedro had music, the music his neighbor had previously called the sheriff pleading for him to make Pedro turn it either off or down. Pedro had an audience, if only a few, who now appreciated his holiday efforts.

"Look, look, Mick, look," Gracie cried out to Mick, pointing to the steadfast discolored Santa with his faithful lit-up crew. Though Mick found the whole scene as distasteful as Pedro's neighbors, he found Gracie's joy and excitement over the display inspiring and sweet. He convincingly pretended to share her excitement.

Pedro quietly and unseen went back into his house and watched through a slight pull of his curtain, taking rare and exceptional pleasure in watching his guests enjoy themselves. It was the reaction he initially tried to elicit from the neighborhood. He received quite the opposite, and he was hurt—though Pedro would never admit that his feelings were hurt and therefore responded with peeve and revenge. Now, it was like Christmas for Pedro and he was enjoying it just like his uninvited guests. The twenty minutes of Christmas spirit was the perfect end to the day for all of them.

"That's them, Roberto," Rosa informed, looking Roberto directly in his eyes. "You need to talk to Scarlet, Roberto."

"Not tonight. Not tonight." He moved his formerly guilty and diverted eyes up to meet Rosa's. "I'll talk to her but not tonight. I'm going to sleep in the rental. Don't mention I'm back. I need to think, okay?"

Rosa nodded; she understood. She knew that Roberto didn't want to spend his life at Rancho Alviso; she knew that he was there due to his sense of obligation. She saw the life dull in him as it had in her only she could accept it in herself. It pained her to see Roberto lose his spirit and zest for life as he once had. It was no surprise that once Roberto had a taste of his old life that he would want it back. Rosa didn't blame him, however, Roberto was a married man and she believed the life he needed would not be the life Scarlet wanted.

Mick headed for the kitchen then to the workshop to go to bed while Scarlet scurried off to find Rosa; she wanted to tell Rosa all about Gracie's trip.

Rosa and Scarlet sat on the front bench and Scarlet told of every detail right down to their stop at Pedro's house. The scenario at Pedro's made Rosa smile to a laugh.

"So, the old guy has a heart after all," she said with a knowing grin.

Rosa was held by Scarlet's blatant and veritable exuberance over the days' events. She was surprised and somewhat taken aback by the typically passive, stand-in-the-background daughter-in-law, who, from her telling of their activities, took initiative. Scarlet apparently stepped out of her shell to make sure the outing was eventful. Rosa was taken by Scarlet's enthusiasm as she described Gracie's reaction to shopping, the birthday cake, the animals at the zoo, the pony ride, and Rosa's thoughts went immediately to the inevitable conversation Roberto was to have with her. Events that thrilled Scarlet and brought her enormous joy would more than likely have bored Roberto. As she listened to the jubilant Scarlet, she knew that their going separate ways in life was necessary for each to be happy but how it would play out troubled Rosa.

"Scarlet," Rosa said once Scarlet ended her sentence, "Frances is in the hospital."

"What happened?"

"I'm not sure. I'm going to see if Bernard will drive me to Los Alamos so I can visit her." That was Rosa's plan, but she hadn't planned on Roberto showing up with news that will change all of their lives.

"Did you call her or call the hospital?"

"I need to go see her. She won't tell me if anything is serious, you know Frances. I call her, and she'll say she's just fine."

Scarlet really didn't know Frances very well but she knew of her and she was known as a very independent, somewhat stubborn and a very private person, so Scarlet understood Rosa's concern.

"Well, Scarlet my dear, I am going to call it a night. I am so glad that the three of you had such a wonderful time. Gracie really needed a time away from here of just fun, all about her; she needed that. It was a good thing you guys did, a good thing. Don't let it be the last." She stood up slowly. She wanted to hug Scarlet but it was too out of character for Rosa and she had no explanation for the hug so she sauntered off leaving Scarlet bright-eyed, alone, sitting on the bench.

Chapter 9
No, You Go...

"No, you go. It's fine. It's better. You go on," Roberto insisted.

"I think I should stay here, now. I think Scarlet might need someone, Roberto; she's not as strong, she's not strong like you, Son." Rosa worried. Roberto was ready to have a talk with Scarlet, a necessary talk that would have to take place sooner or later. They both knew sooner was better.

"It will be fine. Please, I think it will be better...just Scarlet and me, you know. I think it would be better if you weren't here." Roberto looked anxious but determined.

"If you're sure, then I'll go with Bernard."

"I'm sure."

"I'll give Frances your best, okay?"

"Yes, yes; do. Tell her if she needs anything, you know, just give a call." Roberto was quite fond of Frances but at the moment he was preoccupied.

"Roberto," Rosa said, placing her hand on his shoulder, "be kind. Be gentle with Scarlet. Take your time."

"Of course," he said in almost a whisper.

Jeff passed Bernard, Katherine and Rosa as they were pulling out of the parking lot. He was off to Frances's house with a bag filled with meat, eggs and this time a little cheese. Rosa gave him an approving smile and a nod of gratitude. Katherine really didn't want to accompany Rosa to the hospital. She didn't know Frances and hospitals depressed her, in fact, they frightened her. She was fortunate at her age to have never needed the services of a hospital and she wanted to keep it that way. She didn't even want to step foot in one if she didn't have to but when Rosa asked if she was going along with them she gave an automatic yes, which she was now regretting.

Jeff cautiously approached the fence, bending to peek through the slender opening between the slats. He couldn't see Chupi. "Chupi?" He waited. He heard nothing. "Chupi...Chupi," he called out a bit louder. Still he heard nothing. Jeff went for the hose and then pulled the chair up to the fence so he could feed the hose directly over Chupi's water trough. He could see the trough through the fence but he could not see nor hear any sign of Chupi. Worried, and curious, Jeff pulled himself up to the top of the fence to view what he could of Chupi's area. He could feel his heart begin to race, eager to see Chupi and fearful at the same time. If he got out or if something happened to Chupi, Frances would be devastated.

The trough was full and still there was no sign of Chupi. Jeff climbed down and retrieved the bag of meat, eggs and cheese then climbed back up. "Chupi...here Chupi...come get your food. Here Chupi," Jeff called out in a low voice. He opened the bag and dumped the food onto the ground, then waited. He was too afraid to go into the yard to check if something was wrong with Chupi or if he was gone altogether. He hoped that the smell of the food would bring Chupi in sight but began to get more nervous. Chupi might have gotten out of the enclosure in the back and, that possibly, he was in the front somewhere. Jeff stayed on the chair so he could leap over the fence just in case. He continued to glance over the backyard enclosure while looking over his shoulder repeatedly at the front yard area. Without a sound, Chupi appeared in the back, his head peering around corner of the house, staring straight up at Jeff. Jeff's mouth slowly dropped open and his breath disappeared. The two locked eyes, both not moving a hair in what seemed like a timeless freeze-frame.

Chupi made the first move. He took slow steps towards the food scattered on the ground while Jeff tracked his every move as though hypnotized by the creature before him. He grasped in a breath, released his hold on the fence and fell off the chair to the ground.

"*Oh God,*" he said backing away, keeping his eyes on the fencing before he got up the nerve to turn and run, slamming the gate behind him.

Bernard pulled up to the front of the hospital.

"Are you going to park then meet us?" Katherine asked.

"No. I don't know her. I'd rather not go in," Bernard answered then turned to Rosa. "How long do you think you'll be?"

"Give us an hour, maybe a little more."

Katherine was clenching her teeth, *I don't know her either and I sure don't want to go in and you know that, Bernard* she screamed in her head.

"Sounds good. Okay ladies, I'll see you out front here in an hour or so," and he quickly looked forward knowing that Katherine was waiting to give him the squinting glare. Bernard wanted to go visit his former bookstore, say hello to Hank and see how the business was doing.

Katherine walked behind Rosa like a scolded child and Rosa paid no attention: her mission was to check on Frances.

"Aye, Jeff," Lucky hollered.

Jeff was still in a jog heading back to the Alviso, but more so heading away from Frances's place. He turned his direction toward Lucky.

"Hey, Lucky; how's it going?"

"Yeah, ah, I finished painting the wall at the monks' place."

"The monastery?"

"Yeah."

"Is that where you're headed?"

"Yeah, you wanna come see it?" Lucky was proud of this piece of work. He not only impressed the monks but impressed himself. He no longer doubted his artistic abilities in any way. He was an artist. This mural was met with enthusiastic approval from all who saw it and Lucky felt a sense of accomplishment like he'd never known in his life prior.

"I was looking for Rosa. I wanted her to come see it but she's not here."

"Yeah, she's in Los Alamos visiting Frances, you know the old nurse who helped you; she's in the hospital."

"That old nurse is sick? Is she gunna die or something?" Lucky asked in his usual indelicate yet sincere manner.

"I don't know. I hope not. She's a tough old bird; I bet she'll be fine," Jeff answered, hoping that he was right. "Yeah, I'll go see your painting, or mural, it's a mural if it's on a wall, Lucky."

"Yeah, it's on the wall," Lucky confirmed.

The two walked off toward the monastery.

"What's with Roberto?" Lucky asked. He saw Roberto and Scarlet talking and stopped to say hello in passing but Roberto waved him off. "It looked serious, ya know."

"Best leave them be. Married stuff I'm sure." Jeff saw Roberto in the morning and in jest commented about his being fired now that the real chef was back in town but Roberto didn't join in the kidding; he looked at Jeff for a second then said that they needed to talk later. Jeff didn't inquire as to what Roberto wanted to talk about, he just agreed then grabbed his bag of food for Chupi and left for Frances's house although Roberto's demeanor suggested that the talk would be of a more serious nature. He had never wanted to "talk" before. Jeff knew something was up.

"Do you walk this every day?" Jeff asked. "Do ya ever hitch a ride?"

"No, I walk. I like it. I see Granny; she's like a big dog..." and Lucky talked on about his buddy, the faithful gray cow. Then, shocking Jeff, Lucky said, "Ya know that nurse, that old nurse you said is sick, I've seen her up there." He pointed to the wooded area. "I seen her, ya know, like early in the morning and sometimes when gettin' dark when I'm walkin' out here and she's got this dog, man." He looked at Jeff. "Have you ever seen that dog? Ugly thing." He went on describing what he could see of Frances's dog. "Man, have you ever seen that dog?"

Jeff just saw Frances's "dog" up close for the first time. He knew she walked Chupi in the early morning before most would even be up or as it got dark at dusk. And, he knew that she walked Chupi in the forest and places she felt sure to not run into anyone. Lucky's description of Chupi was fairly accurate, though Frances would disagree with it.

"The dog has some kind of skin problem, that's all," Jeff said to protect Frances's best friend.

"Like mange?" Lucky asked, though that didn't account for the odd shape of the dog.

"Yeah, like mange," Jeff answered, resisting his urge to laugh. *Oh Frances, you're one in a million, old lady*, he said to himself. "So, where's your gray cow?"

"Hey, Hank."

Bernard's appearance was more than a pleasant surprise for Hank. Once he relinquished the bookstore, Bernard never came back. Hank had hoped that he would, particularly when he first took over. He could have used his presence in the store many a time but he was reduced to getting help through a phone call. It was too hard for Bernard to see his bookstore in someone else's hands so Bernard preferred to stay away.

"*Hey there, stranger!*" Hank was delighted. "Where the hell have you been? It's about time you came to visit." Hank talked on, inviting Bernard to have a seat and a cup of coffee. Hank talked, asking question after question, not waiting for Bernard to actually answer, which was fine with Bernard: he was more focused on the store itself than what Hank had to say. Hank hadn't changed, nor had he changed much about the store and Bernard was grateful that he hadn't. It felt like home. Old feelings came rushing in. Bernard took a deep breath, held it then exhaled to relax himself.

"The place looks the same," he commented.

It wasn't too long into their visit when Hank made a comment that jolted Bernard's whole world.

"So old man, why don't you buy this place back. I want to see what's in these books for myself. I want to retire again, hit the road. You know, buy an RV and hit the road or take a cruise or maybe even hop a plane and see the world…." Hank carried on about the places he wanted to see before his time was up on this planet while Bernard's racing heart kick started his reoccurring daydream.

"Come on, Mr. Adams, or should I say Mr. Atoms." Hank smiled. He never changed the store name. "You loved this place. I need a break. I'll make you a deal you can't refuse…."

He didn't need to make any kind of deal to persuade Bernard to buy his bookstore back. He regretted selling it from the day it was sold. All that was going through his head at that moment was if Katherine would be willing to move back to Los Alamos and once again make it their permanent home.

"I hate hospitals, Rosa," she said between apologetic and defensive. "I hate going in them." Rosa and Katherine sat on one of the benches in front of the hospital waiting for Bernard. Katherine felt she had to explain her odd behavior though Rosa really didn't pay much attention to either Katherine or her behavior.

"Why?" Rosa asked, not that she was in fact interested but she sensed Katherine needed to clear the air about something. And she did. Frances appeared on death's bed to Katherine. As she stood by her bed, Katherine was beginning to panic, to want to run out of the room and out of the hospital. But the polite and appropriate in Katherine didn't allow her to do so, instead Katherine began to rock from foot to foot, taking in deep breaths with an audibly exhale. She couldn't help herself, and she felt that she was making a minor spectacle of herself even though Frances and Rosa were hardly paying attention. Now Katherine felt the need to explain her behavior while in Frances's room. Rosa listened to Katherine but her mind was on Frances; she didn't believe that Frances would be coming home. Katherine talked on believing Rosa was intently listening. When she finished, Rosa said nothing. The two waited for Bernard in silence.

"Wow, man," Jeff exclaimed, a bit stunned. "You did this?" The mural portrayed a monk sitting by the opening of a cave with birds perched about. The words "He Who Works Prays" artfully scrolled across the bottom. It was beautiful and so skillfully executed. This canvass of stone came alive. Jeff could hardly believe that Lucky, the assumed dimwitted Buck, could have the eye, talent and soul to accomplish such a work of art.

"Of course I did it; I brought you to show what I did." Lucky shook his head. "You think I didn't paint this, man?"

"Wow, Lucky, you're really a talented painter. You're an artist, that's for sure." Jeff stood in awe of the mural while Lucky realized that Jeff didn't doubt his talent but was admiring it. "What does that mean?" he pointed to the writing on the bottom.

"He who works prays," Lucky read it aloud. "I don't know; they told me to put that on there."

"Well, this work is definitely like a prayer, Lucky. It's amazing, man."

"Have you been in the church?" Lucky wanted to take Jeff in the church so he could see if Jesus's eyes followed Jeff around the church like they followed him.

"Nope."

"Come on" and Lucky led the way.

"Isn't anyone around here?" Jeff had expected to see monks roaming about but had seen no monks, no one at all.

"Yeah, but they're busy doing stuff—probably praying or they have a big garden where they get their food. They're always working doing somethin'," he answered, hurrying Jeff into the church.

"Kind of small for a church, isn't it?" Jeff looked around, not much to see, although the display of pastel cliffs though the massive windows was impressive.

"Come look at this carving up here on the cross."

Jeff walked over to below the cross and looked up at the carving just as Lucky was doing.

"Looks like he's lookin' right at ya, huh?" Lucky wanted confirmation.

"Sort of," Jeff replied, not quite as engaged in the carving as Lucky.

"Well, walk around, look around." Lucky had an ulterior motive.

"I can see everything, not much to see. It's not very big in here."

"Go look at that statue in that hole in the wall," Lucky pushed, pointing to the carved saint within the niche. "Go on, go look at it." Jeff gave him a scrunched brow response but did as suggested.

Lucky stood back and watched the eyes on the carved Jesus. They were still looking at him, not following Jeff across the floor to the niche. Lucky stepped back, his eyes still fixed on the eyes on the carving. The eyes fixed right back. They watched him move backward three-four, five-six steps away. Jesus was watching Lucky, not Jeff, and Lucky was convinced it was personal. Jesus was watching him, not anybody who came into the church but *him*.

"I need to head back," Jeff informed a bit loudly to catch Lucky's attention. "You okay?"

Lucky didn't answer but headed for the church doors, watching the carving watching him as he left.

Roberto just needed to walk, and walk. And Scarlet just needed to be alone and cry. Her marriage was over as she knew it and dreamed it. Roberto needed to leave the Alviso and by the end of their conversation Scarlet was convinced of that fact. Like Rosa, she too remembered the old Roberto who, a lot like his father, was always in the midst of plans—he regularly had a project or a goal he was working on. She enjoyed that aspect of Roberto, once foreseeing the two of them sailing on the boat he was working on or traveling—seeking new experiences and adventures together. But Scarlet had grown to enjoy her life at the Alviso; she no longer shared a passion for adventure somewhere else. Scarlet didn't want to leave her home at the Alviso, and at this time she certainly didn't want to leave Gracie. Right now, she just wanted to cry, not entirely because Roberto was leaving but because she didn't want to leave.

Jeff arrived at the kitchen to prepare for the dinner service. He expected to find Roberto in the kitchen when he arrived to work but found only Agnes.

"Have you seen Roberto?" Jeff asked.

"Is he back?" But before Jeff got a chance to answer, "Well, there he is." She smiled at Roberto as he came through the kitchen back door. He gave Agnes a look she couldn't interpret.

"Jeff." Roberto stayed by the door. "I need to talk to you if you could please take a minute." Roberto wasn't smiling and Jeff knew this was "the talk."

"Sure." He looked over at Agnes, whose brow was furrowed, sensing that something was going on of a serious matter that she knew nothing about. "Hold down the fort, Agnes." She watched the two go out the back door.

Roberto briefly explained his situation: he needed to leave and he expected to be gone for an extended amount of time. Though Jeff wanted to ask questions, a lot of questions, he refrained and just listened to Roberto, although he tried to read between Roberto's lines. Roberto wanted to know if Jeff was enjoying his job as a chef (Roberto knew better than to refer to Jeff's job as "the cook." The title of Sous Chef was a boost to Jeff's self-esteem and Chef was a respected title and profession). He wanted to know if Jeff could and would stay on at the Alviso as their chef which also entailed running a good part of the restaurant. Roberto wouldn't leave unless he knew with certainty that Jeff would be there for Rosa.

"You'll have your room and board, like now, but you'll also get a salary, Jeff," Roberto informed. "But, Jeff, I have to know that you will stay, ya know, that you can make a commitment to be here for Rosa. Can you do that? Do you need time to think about it?"

"How long are you going to be away, Roberto?"

The question immediately concerned Roberto. He wondered if Jeff had been on the road for so much of his life that staying in one place for very long may not be workable for him.

"Six months," he answered. "Can you commit to staying and working here for six months?"

Jeff didn't think much about time. He wasn't asking because he was concerned about how long he would be the chef at the Alviso, he asked because he was still curious about Roberto's decision to leave and hoped that the question would inspire more detail about where Roberto was going, and why.

"No problem, Roberto. Yeah, I can be here six months. And don't worry, man, I wouldn't leave Rosa in a bind. Anyway, I'm a damn good cook now. It's like an art, ya know. I'm an artist in the kitchen. Lucky's an artist on walls and I'm an artist on the grill."

The two talked for a few minutes about the logistics of the restaurant then Roberto reached his hand out to Jeff. He shook Jeff's hand like Bernard shook Hank's hand at the sale of the store. Jeff knew Roberto was, without a doubt, on his way out and away from the Alviso. Before Jeff shut the kitchen door behind him he hollered to Roberto, "Can I change the menu?" Roberto nodded a yes, raised his hand in a partial wave and they each continued on to their waiting destinies.

Rosa sat next to Scarlet, wanting to console her as best she could but Scarlet would say little. She wasn't certain if Scarlet may have been angry with her, assuming that she knew all along that Roberto was planning to leave, or at least knew before she did. Or, if perhaps Scarlet wasn't saying much because she was her mother-in-law and what she really needed was a friend to talk to. But, Scarlet, ensconced in the Alviso for so many years, had few friends and none locally. Rosa was relieved when she spotted Mick and discreetly waved him over. She had to try her best to relay to him that Scarlet needed him, but was scantly successful getting her message across. Nonetheless, Rosa got up and Mick sat down in her place, befuddled but willing to help in anyway that he could manage.

Rosa walked over to the house that once was hers and Roberto Sr.'s, the house she gave to Roberto and Scarlet when her husband passed away. Rosa moved into one of the guest rooms and was quite happy in smaller confines. Roberto was packing, and in a hurry, confirming and emphasizing for Rosa his need to get away.

"Where are you going, Roberto?"

He set the large sports bag on the floor. "I'm going with Delmacio and his brothers. We're taking a fishing trip to the Gulf of Mexico," he paused to look at Rosa before continuing, "and then from there, I'm not sure, but I'll be in touch. I'll let you know where I am."

Rosa just stared at Roberto. She could see so much of his father in him at that moment.

"I don't know," he said," I just need to go. Maybe I'll be back after the fishing trip. I just need to get away."

"I know you do. You don't have to explain to me, Roberto. You do what you need to do." There was a minute of silence. "You are, and have been, a good son, Roberto. I trust you like no one else. You do whatever it is you need to do. I'll be fine. Scarlet will be fine. We'll all be fine. The Alviso will be just fine. You go, Roberto. You go and be happy, Son." Rosa didn't wait for a response. She knew that as much as Roberto wanted and needed to go that he also carried guilt for his decision to leave the Alviso. Rosa turned and exited not saying another word, allowing Roberto to continue on without feeling the need to explain further, or to enhance his guilt with her presence.

Rosa hardly had time to sit down in her room when Mick was at her door.

"What's going on?" he asked in a low voice. He sat next to Scarlet on the bench as Rosa had encouraged, and though he could tell that Scarlet had been crying, she insisted that everything was fine and talked about wanting to get a cat or even maybe a dog. Mick was confused.

"I'll tell you later, Mick," Rosa answered. "Just be there for her."

Even more confused he replied, "How? How should I be there for her, Rosa?"

"Just be her friend ... just be her friend." And Rosa got up and went back into her room. She sat on her bed. At first thinking about Roberto Sr. where she said aloud, "He has to do this, Roberto." She knew if he were there that he would be disappointed in his son leaving, leaving his wife and his responsibilities. But, if Roberto Sr. were there his son and his wife would not have been and this would not have been an issue. Rosa sanctioned his decision to leave and hoped that Roberto Sr., in spirit, would also. She put her feet up and laid her head against the pillow but not long enough to rest before there was another knock on her door. Rosa was certain that it was Roberto coming to say his goodbye before driving off.

She sat up, took in several deep breaths before getting up to answer the door. There stood Scarlet. Roberto was nowhere in sight.

"Come in." Rosa opened the door wide and stepped aside, again looking for Roberto outside before shutting the door. Scarlet walked directly to the chair and sat down. "Are you okay, Scarlet? Would you like to talk?"

Scarlet caught her tears before they hit her cheek. It took a few minutes before she could speak.

"I understand, Rosa. I know why he's leaving. I know he needs to get away." She continued to wipe her tears before they could make a massive display. "I don't fault him. I understand; I really do."

"How can I help you?" Rosa didn't know what to do. She had a lot that she could say, but wasn't sure what to do. "Would you like to go take a walk?" was all she could think to offer. Scarlet shook her head no, so Rosa sat back down on the bed.

"I know he has to go, Rosa, but," she held her breath, wiped another few tears, "I don't want to go." The tears began to flow faster than she could catch them.

"He wants you to go with him?" Rosa asked, almost certain that Roberto did not desire her company on this fishing trip.

"No...I don't think so. Does he?" She looked up at Rosa.

"No, I don't think so. I don't think you'd enjoy fishing in the Gulf of Mexico."

"I don't think I would," she responded. She was referring to leaving the Alviso. Going with Roberto hadn't entered her mind or their conversation. "I don't want to leave the Alviso."

"Why would you leave the Alviso, Scarlet; I'm confused."

"Well, Rosa, if Roberto isn't here," she started to explain but her tears took center stage once again. Rosa patiently waited for her to continue. "I'm sorry. I'm sorry for all this crying."

"Now, where are you going?" Rosa asked.

"I don't want to go, Rosa. I don't want to leave the Alviso. And, well, I want to continue on, living here. I don't want to leave but Roberto is going for who knows how long—"

Rosa cut her off. "Oh Scarlet. You don't have to leave here because Roberto is going. This is your home. I don't want you to leave the Alviso. You're like my daughter. You can leave whenever you want to but I don't want you to leave. Please, Scarlet, don't cry about leaving. You're not leaving, not unless you want to. I need you here. I don't want you to go."

She was not only relieved to hear that Rosa welcomed her to stay at the Alviso, but Scarlet had never heard such words from Rosa—that she wanted and needed her. It was as though those words blew away the dark and confusing cloud surrounding her.

"I'll move my things out of the house, Rosa."

"Oh no you won't. I don't want to live in that house. You stay there. I am happy right where I am, and I mean that, Scarlet. You continue to live in that house—whether Roberto is there or not. That is your place, and this is mine." Rosa was resolute; she was not moving back into the house.

"Oh, Rosa, I can't stay there. It's just me. I'd feel bad."

"Well, don't feel bad. You stay there, and I'm staying right here in this room. That's the way I want it, so don't argue with me, Scarlet. If you're uncomfortable being in that house because Roberto isn't there then you can move to the little adobe, but either way, I'm not moving back into that house."

Their conversation was interrupted by Roberto knocking on the door. He was leaving and came to say goodbye to Rosa one more time not knowing that Scarlet was also in his mother's room. It worked out for the best: Rosa and Roberto said their goodbye and Scarlet walked Roberto to his truck where they were able to share a few concerns before his leaving. Scarlet wanted to know if they would be getting a divorce, and she wanted him to know that Rosa welcomed her to stay on at the Alviso. She worried that he may not want her to stay on, though she, at this time, had no desire or intention of leaving. Roberto was pleased that she was staying on, in fact, it eased his guilt about going. And as for the divorce, this was not the time to even think about such a thing as far as he was concerned.

Scarlet watched Roberto drive off, surprised that she did not feel as though she was being deserted, nor did she feel sad; she felt something that was close to happy and an odd sense of independence—feelings she hadn't expected. Scarlet wasn't inclined to investigate her feelings at that moment; she was overcome with relief that she would be staying at the Alviso—and to continue to be near to Gracie.

Jeff wasted no time in revamping Rancho Alviso's menu: featuring *The Town's Best Quesadillas*. Being the town's only restaurant, they indeed were the town's best quesadillas. As he jotted down his new menu and decided on that evening's special, Lucky breezed into the kitchen.

"What's that sound, man?" he asked.

"What sound?"

Lucky held open the door. "That weird sound," Lucky answered. "Is that some kind of coyote or wolf or what?"

Jeff could now hear the howl. Though coming from quite a distance, the howling could easily be heard. Lucky and Jeff remained quiet, listening to the strange howling from afar.

Rosa opened the kitchen door to the lobby, waving Jeff to join her.

"Well, what is that? A coyote?"

"I'm not sure, Lucky. Hold on," and Jeff left to join Rosa in the lobby.

"Did you feed Chupi?" Rosa asked. She knew that howl, though rarely heard, she knew it was the howl of Chupi or one of his kind.

"Yeah, I fed him. I fed him a lot. And he has water. Why?"

"The howling," Rosa answered.

"That's Chupi?" he asked and Rosa nodded a yes. "Have you seen that, ah, dog?" Rosa nodded another yes. "Should I go check on him...but the dinner should start soon, but I'll go check if you want me to."

"No, you go on," Rosa insisted. "I'll go check." She started for the front doors. "Jeff, tell Katherine to watch the desk for me."

Rosa decided to walk to Frances's house. She hadn't walked through the town in some time and a long walk felt like it was just what she needed. As she walked aside the road she strolled down memory lane as well. *A sobriquet.* She smiled. She remembered Roberto Sr. learning that word and having fun with it. He had a nickname for just about everyone: No Butt Evelyn; Pedro The Evil Troll; Loony Larry; Big Bass Crystal, who had her lips enhance to what Roberto found a humorous size. She remembered how much Roberto Sr. enjoyed people and how he had fun with them—and about them.

"Rosa!"

Rosa stopped and turned toward the voice. She couldn't help but chuckle after just remembering her husband's playful way about people and there was No Butt Evelyn shouting out to her, jogging her way over. Roberto would have chuckled too.

"Rosa," Evelyn said, out of breath. "Did you get the word about Frances?"

The smile dropped from Rosa's face.

"Yeah, Rosa, Frances died." Evelyn was catching her breath as Rosa stood silent. "Her niece called..." and Evelyn continued to pass on the information she had received from Frances's niece. Rosa listened but only for a minute then she continued to walk her path to Frances's house at a fast pace. Evelyn trotted along side Rosa, however, Rosa was not responding to Evelyn either verbally or with eye contact so Evelyn stopped and allowed Rosa to be on her way alone.

Frances was somewhat of a loner. She was there to give her professional help when needed but preferred to be left to her own world which involved a lot of wonderful memories, an elaborate garden and her beloved Chupi. Evelyn managed to inform those who were known to be friends with Frances of her passing, and that Frances's niece would be arriving to take care of her affairs.

For those at the Alviso who knew Frances, her death was grievously expected. Not much was said. It was a given that she would truly be missed for the unique person that she was, and for the gracious pro bono service she provided not only for those at the Alviso, but for any person or animal who needed her help.

"What about Chupi," Jeff asked in private. "Do I continue to go feed him?"

She stared at him for a few seconds before answering. Rosa appreciated Jeff's kind heart. Here stood that raggedy hitchhiker, "the bum" according to Sheriff Shelton. Here he stood not as the tie-dye vagrant all the town was familiar with but as a welcome member of the Alviso family and a blessing in Rosa's life.

"I let Chupi go, Jeff."

"But I still hear him howling, Rosa. You gotta hear that...don't you?" Jeff questioned, and Rosa nodded. She heard Chupi like everyone else.

"We need to keep feeding him, at least for a while, Jeff. But, we gotta put the food up the trail, away from the house. Chupi can't be at that house. We have to keep him away from the house, awaaaay from the house. We owe that to Frances, Jeff." She explained that Frances's niece, Charlotte, would be arriving to take care of Frances's affairs and Chupi could not be anywhere near the house, for Chupi's sake.

They put a plan together, just between the two of them. Jeff would hike into the woods and leave food and water for Chupi. He would leave it farther into the woods each time. Jeff believed that they should reduce the food and water so that Chupi would eventually forage off on his own to become self-reliant. But Rosa knew better. She knew the likely results of Chupi finding a meal on his own. Because of the love and respect she had for Frances and knowing the natural tendencies of Chupi, Rosa would continue to provide for Chupi as long as she was covertly able. At dawn and at dusk, the town would hear Chupi's plaintive howl. All but Rosa and Jeff believed that they were hearing the chronic and desperate howls of a coyote calling out to its pack.

Chapter 10
She Stood There...

There she stood, like a vision in tie-dye, watering the garden. An angel of extraordinary beauty to Jeff, and she was wearing a tie-dyed long sleeve tee shirt. He couldn't take his eyes off of her. He stood at the side of the trail watching as Charlotte watered Frances's jungle. Charlotte planned to sell the little house with the amazing garden, although everyone told her that she'd have better luck monetarily if she burned it to the ground and collected the insurance. Who would be buying in a small town with no jobs. This was a town, unless you grew up there, one passed through but not a place one put down roots. Most were like Roberto Jr.; they yearned for more than this town had to offer. Through the years, a few outsiders, "interlopers" as Pedro called them, set up house but they never stayed long. A couple of times individuals purchased a house from a desperate seller to use as a vacation home, but that never lasted long either. Charlotte had quite a wait if she wanted to sell Frances's little, odd shaped house.

"Heeeellooooo."

Rosa looked up from her magazine from behind the counter. A smile drew across her face.

"Did I make it just in time for dinner?" Lena smiled back. "Do you happen to accept a pet here at your fine establishment?" she asked in jest.

"Only if it's a dog named Pepper with funny teeth," Rosa replied feigning seriousness.

"Funny teeth?" Lena laughed aloud. Pepper had a bit of an under-bite which at times made him look as though he were smiling with his upper lip caught behind the protruding bottom teeth. "Come on, you know he has an endearing smile." Lena stepped into the lobby. "This is really looking nice, Rosa; really nice."

Rosa was proud of her new gift shop accented by Lucky's mural.

"So, you here to stay a bit?" Rosa hoped.

"I planned it so I could be here today, Friday, so if you wanted to go to the market again tomorrow you have company and a ride."

"First things first, young lady. Let's get you and that smiling dog of yours set up in a room."

Lena stepped up to the counter, pulling her wallet out of her purse."

"Oh no; put that away," Rosa demanded in a stern voice.

"No way, Rosa; I am paying for my room. If I don't pay, I don't stay." Lena was just as demanding and also used a stern, determined voice.

"Then you'll have dinner with me...as my guest."

"Sounds good."

Lena paid for the little adobe house since it had the fenced in area for Pepper. Rosa charged her for one night, though she fully intended on convincing her to stay longer. Lena left the lobby to pull her car around to park and bring in her suitcases. She let Pepper run a bit through the open field then fed him, leaving him in the enclosed area while she met Rosa for dinner.

Just like before, Rosa told Agnes to bring them sangrias with dinner.

"Aaah, sangria again. And, quesadillas again," Lena commented as she dug right in.

"This quesadilla stuff is getting too much." Rosa shook her head. She wasn't sure if Jeff was actually being creative or that he just found an easy dish to make and was taking advantage of it. If you were passing through town, a well-stuff quesadilla was satisfying but as a regular patron, this dish that was so easy to make at home was becoming quite tiresome. But Jeff basked in the compliments he received for his impressive quesadillas from those stopping for their first and last meal at the Alviso, and Rosa didn't believe that he would retire them from the menu any time soon.

Agnes joined them for a short time since the restaurant had no diners other than Rosa and Lena. She hardly paid attention; she was too busy looking out the window, eagerly waiting for a customer like a dog waiting for someone to throw the ball. Eventually, they threw the ball. Agnes raced to the lobby and escorted the group of five to a table. She was back in her element, happy as happy can be as she recommended the quesadillas.

Lena talked in bits and pieces about her visit at Broken Arrow. Some of what she experienced was personally upsetting so she kept to the light and upbeat of her visit. They talked about going to the market the next day, which had Rosa energized and ordering more sangrias.

"I'll get Katherine to watch the desk," Rosa said. She sipped her sangria and talked about her past sales. Then, all of a sudden, like one remembers in a flash that they left the oven on, Rosa remembered through the fog of the sangria that Katherine and Bernard no longer were staying at the Alviso. They moved back to Los Alamos.

"Oh my," Rosa exclaimed. "I completely forgot that Katherine...you met Katherine and Bernard last time you were here, right?"

"I think so." Lena tried to remember who they were.

"They were here helping out. Bernard bought back his old bookstore in Los Alamos and they moved. I forgot. Oh my." Rosa laughed, a knowing laugh that the sangrias were having their influence. Eventually Scarlet stepped up to the table to say hello to Lena and Rosa requested that she watch the front desk on Saturday so that she and her new friend could go to the market.

"Rosa, I can't. I'm so sorry, but I can't," Scarlet said apologetically, yet firmly. Rosa furrowed her brow, disappointed and curious. "Mick and I are taking Gracie riding."

"Riding?"

"Horseback riding, at Fionn's. He even has a pony for Gracie, that's if she'll get on it." Scarlet smiled.

"That sounds fun," Lena remarked.

"Oh it's going to be so much fun. Mick and I are taking Gracie early in the morning and then we're going on a picnic. It's going to be so much fun. Mick and I bought Gracie—-" she paused, "Did you meet Gracie, Lena? She's the little girl with light brown hair. Sweet little girl." Scarlet spoke about Gracie with such endearment in her voice.

"I don't think I did," Lena answered, while Rosa worried who she could ask next to watch the front desk so she and Lena could go on a shopping trip for the day.

"Pedro had an old Hopalong Cassidy outfit. Do you remember Hopalong Cassidy?" Lena nodded. She vaguely remembered the character; she knew that he was a cowboy. "He had an outfit. It's too big for Gracie but the vest and hat fit her, and the holster. She's going to wear it tomorrow. We'll get pictures...." Scarlet talked on about the next day's event as one would talk about a planned trip to Europe.

"Pedro gave her the Hopalong Cassidy outfit?" Rosa questioned.

"Yes. Gracie told him about going riding on our walk and he came up with the outfit. I don't know whose it was, but he gave it to Gracie so she could look like a little cowgirl on the ride."

"That old grump gave something away? Sure you aren't gunna be charged for it?" Rosa laughed, and laughed, and laughed. And Scarlet knew the sangria was assisting.

"He's been very nice, Rosa. He even turned on all the Christmas lights and music for Gracie. You remember. I told you about that."

"Well who am I going to get to watch the lobby tomorrow?"

"I can watch on Sunday, but I really can't tomorrow. We have this all planned out and——-"

Rosa cut her off, "No, no, you go on your...whatever. I'll find somebody. Don't worry about it. You take Gracie and go have fun."

"It's good seeing you again, Lena. I'm sure I'll see you later. Take care." Scarlet left to meet Mick. Albert sold cowboy hats at the Mountain High hardware store and they both wanted to buy a hat for the next day's ride.

Rosa sipped down the last of her sangria while Lena finished the last bite of her quesadilla. Before going their separate ways, they made plans to meet for breakfast Saturday morning and to delay their trip to the market until Sunday where Rosa was assured that she had someone to work the lobby, though "work" was not quite accurate. Even though this was the season for tourists, their busiest season, still it was a rare few who ventured to stop at Rancho Alviso for a stay or to browse Rosa's gift shop. It was those stopping for a bite to eat that kept the register ringing but Rosa was convinced that her new gift shop would be the new money maker.

Rosa was up early, earlier than usual. She decided to take a stroll by Frances's house. She hadn't intended on stopping to meet Charlotte nor to look for signs of Chupi, but that's just what she did. She could hear Chupi howling and directed her walk in his direction. The smells from the woods were invigorating and very much reminded her of Frances. When they first met, that's just what they used to do. They took strolls in the woods and talked. Mostly Rosa listened. She loved hearing Frances's stories of the past. She was definitely an adventurer and a pioneer of a woman for her day. She had an attitude about, and a way with, people that Rosa found admirably humorous. It was on one of their walks that Frances found Chupi. To Rosa, the youngest and ugliest stray she had ever seen, to Frances, a critter in need of her expertise. Frances's preoccupation with her infant Chupi ended their regular walks. Frances was dedicated to her new companion and Rosa was eventually replaced with Chupi. Rosa understood. Rosa still had Roberto Sr. then but Frances no longer had her long-time love.

Rosa hiked up the narrow trail no longer guided by Chupi's painful howls. She walked and walked but saw no sign of Chupi. Only when she sat down upon a boulder to rest did she get a glimpse of Chupi at a distance. He was watching her, and Rosa was so very pleased to see his distinctive face that only a mother could love. So very pleased that Chupi was making his way without Frances and so very pleased that she could be there for Chupi in the only way possible. As she looked back at Chupi she swore she could feel Frances. "Don't worry, my dear, we'll look after Chupi for you," she said as though Frances was standing beside her.

Chupi stepped out from behind the trees. Rosa watched, surprised that he was showing himself. She could see his tail wag. *Was he wagging his tail because of her, or did he also feel the presence of Frances.* She was happy to see Chupi's tail wag regardless.

Rosa made her way back down the trail to France's house. Charlotte was in the window, staring out when she noticed Rosa. Rosa waved and Charlotte immediately came out to talk with Rosa. Charlotte wasn't sure what to do with all of Frances's possessions. There were few that she herself wanted. There was not an organization nearby that Charlotte knew of to donate the array of items, including the furniture. She was at a loss. She also did not anticipate Frances living so far away from "civilization" and the prospects of her house selling were obviously miniscule. She wondered if Rosa could be of help. And of course, she would; but not in a hurry. She would take her time, for Jeff's sake. Love opportunities are lean in a small town. Yet consuming when hinted upon and Rosa would give this light in Jeff's possibilities as much time as she could manage.

Rosa could see through the dining room window, between the pulled-back lace curtains, Lucky sitting with Lena. She sped up her pace and cheerfully joined them. She was happy to see Lucky, she saw so very little of him as of late. Though proud that he was devoting so much of his time and skill to the monks, she did miss him. She invited them in for a bite to eat. Agnes took their order then scooted in to have a cup of coffee with them as she yearned for more customers to arrive.

"Feuw," Lucky expelled a puff of air. "Look at that," he said staring out the window. It was Mick, Scarlet and Gracie: Gracie in between Mick and Scarlet, each holding a hand. All three were donning cowboy hats.

"They're off to go horseback riding; they're taking Gracie riding," Agnes commented, mostly to inform Lena.

Lucky shook his head and scrunched his mouth.

"What?" Rosa responded to Lucky's rather disapproving expression.

"Look at Mick," Lucky mumbled. "Look at that outfit."

"I think they look cute," Agnes added with her usual upbeat positive demeanor. Agnes was one happy human and so viewed not only her life as delightful since coming to the Alviso, but the life around her and not much was going to change that. The three could have been wearing potato sacks and Agnes would have nothing but compliments.

"He looks corny. He ain't a cowboy, Agnes. He just looks stupid with that hat on."

Lena giggled. She thought they looked fine in their matching cowboy hats but found Lucky's scowl humorous.

"You leave them alone, Lucky. Don't you say anything hurtful to them. You hear me, Lucky?" Rosa was charmed by their devotion to the little girl who lost not only her mother but her father. Until Scarlet, and now Mick, little Gracie was left with only an old man who favored nothing more than fishing to fill her needs in life.

Lucky turned from the window, raised his eyebrows and said, "corn-ball" then dropped the subject.

Eventually Agnes got her wish when a family passing through stopped at the Alviso for a bite to eat. And, Rosa got her wish when they also browsed the gift shop and made several purchases. The day started out quite eventful and Rosa was pleased. Even with Roberto Jr. away, Rosa couldn't have been more pleased with her life and life at the Alviso.

Sunday morning was off to a planned and good start. Scarlet agreed to work the lobby—escort guests to the dining room and do her best to sell items from the gift shop. Jeff was off early with Chupi's food and hopes that Charlotte would again be in the garden. Lucky was up early, per usual, to head off to the monastery. That day he volunteered to help the monks with fencing for their garden, and, as he did every visit to the monastery, he stopped to exchange stares with the carved figure on the cross. Lucky swore that there was communication far beyond the mutual gaze. Mick was also up early, repairing the roof on the little adobe. At first Pepper gave Mick a hard time but soon calmed down once Mick retrieved a bone still rife with fat and meat.

"Did you like that hat, that cowboy hat?" Rosa asked Lena as they pulled out of the parking lot and onto the road leading to Santa Fe.

"You mean the cowboy hat that Scarlet was wearing?"

"Yeah, did you like it?" Rosa watched Lena's hair whipping around her face as they drove with the top down. Rosa long knew how to spray her hair into place where nothing was moving it, and it would last for days.

"Yeah, I thought they looked good on them," she answered, wondering if Rosa was going to now take Lucky's side.

"Pull in here," Rosa said, pointing to Mountain High. And, Lena did as she was told. "I'll be right back."

"Should I leave the car running?" Lena asked.

"You can; I'll be right out," she answered though Rosa never moved very fast. Lena was curious as to why Rosa needed to stop at the hardware store, but it was none of her business so she left the car running and waited.

"Albert," Rosa shouted. She wasn't going to hunt him down. "*Albert.*"

"Coming, coming," he shouted back, shuffling down the aisle making haste to the front counter. "How can I help you, Rosa?"

"Get me one of those cowboy hats," she demanded. She wasn't going to make small talk since Albert knew how to chew on small talk just a bit too long for Rosa's taste.

"Okay," he said, perky and accommodating. "Is this for you?"

Rosa found Albert too nosey. It was none of his business who it was for so she didn't answer.

"Well?" he asked again. He stared at her for a few seconds. "I need to know what size, Rosa. Is this going to fit you or somebody else?"

"Oh, yes. You're right." She felt a tiny bit guilty for prejudging his intent. "My size; give me one that would fit me."

Albert stepped down from the ladder with a tan woven cowboy hat in hand. He reached over to place it on Rosa's head.

"Aye, Albert," she swatted him away. She didn't want that hat denting her hair. "Just give it to me."

"How ya gunno know if it fits, Rosa?"

"How much do I owe you?" she asked and grabbed the hat from Albert's hand.

Rosa rushed, as much as Rosa rushes, out the front door. She got back into the little car and held out the hat to Lena. "Here, this is for you." Rosa placed the hat on Lena's head. "It looks good on you." Rosa grinned.

At first Lena didn't know if she was joking, but Lena liked the hat—joking or not.

She gave Rosa a huge smile. "Thank you." Lena pulled the hat down so that the fit was tighter. "I love it, Rosa. Thanks."

"It'll keep the hair out of your eyes, and blowing all over your face... *let's go.*"

Lena shared Rosa's optimistic enthusiasm for her new gift shop which helped fueled Rosa's determination to keep the shelves full and to expand her new enterprise. This was Rosa's, all Rosa's and she loved that. It wasn't something that another person started or something that she was obligated to participate or to keep afloat. This was her idea, her baby, and so far, it was doing okay.

"Look," Rosa shouted over the wind. She pointed to a sign on the side of the road declaring a flea market in White Rock.

"Should we go?" Lena slowed the car. Rosa nodded a yes and they flew from one lane to the next and off the main road to follow the crudely made signs for the flea market.

The market was large, not as large as the Santa Fe market, but big enough and surprisingly busy for White Rock. They parked on the dusty flat area next to the other cars. Rosa was out the door immediately. Lena adjusted her hat, grabbed her leather backpack then hurried out of the car to catch up to Rosa. She walked along side Rosa scanning the items and making a comment here and there, though Rosa didn't respond to any of her comments.

By the third row Lena stated, "I don't think you're going to find new things for the shop here, Rosa."

Rosa didn't reply but kept on scrutinizing the array of items displayed on tables, the hoods of cars, the tailgates of trucks and on blankets spread out on the ground.

"Let me see those rings," Rosa asked one of the vendors. He obliged and pulled the black velvet display tray from the case. Rosa pulled out a ring and examined it then placed it back. Pulled another out and examine it, then put that one back. She did this at an annoyingly slow pace all the while the seller gave a material breakdown and supposed history of each. Lena became impatient.

"I'm going to continue looking around. Holler to me if you need me," she said then walked off. The weather was nice and Lena was enjoying the stroll and minor interaction with those selling and buying. She purchased a jacket made with Chimayo weaving whose seller claimed was from the 1940's. She was excited about the treasure with the perfect fit and headed off to find Rosa. She located Rosa rows back pulling an upright metal basket on wheels.

"Where'd you get the basket?" Lena asked.

"Nice, huh? It folds down flat," she explained, quite proud of her acquisition.

"Excellent. Perfect. That's a great idea."

"Yes it is," Rosa agreed. "So, what did you get, young lady?"

Lena held up the jacket. "And it fits perfect."

"Chimayo," Rosa informed and Lena nodded. The seller gave her a more than apt description and history of the jacket.

"Yeah, I got the jacket's full bio." She looked in Rosa's basket which contained a cardboard box. "So what did you get?"

"You go on, you go shop and I'll find you when I'm done." Though Rosa enjoyed Lena's company, she was particularly enjoying making decisions about the shop items on her own this time.

They put the purchased items in the trunk of Lena's car and placed the folded shopping basket on the stunted backseats then strolled over to a weathered concession trailer painted a dark pink. Each ordered an Indian taco and an ice tea then found the shade of a tree on a rickety bench. Rosa was quiet, something everyone at the Alviso was used to but Lena's experience with Rosa was quite different.

"I guess I should have ordered you a sangria with your taco to get you talking," Lena noted in jest. Rosa grinned to a laugh. "Really," Lena continued. "You've been pretty quiet today, Rosa. Is everything okay?"

"Thinking," Rosa said. "I've just been thinking, thinking about a lot of things." She shifted to face Lena. "Do you have a boyfriend Lena? Someone you're in love with?"

"Well that's an interesting question out of the blue, Rosa." Lena wanted to laugh, but refrained. "That's something you've been thinking about?"

"No, but do you?"

"No."

"You haven't been in love?" Rosa questioned.

"Yes…but why are you curious about this? Don't tell me you're going to set me up on a date or something."

Rosa gave a quick giggle before answering. "No. I was just thinking about, oh I don't know." She paused for what seemed like a very long time before finishing her thought aloud. "I miss Roberto, my husband, Roberto Sr."

"How long has he been gone?" Lena asked, hoping that she wasn't furthering a subject that would sadden Rosa.

"A very long time, Lena; sometimes it feels like a hundred years; sometimes it feels like the other day, that I'll walk out front and he'll be talking with somebody. He'll be coming into the kitchen to tell me a story about somebody. He'll be making me laugh." She looked directly at Lena again and asked, "You never been married or in love?"

"I've never been married, Rosa, but I've been in love."

"So where is he? In California?"

"No, he's here in New Mexico, Rosa. He's here, buried here. Jose was killed in an accident. He's buried in Pista."

There was another rather long silence.

"Did you come to visit his grave, or his family?"

Lena nodded. She had visited his grave while in Pista—impressed that it still displayed mementos of love from those in Jose's life—and Broken Arrow where Jose found solace and family.

"We lost our men, Lena," Rosa uttered.

Lena took in the solemn and sad truth of her statement then looked directly at Rosa. Rosa smiled, opened her mouth wide and shoved a quarter of the Indian taco into her mouth. The visual incongruity made Lena laugh, and Rosa joined in.

"Two widows on the bench," Rosa added with a beam of a smile. "So, tell me what you loved best about——"she paused, trying to remember his name.

"Jose." Lena helped.

"Tell me what you loved about Jose..." and the two talked as if their ice teas were sangrias. By the time they got up to leave, Lena felt as though she knew Roberto Sr. and understood his influence at the Alviso—as Rosa came to know Jose, his humor and heart. The best, the worst and the delight of both men were shared, and how they were so dearly loved—and missed.

By the time their conversation naturally ended, both satisfied that they had shared the depth and highlights of the men they had lost, it was too late to continue on to the Santa Fe market. They drove out of White Rock and headed back to the Alviso.

"You found new things for the store?" Lena asked in a raised voice. They preferred the top down on the little car so communication was at a minor shout.

"I bought all those rings, the tray and all," Rosa shouted back. "And I bought a couple of bracelets, and necklaces. He threw in a case for free."

"As well he should. Was it all new?" All that Lena had seen at the market were used items.

"Naaah, not new; the guy said to tell customers that they're pawn. I can raise the price."

"Pawn?" Lena wasn't sure that she was hearing Rosa correctly.

"Pawn pieces, that's what he said. He said to say that they're pawn pieces—to say the old used jewelry are pawn pieces."

"What does that mean?"

Rosa shrugged. "I guess they came from a pawn shop," she speculated aloud. Rosa really wasn't sure why she was supposed to say that the used Indian jewelry was "pawn."

"It makes it more valuable if it came from a pawn shop? But why?"

"You had an antique store, you tell me." Rosa grinned with her eyebrows raised as though she were about to laugh. "Aren't you an expert, Lena?"

"Have, Mz. Rosa, I had and *have* an antique store, but I'm definitely no expert. I just love the stuff, the decorating, the hunt, all that goes with the store. I love the customers; they're the experts, not me. Most, I really like the customers, you know what I mean?"

"No."

"Well, I rarely sell Indian jewelry and when I think of pawn I think of TVs or cameras and wedding rings and things like that."

"If you don't know nothin' 'bout antiques," Rosa kidded, "then I'll have to ask Roberto." He solved most of Rosa's dilemmas. Until then, she was putting the old jewelry in a display case with a sign announcing "Pawn Jewelry;" she trusted that the seller was far savvier than she with making sales so she was going to follow his lead. And he was, and his advice was a common ruse used on tourists and others who were innocently impressed and taken by such retail folklore.

"I got something for you, Rosa." She asked Rosa to hand her the backpack from the backseat. Rosa had a heck of a time turning even the slightest much less turn to reach in the backseat. She managed to hook her hand on a strap and pull the backpack to the front. "Here, steer for me for a second." Rosa grabbed the steering wheel with her one hand while Lena opened her backpack. She pulled out an antique Spanish fan. She tossed back the backpack then regained control of the steering wheel.

"Here." She handed the fan to Rosa.

Rosa opened the fan, ran her fingers across the painted surface then held it up and away to admire it. "This is…beautiful, Lena, beautiful."

"It reminded me of you." She watched as Rosa examined the fan, running her fingers over the ornately carved base then across the hand-painted silk and lace. "For Alviso's Spanish Senorita."

"Senora," Rosa corrected holding the fan open across her face while batting her eyes at Lena. "Gracias."

"You're welcome."

Rosa suggested that they stop at Pete's for a drink before getting back to the Alviso. She wanted to spend more friend or social time. Conversation was easy with Lena, as was laughter—something she so dearly missed. Lena was a lot like the girlfriends Rosa had in her past where she could be silly and talk without reservation—something she had been without for too many years and, at this time, dearly missed. Most noteworthy for Rosa, Lena didn't bore Rosa—something exceptional and greatly appreciated. She was aware that Lena was eager to get back to Monterey and Rosa's new pal would soon be gone with the likelihood of a replacement anytime soon, if at all, a slim prospect. Lena enjoyed Rosa's company as well, but declined the offer. She was concerned about Pepper being locked up in an unfamiliar yard for so long. Unlike at Broken Arrow where Pepper had made friends, where Penny or Bella or many others would look after him as if he were their own, he had yet to win a heart at the Alviso. He was alone in the confines of a foreign place and Lena wanted to get back to her buddy. Though disappointed, Rosa understood and the disappointment didn't put a chink in their chatter. They talked, and shared several bouts of laughter the remainder of their long and winding ride back to the Alviso.

Lena helped Rosa unload her new "pawn" merchandise into the lobby where Scarlet was busy polishing the carved wood counter which obviously pleased Rosa.

"Jewelry," Scarlet observed aloud. "People love to look at jewelry, Rosa." She craved positive responses, however, Rosa's personality didn't tend to accommodate Scarlet's emotional needs. She loved Rosa, and felt certain that Rosa cared for her but Scarlet needed the type of reassurance of affection that just wasn't in Rosa's comfort zone. "Let me help you," Scarlet offered, reaching to take the rectangular display case from Rosa's grip.

"Hey Scarlet, how's it going?" Lena found Scarlet to be one of the sweetest women she had ever met.

"Hi Lena. Did *you* buy anything?"

"Yes, I did; I found a really nice old woven jacket. I'll show it to you in a bit if you'd like to see it." Lena turned to Rosa. "I need to go walk Pepper, Rosa. I'll talk to you later." She smiled at Scarlet. "I'll see you later and show you my jacket, or coat, not sure which it is. You'll like it."

"Okay, Lena; I'd love to see it." Scarlet was sincere; she truly did want to see the jacket and she also wanted to visit with Lena. Scarlet didn't have much of a social life outside of the Alviso. Scarlet enjoyed Mick's company and adored the company of Gracie, nonetheless, having a female around closer to her age to talk with was unusual and special for Scarlet and something she wanted to take advantage of.

"Hand me that box of tags under the counter," Rosa ordered.

Scarlet reached down and brought up the white box of tags.

"Let's get these priced right now."

"Sure, I can help you with that, Rosa." Scarlet was more than happy to help Rosa get her jewelry priced and set up. She waited for Rosa to open the display case and to remove a ring before she dared to start pulling rings from their designated slot. "Rosa, they already have tags on them."

"Yeah," Rosa said, pulling tags from the box. "Cut the tag off and put the same information on the new tag and double the price."

"Double?" Scarlet thought Rosa was surely kidding.

Rosa stopped, looked directly at Scarlet. "Double the price and if he has information on the tag, write the same thing on the new tag and we have to make up a sign that says 'Pawn'."

"Pawn, like we're a pawn shop?" Scarlet was bewildered by Rosa's instructions.

Rosa was repeating what the salesman at the market had told her when she heard voices from the kitchen.

"Who's that?" she asked Scarlet.

"Bernard and Katherine are here."

Rosa at once put down the tags in her hand. With a smile on the inside she made her way through the kitchen door.

"Well, did you sell that bookstore again already?" she asked Bernard in stern jest, so delighted to see Bernard and Katherine standing in her kitchen.

"Hello, Rosa," Bernard said immediately echoed by Katherine. "I have to have a day off, ya know. We thought we'd come by and visit our old homestead, see what kind a chef Jeff's turned into and have dinner."

Rosa noticed Agnes sitting at the table reading the paper and that the door was open to Lucky's artist den.

"Is Lucky here?" she asked and Jeff nodded a yes. Rosa whispered, "You're all here." She walked over to the open door on the floor. "Lucky," she shouted.

"Yes; don't have to shout. I'm down here, Rosa, in my room, the artist den. I can hear ya," Lucky returned, making both Jeff and Rosa shake their heads and stifle a laugh.

"Don't you go anywhere, Lucky," she barked her demand. "I mean it. Don't you leave the Alviso. Do you hear me?"

"I hear ya," Lucky confirmed. "I'm not going anywhere."

She turned to the others in the kitchen. "We are all here together. Katherine and Bernard, you are having dinner with me tonight." She turned to Agnes. "Agnes, you are not serving dinner but you are having dinner with us tonight."

"What about the restaurant? Who's going to serve the customers?" Agnes worried.

"Don't you worry about it."

Agnes was the belle of the ball in that restaurant even if there were only a few tables audience. Closing the restaurant for the night was not a vacation for Agnes but an emotional hardship.

"One night, Agnes. You are having dinner with us." Rosa looked at each. "Tonight is my night. You are all here and I'm going to enjoy it... whether you like it or not!" Everyone smiled a response, even Agnes. Rosa turned to Jeff. "Jeff, let's plan a dinner."

"Sure, just tell me what you want, Rosa."

"You're the chef, but Jeff, tonight, you're eating with us. We are all going to have dinner together...all of us; you included."

"Should I fire up the grill now, Rosa?" Jeff wanted to accommodate Rosa's wishes but still wasn't sure what she wanted.

"You put out whatever you want. You make your best, Jeff. Make it a special dinner. I'm counting on you; I know you won't let me down."

"Yeah, sure, Rosa, but, aaah, ya gotta give me a bit more, like how many people? How many courses? What do you feel like tonight for your dinner, Rosa? Give me something to work with."

Rosa thought for a minute, counting in her head who she would demand be at the table. "Make it for ten people, and make your best, your gourmet dinner." She turned to Agnes. "Agnes, can you make the sangria?"

"Of course I can. And I do make the best sangria ever, don't I Jeff?" She fixed her eyes on Jeff waiting for his response.

"Yep, she can make a mean sangria."

"With real fruit, Rosa," Agnes added to bolster her claim.

"So Rosa, when do you want this ready to serve?" Jeff asked his final question but Rosa's attention was on Katherine and Bernard.

"Will you both stay the night?" Rosa asked. "You're my guests?"

"Yes, we can. I mean if you have a room available. We don't want to take one of your rooms——"

"You two go take one of the rooms and we'll meet in the dining room at about...about seven-thirty." Rosa looked at everyone and added, "How does that sound?"

"Sounds fine," Bernard answered.

"What's the occasion, Rosa?" Katherine asked.

"Are we supposed to dress up?" Agnes added.

"Dinner, we're having dinner. If you would like to dress up, wear whatever you like, Agnes," Rosa responded as she walked over to Lucky's open door and informed him that he was to be in the dining room at seven-thirty, and not to be late and "don't even think about escaping to the monastery tonight, Lucky. *You are eating here with us. That is an order.*"

"Yes Ma'am," Lucky shouted back, and Rosa left the kitchen.

"Scarlet," Rosa said in a firm voice which, of course immediately had Scarlet believing that she had done something to displease Rosa. "You are having dinner with us in the dining room tonight. No other plans. Not tonight. I want you to be in the dining room. You're having dinner with me and the others tonight at seven-thirty."

"Okay. Of course. Is it a special occasion of some kind, Rosa?"

"Yes, it is. It is a very special occasion. This is *my* night, Scarlet. *My night.*"

Rosa detected a look of worry in Scarlet's eyes. She figured that Scarlet believed she had forgotten some significant day. "It's not my birthday or anything else. It's just going to be a special dinner, Scarlet, and I want you there."

Scarlet was at once both relieved and complimented.

"I'll be there, Rosa. Should I bring anything?"

"Yes. Mick. Would you find Mick for me and tell him that he *must* be there: seven-thirty tonight in the dining room."

Rosa left the lobby to find Lena. She found her standing, grinning, watching Pepper run through the woods. Like with the others, Rosa wasn't taking no for an answer as she insisted that Lena be in the dining room for dinner at seven-thirty. She also insisted that Lena stay over another night as Rosa's guest.

"Well, if you insist; no problem, it would be my pleasure, Rosa. Should I dress up for dinner?"

Rosa gave her rare open-mouth smile. "Wear whatever you want." She then asked, "You packed formal clothes with you, Lena? You expect to meet the queen?"

"Never know. I can forgo the chiffon gown and just put a bow in my hair if you like."

Rosa laughed, "Put a bow on it," and walked away, turning to reiterate the time and the fact that Lena's presence was mandatory, not an option.

"Why, what's up with tonight?"

"I'm not really sure, Mick, but Rosa was more like demanding that everyone be there, not asking if we would be there." Scarlet felt it her duty to make sure Mick did as Rosa instructed. She wanted to please Rosa and she also would enjoy Mick being there for this special dinner, for whatever reason Rosa was having it. "It's important to her...for some reason."

"Well, yeah, I'll be there. You're going right?"

"Yes, yes, of course. Bernard and Katherine will be there and Lena, the one with the dog. I'm not sure who else will be there but it's important to Rosa that we're there at seven-thirty, Mick."

"No problem; I'll be there. Seven-thirty."

They stood by the wavy adobe wall and within the silence Scarlet felt certain she knew what Mick was thinking.

"No one knows, Mick. I'm sure of that," she responded to his silence.

"Maybe...ya know, maybe this would be——"

Scarlet cut him off, "No, Mick. Just be there, okay?"

"Yeah, I'll be there, Scarlet."

"Rosa will be very upset if you're not. It's some special night for her, but don't ask me what it is because I have absolutely no idea. It's not her birthday. I don't know what's up but whatever it is, it's important to Rosa."

Mick reached up and gave Scarlet a closed fist tap on the upper arm, smiled and said, "Seven-thirty. See you, and Rosa, at seven-thirty."

Chapter 11

Closed For The Night

Scarlet arrived early to help with the evening's event. Only Agnes and Jeff were in the kitchen. Katherine and Bernard had taken a room and had yet to arrive for dinner. The door to Lucky's room was open but no sight nor sound of Lucky.

"Can I help out?" Scarlet asked.

Agnes quickly grabbed her hand. "Come look, Scarlet."

She was taken by the deviation in Agnes's demeanor and fascinated by her girlish enthusiasm. Scarlet followed her lead across the kitchen to the doors opening into the dining room.

"What's going on, Agnes?"

Agnes slowly opened the doors to expose the splendor.

"Oh, Agnes, this is beeeeeautiful." Scarlet placed her open hand over her heart. She had never seen the dining room look so elegant. "Ooooh, it looks so nice, so beautiful. Did you do this?"

"With help from Rosa," Agnes replied with pride. This was not the dining room any had experienced before; it was like stepping into an entirely different restaurant, in fact, it didn't look like a restaurant but the dining room to a home from another era: white crochet-lace tablecloth covered the tables set together to make one long table; Rosa's old and savored blue lace china fashioned ten table settings adorned with ornate sterling-silver flatware. Candelabras with crystal prisms made the light from the candles dance on the table. The rather dusty lace curtains perpetually pulled to the side now hung like a veil over the old wavy glass and delicately cordoned off the outside world, enriching the ambiance of the room.

"Like it?" Jeff asked as he passed the two to set his culinary works of art on the dining table. He wasn't presenting his dishes in the usual manner (Mexican pottery set in woven baskets), but in glass with sterling silver casing.

"What is going on?" she asked Agnes. "What's this all about?"

"Truthfully, honey, I don't know. This is all Rosa's doing, though...I've been thinking about it and I think maybe she has some kind of announcement. Maybe this is some kind of anniversary. How long has the Alviso been in business?"

"Rancho Alviso has been in the family for over a hundred years but I'm not sure how long the hotel's been in business. But ya know, maybe that's it. Maybe it's some kind of anniversary for the Alviso."

"When did her husband die?" Agnes wondered if this could be the reason for the evening's gathering but before Scarlet had a chance to answer Jeff shouted to Agnes, "I could use some help, Agnes." She was off in a hurry, leaving Scarlet not only wondering about the impetus for this spontaneous and relatively formal occasion but mesmerized by the atmosphere—redolent with a rather haunting feeling about it.

"Good evening, Scarlet."

Scarlet turned toward the entranceway to the lobby. There stood Rosa, dressed in a way Scarlet had never seen in all the years she had known her. Her hair was coiffed into a Spanish chignon with a high and decorative comb. She wore a black satin and lace dress with a black lace shawl draped around her shoulders. The red roses adorning the shawl delicately vined down the front of her dress. She looked regal, stately with grace and purpose.

"Rosa," Scarlet softly exclaimed, "you look so nice." She wanted to say more but she didn't know what to say—the enchanting dining room setting plus Rosa in a formal black-lace dress was perplexing. Agnes entered the dining room with a large salad in what looked like a cut-crystal punch bowl.

"Oh my, Rosa, don't you look...spectacular." Agnes placed the bowl on the table. "Is it time already; I'll be back," she said and left the room as Jeff entered.

"I'll be back too," Scarlet announced and quickly left the room behind Agnes. She felt terribly underdressed after seeing Rosa.

Agnes stopped at Lucky's door and shouted down, "Lucky, it's time for the dinner and Rosa is dressed up. It's sort of a formal dinner so—-"She realized while speaking that Lucky didn't really have much of a selection of clothing so she finished with, "Make sure you brush your hair."

"Brush my hair?" Lucky mumbled to himself. He always brushed his hair. He shouted back, "I'll be up in a minute." Agnes scurried off to find something to wear more appropriate for the occasion.

"Wow, look at you!" Jeff was as taken aback as the others.

Rosa stepped towards the table and Jeff immediately put down the dish and said, "Wait, wait." He hurried to Rosa's side, slipped his arm through hers and escorted her to the table, pulling out the chair at that the head of the table, "For you, Ma 'dame."

"Why, thank you, Jeffery," she replied in pace. He pushed the chair in for her in gentlemanly fashion wherein Rosa pulled the fan that Lena had given her (and that matched her black-lace dress perfectly) from her sash, opened it across her face then coyly batted her eyes at Jeff. He responded with the biggest smile Rosa had ever seen on a face that typically maintained a neutral expression.

"Well, they'll be back but I'm here to stay," Jeff said. "Where do I sit?"

"Anywhere you like," Rosa answered but when Jeff pulled the chair out to her right she reached for the chair and said, "No, not in that chair; this place is saved for someone special."

"I'm not special?" Jeff joked then seated himself in the next chair over.

Scarlet found Mick and told him about the change in the dining room and about Rosa wearing formal attire.

"It's not like I have a tux, Scarlet."

"I know, but I'm going to go to the house to find something better to wear. This dinner is something special, Mick. Something is going on."

"Are you worried about it?" Mick was surprised by Scarlet's apparent concern and her stress over the changes she had witnessed in the dining room, and Rosa.

"I don't know, sort of. I mean, why would...oh well, never mind. I'll see you at dinner; I have to change." Scarlet hurried off to the house.

Katherine and Bernard arrived and were as impressed and puzzled as the others by the changes before them. Soon Lucky entered the room with his hair not only brushed but brushed with an exaggerated part to emphasize to Agnes that his hair was indeed brushed. Agnes was the next to show up followed by Mick who understood Scarlet's bewilderment once seeing the dining room, and Rosa, for himself. It wasn't long after when Scarlet entered the room. She caught everyone's eye. She was wearing a dress—not a formal dress such as Rosa's, but a sundress from her past, something she hadn't put on in years: a white cotton strapless dress with embroidered flowers across the bodice, tight on the top with a slight flare ending several inches above her knees. A bit self-conscious, she added a petite summer sweater. There were three unoccupied chairs: one on each side of Rosa and one between Mick and Bernard. She hesitated before choosing her seat and chose the empty seat to Rosa's right.

"Nope," Jeff said as soon as Scarlet placed her hand on the back of the chair. "That's reserved for someone 'special' unless your that someone special."

"Oh, oh, okay." Scarlet withdrew her hand from the chair. Mick stood up and pulled out the chair next to him which she swiftly accepted.

With the exception of Lucky, everyone was teeming with anticipation, waiting for Rosa to speak up—about something. They waited for some kind of explanation for this impromptu and distinctively different get-together. But she said nothing, elevating the suspense.

"Are we gunna eat?" Lucky asked, wondering why no one was saying anything nor eating. It appeared to him that all of the food was on the table and he couldn't figure out what everyone was waiting for. He looked around at everyone and in turn everyone looked at Rosa.

Jeff spoke up. "We have a few more people coming."

"Did you cook all this?" Lucky asked Jeff.

"With the help of Agnes," Jeff replied, looking Agnes's way with a nod.

"So, you're a sous chef too now?" Bernard teased.

Agnes began to respond to his teasing but silenced when Lena walked through the lobby doors into the dining room. Lena stopped in her tracks. Observing the ambiance of the room then seeing Rosa in her beautiful lace dress and shawl, Lena felt immediately embarrassed, though she elicited a huge smile then a chortle from Rosa. Lena was wearing her usual casual attire of jeans, cowboy boots and a blouse but, as a joke, in accordance with her comment to Rosa earlier, she had brushed her hair up into a ponytail that resembled a palm tree sitting on the top of her head with a large bow at the base. It looked ridiculous but that was the point—to make Rosa laugh. It hadn't occurred to Lena that others might be attending what she believed to be a casual dinner for two.

"Here, Lena, sit here," Rosa said with a smile indicating the chair to her left.

Lena said nothing. She took her seat, not making eye contact with anyone but Rosa, who was still smiling and loving the bow-based palm tree.

"Who else we waiting for?" Lucky asked, ready to eat and tempted by the aromas wafting from the dishes before him.

"Yeah, who's the 'someone-special'?" Jeff added.

"*Oh...I* need to get the sangria," Agnes announced as she jumped from her chair and hurried off to the kitchen. Then there was silence: Lena from embarrassment and the others who were waiting for Rosa to make some kind of announcement.

Agnes entered the dining room with a pitcher of sangria in hand and by rote began serving everyone. Once everyone's glass was full, Rosa asked Agnes to "please sit down." The silence continued. For a group that was characteristically chatty, such quiet was verging on uncomfortable—for everyone. Rosa lifted her glass. The others followed.

"What about our 'special' guest?" Jeff interrupted.

Rosa lowered her glass; the others followed.

"Who would you like the special guest to be, Jeff?" Rosa asked.

"Whoever you want," he answered, not understanding Rosa's question.

"No, whoever *you* want, Jeff." Rosa's question was straightforward and sincere. "If you could have anyone in that chair for dinner tonight, who would it be? Who would be *your* special guest, Jeff?"

Jeff looked up at Rosa figuring he'd play along. "Well, you know who I'd have sitting in that chair next to me." Jeff had a glimmer of hope in his eyes.

"And, that would be?" Rosa urged.

"Charlotte. I'd have Charlotte sitting there." He was being entirely honest, flippancy aside.

"What about you, Lucky? If you could have anybody, someone special, sitting in this chair having dinner with us, who would it be?" Rosa inquired, curious who would be that special guest for Lucky.

Without missing a beat or hesitation Lucky answered, "Jesus." His answer was genuine and a surprise to most, but not to Rosa.

Rosa's question didn't seem to be a social or dinner pastime; she was asking in earnest.

"What about you, Bernard?" she continued.

He was sitting at the other end of the table donning a serious expression instead of the former look of anticipation. He thought for a few seconds. He saw Ralph sitting in the empty chair next to Rosa. He was in his uniform. "I'm not coming back, Bernie. I know it. I ain't comin' back." Those words haunted Bernard. And Ralph was right. He didn't come back. Bernard jumped back into the foxhole. It was dark. Ralph was catching some much needed sleep. The sun rose but Ralph didn't. It was the worst part of the war for Bernard. "Ralph," Bernard said, gazing at the empty chair next to Rosa.

Katherine knew of Ralph, knew how important he was to Bernard and knew how serious his answer was to Rosa's unusual question.

Rosa looked around the table then set her eyes on Mick. "And you, Mick? Who would you put in this chair?" Rosa believed that the person Mick would choose would be related to the reason How went to prison. And she was correct.

Mick didn't respond immediately. He wasn't sure that he wanted to participate in what would require mention of his past. But, with all eyes upon him, Mick said, "Ronnie." He said nothing more and looked away from Rosa.

"Scarlet." She was next. "How about you? Who would you put in this chair?"

Scarlet questioned to herself if Rosa expected her to say Roberto. She wanted to please Rosa, and say Roberto but it wasn't true. Roberto was gone to a life that better suited him. The Alviso was not where Roberto wanted to be nor did Scarlet yearn for him to be there. As the others waited for her to answer Rosa's hypothetical question, Scarlet stared at the empty chair and envisioned her own baby sitting in a highchair next to her proud Grandma Rosa. She was smiling on the inside, not sure if that smile was exposed on the outside.

"Well, Scarlet?" Rosa asked again.

"I don't know," is all she would say. Scarlet was terribly uncomfortable and Rosa, along with everyone else, could see it.

"Lena, you're so quiet," Rosa commented, ready to ask Lena to fill the empty chair.

Lena looked up at Rosa then scanned her eyes down the table. "I feel so embarrassed. I did my hair like this as a joke, to make Rosa laugh. I didn't know other people would be here, that it was going to be such a nice, you know, more formal dinner. I apologize."

"I think the bow is pretty." Scarlet felt bad that Lena was so uncomfortable.

Lena gave Scarlet a look as if to say *Are you serious?* The group broke out in a chuckle which made Lena far more comfortable about her comical look. She would have pulled out the ponytail and bow except she had hair-sprayed it into place. That silly-do would go from the comical-look to the crazy-look if she tried.

"So Rosa," Lena said taking the lighthearted atmosphere back to Rosa's candid and probing inquest, "who would you have sitting in that chair?"

Rosa turned to Lena, leaned a bit forward resting her chin on her palm and answered, "So many people, Lena."

"Such as?" Jeff chimed in.

"My Robertos," Rosa answered first, then took a long pause. "My brother," she continued. The evening howl caught her attention. There was a quiet anticipation for Rosa to continue her personal choices to fill the empty chair beside her. Rosa said nothing, just listened to Chupi announce to the world his pain for the loss of his best friend.

Rosa looked at Jeff and said, "And Frances."

"What the hell is that animal?" Bernard asked to anyone at the table who might have an answer or even some speculation. "That's not a coyote, or not one like I've heard before." He was certain.

"Who knows," Jeff replied with a shrug, while both he and Rosa knew just who and what cried out each day a mournful wail, and each vowed for the safety of Frances's beloved Chupi.

"Yeah, it howls like every day. Maybe it's a wolf or somethin'," Lucky contributed.

"Go on, Rosa, who should be sitting in that chair," Lena implored.

"No," she calmly retorted. "You tell us who you would put in that chair, Lena."

Lena gave the prospect serious consideration. She, like Rosa, had several people of equal importance that she would relish the chance to have sitting across from her at that moment. Being in New Mexico and on her way back to Monterey, it was Jose who should be sitting in that empty chair enjoying the evening of good food with good people then joining her, joining Scout, on her way back to Monterey.

"Jose," Lena answered.

"Agnes," Rosa continued on, "is there someone you would love to see sitting in this empty chair tonight?"

Agnes had already been thinking of who she would enjoy having to dinner and answered Rosa straightaway, "Gretchen." Everyone waited for Agnes to inform them of whom this Gretchen was and how and why she was significant to Agnes—Agnes, whose past was somewhat of a mystery. Rosa realized that she had never asked Agnes about her life prior to coming to the Alviso; she, like everyone else, knew very little about Agnes pre-Alviso. It occurred to Rosa that she actually knew little about anyone's past at the Alviso. She didn't know why either How or Buck was in prison. She didn't know much about Bernard and Katherine other than they had closed their bookstore in Los Alamos and were searching for new meaning in the last years of their life, which she believed they really never found. They went back to where they left off when Bernard bought back his bookstore and it appeared that the bookstore gave the desired meaning to Bernard's life. Agnes never explained who Gretchen was or why she picked her to sit in the special guest's chair.

Katherine avoided eye contact with Rosa. She didn't want to be included in this table game, though she had placed that special person in the chair several people back. She didn't know what he looked like. She knew his age only, *if* he was still alive. She brought him to life and he was out in the world somewhere, yet she knew nothing about him, nor did anyone else, including Bernard. Rosa's hypothetical question brought him back up in Katherine's heart. Through the years she deeply regretted giving him up but the time and the circumstances gave her little choice, or so she thought back then. Times had changed and Katherine would now have made a very different decision. But this night—at this table, in that empty chair—she fantasized his handsome appearance and saw him looking at her with love.

"Katherine?" Rosa asked.

"No one," Katherine sternly proclaimed as she saw him smile at her. She smiled back.

"So do we have to wait for the pretend person before we can eat?" Lucky asked. He was hungry but he was also now a vegetarian and before Rosa could answer he grilled Jeff about which dishes were meat-free.

"A toast before we eat?" Rosa politely asked Lucky, and the rest at the table.

"A toast," Bernard said lifting his glass.

Rosa slid back her chair and stood before the table holding her glass of sangria up and out before her. Everyone lifted their glass in response.

"Thank you all for coming tonight." She turned toward Lena. "Thank you, Lena, for staying an extra night, and for your lovely hairdo."

"You're very welcome."

Rosa continued, "Each one of you has brought something special to my life, to the Alviso. I appreciate...all of you." Emotion began to well and this time Rosa did not want to stifle it but wanted to be able to express it—a rather difficult undertaking for Rosa. "I thought when Roberto left me, well, I wanted to close this place. I wanted to walk away and maybe never come back. But I couldn't, for many reasons. I quit enjoying my time here." Scarlet looked hurt by those words, yet she understood. The bell from the lobby sounded, interrupting Rosa's attempt at the difficult task of expressing her emotions.

"Customer," Jeff said in a low voice. Everyone set down their glasses.

"Lucky, could you please go tell them that we are closed, the rooms are full. Then, please make sure that the door is locked and that the closed sign is up," Rosa quietly requested.

"Sure," he replied then got up from the table.

"Déjà vu, Rosa," Mick said with raised eyebrows and a slight smile.

It took Rosa a good minute to understand Mick's remark and when she did, she continued her toast, not waiting for Lucky to return. "Yes, yes, a very déjà vu moment, Mick. It was that night that changed life here at the Alviso, Mick. We were all brought together that night—-"

"With a gun," Bernard interjected.

Lucky sat back down at the table and raised his glass with the others.

"Yes, with an empty gun. I'm grateful that you picked this restaurant to wave your gun, Mick. And Lucky, I'm glad that we had no potatoes that night." Rosa focused her eyes on Jeff's garlic potatoes for Lucky's benefit then pointed out, "We have them tonight."

Lucky felt embarrassed by his former attitude and actions, and his face showed it. He looked around the table then at Rosa. In a whisper he said, "Sorry, Rosa."

Rosa openly retorted Lucky's apology, "No, Lucky, there's nothing to be sorry for; it was meant to be. I truly believe that. You're an artist now,

Lucky. You're here where you're meant to be and *who* you were meant to be—an artist.

"Did you all know that Lucky sold two paintings in Santa Fe?" The response was more of a group congratulations than surprise. Everyone had seen Lucky's work and was duly impressed, so the selling of his paintings was not unexpected in an art mecca like Santa Fe.

Mick couldn't help but ask, "What name did you sign on your paintings?"

"Lucky," Lucky answered.

"Just Lucky?" Mick inquired further.

"Yeah, I signed my name, Lucky."

Mick figured that Lucky couldn't remember his new last name much less spell it.

"You Lucky's agent?" Bernard teased.

"He doesn't need one, Bernard. His paintings sell themselves," Rosa proudly exclaimed.

"Are we going to eat?" was Lucky's only input. He was hungry and tired of holding up his glass.

"Rosa's toasting, Lucky. Come on," Jeff quipped.

Rosa smiled at Lucky then gazed once again at everyone at the table.

"A toast to the many blessings you have all brought to the Alviso, to my life." Rosa lifted her glass higher. The others followed and in unison they took the first sip of Agnes's prize sangria then all joyfully began passing the dishes with Lucky grabbing the garlic potatoes first.

Conversation was at first taken up with compliments aimed at Jeff for his accomplished culinary skills. A year ago his attempt at omelets turned into scramble eggs; his steaks were burnt crisp on the outside while bloody red on the inside. There wasn't much that Jeff cooked at Roberto's request that didn't get delegated to a non-customer. Now, he outshined Roberto by far, even Rosa had to admit that. After the appreciation-fest for Jeff's delectable offerings, the conversations were light and varied. Katherine had everyone's, except Rosa who was more observing the ambiance of the gathering, attention when she talked about being a swimmer in her younger days. She had them smiling and laughing when she talked about being one of the few female surfers of her day. No one would have imagined it and Katherine was pleased and proud to speak of her past feats and triumphs. She inspired others to reveal their own unproclaimed exploits from their past. Even Mick joined in. Though the majority at the table hoped that he would disclose the reason for his incarceration, Mick avoided that topic altogether. Although, his escape would be toted as quite an accomplishment and a small part of Mick wanted to share that triumph with his new friends. Yet, he wasn't quite ready to do so—even a bit uneasy that Lucky might find their breakout an accomplishment to brag about and share the details with everyone. He knew what to expect from Buck, however, he couldn't predict this Lucky. There were only traces of Buck left, which was a relief to Mick. Whatever changed Buck—whether it was the blossoming of his artistic talents, his time at the monastery or his finding a home at the Alviso with several mothers by proxy—the others should count their blessings for the change.

Rosa watched as the others chatted, exchanged life stories and listened patiently with mixed responses while Bernard tested out his jokes. The lighted candelabras on the table were charming but a bit lacking in illuminating the room. Rosa relished the task of lighting the dusty candles placed in sconces what seemed like ages ago. She remembered eating in this very room by the light of these same half-spent candles. The rustling sound of her grandmother's full black dress as she moved with short unsteady steps, her stern face wrapped in a black veil of a scarf—all came back to Rosa, as though she were following her grandmother's steps across the room to light each waiting candle. Looking at the Alviso's many-years familiar landscape through those old lace curtains held Rosa still and immersed in a private past. In her mind she could see the horses tied to the posts, and hardly an engine driven vehicle would pass their way. Milling about were the hardworking men conversing about things scarcely shared with the women. Sounds, smells, emotions all whispered through Rosa like the breeze stirring the branches and leaves of those very same trees that stood guard at the Alviso for as long as she could remember. This had always been her home, as it was to so many others now gone. It would always be her home. But she would not always be around to ensure the life of the Alviso.

The sounds of booing brought Rosa back to the present and to her dinner guests. Bernard's jokes were getting worse and there was a unanimous vote that he terminate his attempt at being a comedian.

Agnes looked at the near empty pitcher. "I'll make another pitcher. Okay?" Everybody was in agreement and Agnes sped off to concoct her praised sangria. Rosa took her seat at the head of the table and next to the notable empty chair. Lucky was now talking about the garden at the monastery, suggesting that the Alviso should have a garden. The idea was appealing to Jeff: having fresh vegetables for the kitchen was a sensible plan.

"Do they have chickens?" Katherine asked.

"For the eggs," Lucky answered. He didn't suggest chickens for the Alviso for fear that they might be used for food.

"Here we go, just as good as the first one—*if not better,*" Agnes declared as she set the pitcher of sangria onto the table. "Scarlet, don't you like the sangria?" she asked once noticing that Scarlet hadn't touched her sangria other than to lift it for Rosa's toast.

"Oh, aaah. " Scarlet looked up at Mick. She seemed at a loss for words, which, of course, grabbed everybody's attention. "I like your sangria, Agnes. I just," Scarlet paused looking around at everyone then looking directly at Rosa. "Excuse me," she said turning her head as though hiding it while she stood up from her chair. Scarlet scurried off through the kitchen door.

"What was that all about?" Bernard was the first to speak up.

Instinctively Rosa looked to Mick for the answer. He acknowledged Rosa's silent inquiry but was tight-lipped.

"I'll pour," Agnes was doing what she loved, she was serving, being the quintessential hostess.

When Scarlet returned to the table and took her seat, it was obvious to all that she had been crying. This was something that no one could ignore. Something no one was willing to brush off, however, no one actually knew what to ask other than *Why were you crying?* and that somehow seemed too direct and insensitive. So, the gathering was once again in a pause.

"Scarlet," Rosa decided to speak up. This wasn't something she was willing to ignore either. Scarlet looked her way and appeared as though the tears were welling and about to fall again. "Are you alright, honey."

Rosa had never called Scarlet honey before. And that simple and common term of endearment pushed the tears right out. To everyone's, but Rosa's, astonishment, Mick placed his arm around Scarlet's shoulder to comfort her.

"I'm sorry," Scarlet apologized for her curious outburst.

Mick whispered into her ear. Scarlet's expression showed how intently she was listening to whatever it was that Mick was saying. When he pulled away, finished with what he had to say, Scarlet looked him in the eyes and nodded. The anticipation at the table was as penetrating as when they waited for Rosa to make some unforeseen announcement.

"Are we expecting her to say somethin'?" Lucky blurted out, so matter of fact that it was hard for some others not to snicker. Much to everyone's surprise, Scarlet did snicker at Lucky's rather abrupt question.

"Expecting is correct, Lucky," she said. No one but Rosa grasped what Scarlet was saying.

"That's wonderful, Scarlet." Rosa's response was genuine, something Scarlet did not predict when rehearsing the inevitable revelation. Again, there was a silence at the table.

"Do we have a dessert, Chef Jeff?" Rosa asked, taking the focus off Scarlet and ending the awkward stillness at the table.

"Of course we have dessert, Rosa. Of course we do. This is a multi-course meal, Ma 'dame."

"Let me get it, Jeff. I'll get it," Agnes was quick to offer. She discovered a side of herself while waiting tables that had lain dormant for so many years: she could take charge instead of sitting in the background. Customers enjoyed her friendly service and how she openly cared that they were enjoying themselves. Agnes felt in charge, and mostly, Agnes knew she was appreciated and needed.

"So what was this dinner all about anyway?" Lucky asked before stuffing a quartered meatless quesadilla in his mouth. It was a question everyone still had on their mind only Lucky was brazen enough to ask it, and so bluntly.

"The celebration is you. Is all of you." She turned to glimpse at Lena. "You included, Lena." Rosa had more to say but Agnes entered the dining room with a stunning cake on a crystal platter.

Agnes set the platter down on a separate table. "I'll be right back with the plates."

"What kind of cake is that, Jeff?" Katherine wanted to know.

"Chocolate with espresso-buttercream frosting," Jeff proudly answered. He leaned forward at the table to see Scarlet. "You can have cake, right?" It took him a little while but he caught on about Scarlet's condition. He had a feeling that Mick had become more than a friend to Scarlet. He believed that it wasn't just little Gracie that put that spark in Scarlet. Jeff felt that the

Mick situation was precarious; all the same, he was happy for her, for both of them.

Agnes placed a piece of cake before each at the table including the phantom guest next to Rosa.

"Oh," Agnes exclaimed, "does anyone want coffee?" No one did. "Okay, sangria and chocolate cake. I hope no one is on a diet," she joked. The sangria paired deliciously with the chocolate-espresso cake.

Even though it was getting late, and they were on dessert, this dinner felt nowhere near being close to ending. As the night went on everyone at the table, with the exception of Lucky, recognized the relationship between Scarlet and Mick. With the pressure of secrecy now lifted, Scarlet was participating in the conversations comfortably and speaking of her pregnancy with joy. Several times she looked Rosa's way and was met with the look she had always sought from Rosa. Mick had no worries regarding Rosa. They liked each other right off. There was no question, no emotional quandary as there had been between Rosa and Scarlet.

"I helped my best friend commit suicide," Mick said aloud and distinctly at a volume above the others, and without any prompting.

Scarlet's heart began to race. She wasn't sure she wanted or even should hear about this, nor that anyone else wanted or should either.

"Do you want to talk about it?" Rosa asked, giving Mick an out if he chose to go no further.

"I just thought," Mick paused, "I figured you all probably wanted to know what I had done to be sent to prison."

Lucky put down his fork. He stared at Mick, worried. He didn't want to confess to those at the table what he had done to be sent to prison. Lucky had become ashamed of his former self. He believed that God had forgiven him, and that Jesus was now always watching him, still, he wanted to leave his past dirty deeds buried along with Buck.

"Why did he want to kill himself?" Bernard questioned, then added, "If you don't mind me asking."

Scarlet placed her hand on Mick's thigh. He glanced appreciation for her concern then answered the best he could at the moment.

"He was in a lot of pain. He was in a chair, wheelchair—had been for a long time. He wasn't getting any better. He'd never get better, only worse. Life was...agonizing, more like excruciating. His life became unbearable for him and he couldn't handle it anymore and he was going to do it one way or the other...but, he was pretty much helpless, ya know. He was desperate. It was a mess." Mick stopped. He could feel his eyes welling and he wasn't willing to go there. He could go no further with that final goodbye.

"Was that who was in our guest chair?" Agnes softly asked, and Mick nodded.

"My best buddy, Ralph—hell of a friend—we went to war together... died right there beside me, Mick," Bernard contributed, showing his understanding of how watching a friend die is an experience that makes the strongest of men weep.

"You put Ralph in that guest chair," Agnes commented. He nodded. "I guess we all put someone who is now gone in that chair," she added.

"Not me," Scarlet said. "I put someone who will be, someone on the way, in that chair—in a highchair." Her comment lifted the mood at the table.

"Let's toast to our new arrival," Rosa said, lifting her glass in the lead. "And, might I ask when that might be, Scarlet?"

Even with the lighter and accepting environment, Scarlet felt uncomfortable answering the question which, of course, revealed when she and Mick had become intimately involved. Seeing how uneasy Scarlet was in answering the question, Mick jumped in, "About six months." Both he and Rosa were amused by the obvious calculating going on within the group.

Rosa lifted herself to a standing position along with her glass. She waited for the quiet instead of insisting on it. Rosa was taking in the intimate exchange among her guests. She would wait for the silence to come by their choosing. Rosa's standing position slowly came to notice and a respectful silence moved down the table like gently tipped dominoes.

"I am so honored to have each one of you at my table this evening," Rosa began. She raised her glass up and out to them all, then she turned to face the empty chair. She bowed her head slightly while holding the glass in the direction of the empty table setting. "To Frances, I hope that you are here in spirit." In a whisper that only Jeff understood she added, "I promise we will look after Chupi." Rosa turned to the others at the table with her glass still raised. "To Ronnie," she said looking at Mick for approval.

"To Ronnie," Mick responded. "I wish you were still around, buddy."

Rosa looked at Bernard and again lifted her glass.

"To Ralph," Bernard was quick to react. "Yeah, he should be here. He'd have all you guys laughing if he was sitting in that seat. You'd have to make a few more pitchers, Agnes." When he looked to Agnes for a light response, Agnes could see the shine in his eyes from waiting tears.

"To Jesus. I'm toastin' to Jesus," Lucky contributed with his glass held high. "He watches us all, so he's already here anyway."

"To Jesus," Rosa confirmed his toast.

Scarlet spoke up, "To our new baby."

Without further prodding the others joined in, some repeating their first choice and some adding to their first nominee for the empty guest chair.

"Jose and Lauren," Lena said, then added, "And Sam. Oh Sam would have loved being here. I need three chairs there." She smiled at Rosa.

Only Katherine stayed silent, still keeping her desired guest to herself. When they finished, Rosa continued adding those she pained to be at the table that night: her grandmother, her grandfather and her father. When she spoke her father's name aloud, the old lace curtains—the very curtains made by her grandmother and installed by her father—moved as though a breeze from an open window quickly passed through them. Only Rosa and Lena noticed the curtains move and only Rosa knew that the windows were shut tight, not a whisper of breeze could make its way through them. Rosa continued to add a few more people no longer with her whose company would have been a precious gift that evening. She looked around the table welcoming others to contribute to the list of imaginary occupants of the hallowed empty guest chair.

"Aaah, Rosie, we could fill this room, not just a chair, you know that," Bernard unceremoniously shouted across the table. "Let's toast this sangria right into the old kisser." And that they did. Scarlet joined in with her glass of sparkling cider.

"Are you excited about the baby, Scarlet?" Agnes asked from across the table. She was quite sure that Scarlet was excited but the question opened the door to the good news. As far as Agnes was concerned, she was now going to be a grandmother.

Though Agnes felt comfortable almost instantly around Mick, with or without a gun, Scarlet was a different story; she was more distant and harder to figure out. Scarlet behaved like a perpetual employee. She appeared preoccupied, even a bit nervous at times. Agnes didn't realize that all Scarlet wanted to be was a good wife, and a good daughter-in-law, and that meant, in her view, a good employee. She wanted to fit in at the Alviso and excel in whatever it was that was expected of her, though she often wasn't sure what was expected of her. She wanted to please Roberto. She wanted to please Rosa. She wanted to be happy in her new family even though neither Roberto nor Rosa seemed to be all that excited about anything at the Alviso. Nothing Scarlet did, or could do, would change the hollow feel looming about the hacienda. The Alviso lost its luster and life when Roberto Sr. died.

Scarlet's enthusiasm upon arriving at the Alviso was met with a rather empty response. She believed initially that it stemmed from the passing of Roberto Sr., but time changed nothing. From where she came, the old hacienda was legendary. It was near to a mansion to Scarlet and an honor to call home. No one complained; they did their jobs to keep the Alviso with the restaurant in order and running. No one spoke of possible improvements other than the necessities, nor did they speak of Alviso's future. Though both Roberto and Rosa gave the impression that they desperately needed one, a vacation was never in the picture. After enough time had passed, even Scarlet took on a noticeably lackluster attitude towards her days at the Alviso. It was when the Alviso was taken over that Scarlet's emotions became visible—from the fear How and Buck introduced in the dining room to the spark of joy little Gracie brought to her life. Agnes had yet to witness Scarlet interact with a single friend, until Mick became her friend and now she knew he had become more than just a friend to Scarlet.

Scarlet leaned past Mick directing her attention to Lena.

"Lena," Scarlet raised her voice to get her attention.

"Yes," Lena responded and added, "Congratulations, Scarlet, on your new little one. You too, Mick."

"Thank you."

Mick smiled.

"Do you have children, Lena?" Scarlet hoped that she had. She wanted someone to talk with, to share, to learn from but Lena had no children. She gave no explanation why she was without children. Lena felt it terribly inappropriate to voice her reasons: she just plain never wanted any. Her four-legged canine kid with the bad attitude was plenty for Lena.

"Well, Lena, Katherine and I don't have kids. Yep, no kids for us," Bernard announced. He didn't take notice that Katherine didn't don his same

expression of satisfaction. Nor did he know that Katherine did have a child...
somewhere."

"Yeah, me and that Charlotte are plannin' on havin' a lot a kids," Jeff
kidded to Rosa. "We're gunna have to open up one of those Montessori
schools out here so we can take care of all my youngin's."

"Who's Charlotte, Jeff?"

"She's staying over at Frances's house, her niece," Jeff answered. "I think
she's going to be here a long time."

"What does she do?" Scarlet wanted to know more. Maybe she would
have a friend in town after all.

"She stands around the garden looking good," Jeff said as though he
were serious.

"She's in charge of Frances's estate, her house and belongings. She's trying to sell the house and land, but it's going to take some doing so I suspect
she'll be here awhile," Rosa further explained. It hadn't occurred to Rosa
prior that Charlotte could be a friend to Scarlet, in fact, would very likely
enjoy having a friend like Scarlet while in this small town. Rosa became sadly
aware that she didn't give Scarlet and her predicament at the Alviso much
consideration over the years. Scarlet was just there, just like she and Roberto
Jr. were *just there*. They were the three pieces of the Alviso machine grinding
to keep it moving.

"How old is she?"

Before Jeff could reel off the expected flippant remark, Rosa quickly
answered, "I believe she is in her thirties, but that's just my guess." It was a
guess that made Scarlet happy. She would make it a point to visit Frances's
old home. Maybe this Charlotte would be the girlfriend she longed for.

"Jeff," Agnes called across the table. "Didn't you make that cactus gelatin dessert too?"

"Yeah, it's in the fridge. Does anybody want to try it?" Jeff perked up.
It was Jeff's original creation and he believed quite tasty.

"Cactus gelatin?" Lucky scrunched up his face. It sounded awful.

Jeff got up to help Agnes prepare the gelatin dessert. He knew cactus
gelatin didn't necessarily sound appetizing. He would have to think up a
more appealing name. Together they scooped the candy-like gelatin made
from prickly pears, ripe off the local cacti, into small dessert dishes. Jeff
added a touch of jalapenos and finely chopped nuts to add some kick and

texture. They placed a cloud of whip cream on each and together delivered the offbeat final course. And, they all loved it—even Lucky.

"It's late, Rosa," Scarlet softly commented. "I need to get to bed." As soon as she began to rise, Mick pulled out her chair for her.

"Mick, would you please walk Scarlet out?"

"Of course, Rosa." Mick then stood up from his chair.

"This has been so nice." Scarlet looked at each person still sitting at the table. "This has been a wonderful dinner, a really nice get together. I hope we do this often. I really do. I hope we get together like this again and again." She stood there, wanting to say more but felt a loss for words other than what she just expressed: how much she loved getting together and how she wished that there would be more such dinners.

"We most certainly will Scarlet," Rosa replied, thoroughly satisfied that Scarlet had truly enjoyed herself with everyone, and that she was no longer burdened with their secret. As they passed, Rosa called Scarlet to her side. In a whisper for only Scarlet to hear, she said, "You and Mick take the house now. You set up a nice home in that house. You make it nice for my new grandchild, Scarlet."

Scarlet was glowing. Life hadn't had a better moment. Mick had no idea what Rosa had whispered to Scarlet but seeing her look so joyous touched him profoundly. He loved Scarlet; he had fallen in love with her too.

"I'm goin' ta bed," Lucky announced. "Thanks for the dinner." He looked to Jeff. "Thanks for the food, Jeff. Don't throw anything out; I'll finish it later." Lucky said goodnight to all at the table then excused himself. He was expected at the monastery early the next morning. He wasn't used to late hours anymore and though he enjoyed dinner and the company of everyone at the table, Lucky's heart was always somewhere within the monastery. His visits and communication with Jesus on the cross were faithful. He enjoyed working and learning from the monks. He looked forward to seeing Granny on his trek to and from. His "off" days were devoted to painting, something Rosa encouraged. Occasionally Lucky helped out at the Alviso but Rosa's support went to his time at the monastery and his painting, of both she was most proud.

"Well, Katherine, ya ready to turn in? It's pretty late for us old folks." Bernard was ready to call it a night.

"I'm going to help Agnes clean up," she replied.

"Oh no, Katherine——"Agnes began but Katherine cut her off and insisted on helping. Agnes could see that it was not obligation but something Katherine needed to do.

"Okay, thank you, Katherine."

Jeff stood up. He grabbed onto the empty chair of the phantom guest and slid it back. "Are you ready, Charlotte?" he kidded, waited for the invisible guest to rise from the chair and together with his imaginary lover Jeff left for his room.

Bernard left the dining room to go to bed, nodding at the empty chair that earlier held his army buddy, Ralph. Agnes and Katherine, like two teenage girlfriends, cleared the table chatting the whole time. That left Rosa and Lena. Neither was tired and neither was ready to leave the table. The candlelit ambiance, the sangrias, the depth of the evening was still with them. They couldn't help themselves, they both wanted and needed and utterly rejoiced in talking about Roberto Sr. and Jose. It wasn't the endearing or loving deeds of each that they delighted in, it was their pranks, their antics and outlandish comments, ideas and behaviors. Like Rosa and Lena, they knew they would have become instant friends. After the shared amusement from stories of the men they loved, an overpowering sense of emptiness enveloped them both. Rosa rested her chin on her palm and gazed at the empty chair. Lena looked past the chair focusing on the aged lace curtains, remembering with a smile the ruffle curtains used to spruce up Jose's RV. That smile spread to the image of Jose's love-laced grave.

"So much has happened, Rosa." She placed her hands to cover her face. "It all doesn't seem real sometimes."

"I know...I know."

Katherine confessed to Agnes. She told who she had put in the empty guest chair. She and Agnes sat at the kitchen table and over coffee Katherine released her age-old secret and all that went with it. Katherine cried and Agnes held her like a sister.

Lena couldn't sleep. She wasn't the least bit sleepy, but was wide awake—too awake to even attempt sleep.

Rosa wasn't ready to call it a night herself. She took a short stroll around the Alviso which stirred up memories of all kinds. She placed her shawl tightly around her shoulders and sat in the dark outside her room. The scents about her felt eternal. She remembered them as a little girl. She remembered so much that took place on the grounds before her though for so many years Rosa walked the grounds feeling hollow. The quiet was interrupted, but not intentionally. She saw Lena packing her car. Quietly she shut the trunk. After putting Pepper inside the little car, Lena slowly and quietly closed the door. Lena was heading toward Rosa. She had a piece of paper in her hand. She didn't see Rosa sitting in the dark in her black dress and shawl until she was at the walkway.

"Oh God," Lena exclaimed in a controlled whisper. "I didn't even see you there. I was going to leave you this note."

"You're in a hurry to get home, Lena?"

"Yes. I can't sleep so I may as well head out," she answered. "What about you? How come you're sitting out here?"

"I can't sleep either," Rosa answered.

"Dinner was something else, Rosa. It was great—the food, the people. I really enjoyed myself. Thank you."

"It was nice, wasn't it."

Lena stepped up onto the walkway and sat down next to Rosa on the bench.

"Maybe I'm wrong, Rosa, but I got the feeling that the dinner had some other meaning. Was it some kind of anniversary or something?" Rosa didn't respond. "Am I being too nosy? Sorry. It just felt like it was a special occasion of some kind. You look beautiful in this dress too, like royalty. Well, it was a special dinner, at least for me. Thank you for inviting me."

"It was a special occasion, Lena."

Lena waited for Rosa to explain the significance of the occasion but an explanation never came. She sat with Rosa a little longer, worried that Pepper might start barking, waking those fast asleep at the Alviso. Eventually, he did.

"I gotta go, Rosa. Can I give you a hug?" she asked but fully intended on hugging Rosa regardless of Rosa's response. They hugged, and Lena left her note on the step.

"You coming back?" Rosa asked as Lena stepped off the walkway.

"You bet I'm coming back, Rosa. And, I'm gunna bug ya with letters, cards and phone calls." She extended her arm, pointing her finger at Rosa.

"I'm not kidding. You haven't seen or heard the last of me, Rosa." She turned, took a few steps toward her car confining the waiting and eager Pepper then turned back to face Rosa. "Hey, Rosa...*I love you.*"

Lena was tempted to honk the horn as she exited the Alviso. She waited until she was a bit down the road then gave a goodbye blast of the horn.

Rosa remained sitting in the dark. Her eyes set on the house now occupied by Scarlet and Mick. She was going to be a grandmother. That longtime vacuous place would become a home, full of life—a new life. She looked up to the blue-black sky, to the thousand stars above her.

I miss you. You know I miss you, old man. And I know it was you who brought this crazy family to our Alviso, to make it a home again for me. Only you, Roberto; only you would bring me two convicts to give me a family again. Now don't you be hard on Roberto Jr.; he's happy now. This life wasn't for him; you know that. I know he misses you. You're going to be a grandpa, old man. Abuelo...I know, I know, but they'll give the baby a family name; the baby can be as white as a sheet, but that's our nieta o nieto, Grandpa.

Eighteen months later Rosa passed away from a heart attack. Roberto came home but this time he didn't have to stay. He kept a distant hand in the goings on at the Alviso while he lived the life he was meant to live. The Alviso was running like precision clockwork with Jeff as the full time chef, assisted by Agnes and occasionally Katherine; the two had become best of friends. On the busy nights Albert's nephew came to help out. Charlotte had yet to sell Frances's old house which gave Jeff more time and hope for her affection. Scarlet became quite adept at selling Rosa's "old pawn" jewelry. Lucky's artwork sold itself. Mick was a great dad to Benicio and Gracie made the perfect older sister. Rosa left the Alviso as alive and flourishing as it had been in generations past. This new generation was of the same spirit, only different blood.

Made in the USA
Charleston, SC
08 October 2012